"What happened?"

"Fontaine and Baptiste brought in a DUI. Guy was weaving around on Nantier and running red lights, they pulled him over, and he practically melted the breathalyzer. He had no ID and apparently couldn't remember his name. So they brought him in to sleep it off. I swear, I was actually *reading* Fontaine's report on it when I heard the boom."

Rubbing the bridge of his nose between his thumb and forefinger, Garcia said, "He was a costume."

"Well, either that or he was hidin' a cannon up his ass." Taylor shook her head, and took her glasses off her nose, letting them dangle over her chest by the chain. "According to these other fine, upstanding citizens, he shot a ray-beam of some kind out of his hands, blew the hole in the wall, and walked out. Followed by six other people. I already got their sheets together, and I'll put the word out at roll call for the day shift."

The Case of the Claw

by
Keith R. A. DeCandido

This book is dedicated to the memory of Gene Colan.

ACKNOWLEDGMENTS

In general, this book owes its inspiration to all the comic books and cop shows and books on police that I've consumed over the years. Some of the more obvious inspirations include *Kurt Busiek's Astro City*, *The Wire*, and David Simon's *Homicide: A Year on the Killing Streets*, but there are plenty more beyond that, far too numerous to list here.

Many thanks have to go to Wrenn Simms, Laura Anne Gilman, Tina Randleman, Lucienne Diver, and GraceAnne Andreassi DeCandido, who all provided tremendously useful feedback that made this book far better than it would've been if they hadn't read the book first.

Also to David Niall Wilson for publishing the book, Glenn Hauman for creating the cover, Mike Collins for designing many of the characters and for the artwork that graces the cover, Aaron Rosenberg for his excellent design work, and Darick Robertson for Knight Dude.

Finally, thanks to them that live with me, be they human, feline, or canine, for the continued support.

PROLOGUE
SUNDAY

11.45pm

A yellow streak flew overhead, stirring up the litter on 20th Street. Officer Sean O'Malley didn't even notice it until the sonic boom rattled the windshield of the blue-and-white police car he was driving.

O'Malley steered the cruiser down 20th. From the seat next to him, Officer Paul Fiorello stuck his head out the window. "Was that Spectacular Man?"

Shaking his head and hitting the brake as the cruiser approached a red light at Jaffee Avenue, O'Malley said, "Christ, Paulie, how long you been livin' in this town? If it was him, it'd be blue and red. It was yellow, so that means the Flame."

This late on a Sunday night in the Simon Valley neighborhood, the streets were dark. Nothing was open, plus the street lights hadn't been repaired since the Bengal tangled with the Dread Gang last month.

"I can never remember," Fiorello said, "is he Ms. Terrific's brother or husband?" Flame and Ms. Terrific were two-thirds of the Terrific Trio.

O'Malley grinned as the light turned green and his foot moved from the brake to the accelerator. "Hope it's her brother, 'cause that lady's *hot*. I'd do her in a cold minute. Y'know, there's nude pictures of her on the Internet, right?"

"Gimme a break, Sean." Fiorello shook his head. "That's some skank they found at Bitches With No Brains dot com and Photoshopped the Terrific lady's head on it."

Frowning, O'Malley asked, "Seriously?"

Fiorello rolled his eyes. "Yeah. And Santa ain't real, either."

"Damn." O'Malley let out a long breath. They were some *fine* pictures.

"So yellow's Flame?" Fiorello started counting on his fingers.

"Spec Man's, like you said, blue and red."

"Nice rhyme."

Fiorello gave O'Malley a nasty look before continuing. "So green's who? Major Marine?"

"Yeah. And purple's Amethyst and if it's all rainbow-y, then it's the Prism."

Shaking his head, Fiorello said, "I don't know how you keep track of the costumes like that."

"In this town, it's the job." O'Malley couldn't believe that his partner was still having trouble keeping it straight after all these years.

Fiorello's face looked sculpted: perfect Roman nose, dark hair that never got mussed no matter how crazy things got on the street, and friendly brown eyes that always calmed down the craziest of citizens. Which meant, of course, that women paid more attention to him than to O'Malley with his bad skin, messed-up nose thanks to an attempt to stop a bar brawl when he was a rookie, and crappy hair.

Still, Fiorello was good police, and he always had O'Malley's back—certainly more than the other assholes he'd been paired with over his six years on the job—so O'Malley put up with him as best he could.

Even if Fiorello always left Manny's with someone on his arm while O'Malley went home alone to an empty apartment.

The next street was Ayers, and O'Malley slowly turned the wheel to the right. Even on a Sunday night, there was always *something* happening on Ayers.

Sure enough, there was movement to O'Malley's left, as well as the sound of metal grinding against metal, though still no lighting. It was the Tavares Pawn Shop, which stayed open until midnight, though it looked like they were closing a few minutes early. The sound had come from a man pulling the grate shut; a woman was crouching down and pushing a padlock shut. O'Malley didn't know their first names, but he knew the Tavareses had always cooperated with the cops, reporting stolen merchandise and such.

Slowing down the cruiser, O'Malley leaned out the rolled-down window. "You guys all right?"

Mr. Tavares looked over and smiled when he saw the cops. "Yeah, we're good, Officer. Headin' home."

His wife, having applied both padlocks, stood upright. "Hey, guys, if you see the Bruiser tonight, could you do me a favor and thank him? Some guy tried to jump me on the way in to open this morning, and he drove 'im off."

"If we see him," O'Malley muttered. "Get home safe."

"Thanks!"

"What the hell?" Fiorello asked as they continued down Ayers. "'If we see him'? Sounds like DeLaHoya saved her ass."

"I guess."

Fiorello stared at his partner. "C'mon, DeLaHoya's one of the good guys. And you know how I know that? *You* said it when we first partnered up. 'Most'a the costumes,' you said, 'they're assholes, but the Bruiser's okay.' So what the hell?"

O'Malley sighed. "You know that double MacAvoy caught last week? DeLaHoya fucked with the evidence—they had to toss the case 'cause'a him."

Fiorello shook his head. "He doesn't usually do that."

"Yeah, well, he ain't police. None'a them are." O'Malley went through an intersection, ignoring the octagonal stop sign.

His heart suddenly hammered into his chest as he saw a square block of a man dressed all in black jump into the middle of the street right in the cruiser's path.

"Dammit!" O'Malley slammed on the brakes and tried to get

4

his breathing under control. It wouldn't do to run down the Bruiser, since in that confrontation, the costume would still be standing, and the front grille of the blue-and-white would be smashed in. The last thing O'Malley wanted to do was call in a damaged cruiser *again*—not after that time the Brute Squad totaled the unit, and he had to ride a desk for a week.

Fiorello smirked. "Hey, now you can give him the Tavares lady's message."

"Kiss my ass," O'Malley said.

No one knew what exactly happened to Jesus DeLaHoya to make him super-strong, invulnerable, and big as a house, but ever since it happened, the former amateur boxer—who'd acquired the nickname of "the Bruiser" when he was a Gold Gloves champ back in the day—had taken it upon himself to clean up Simon Valley. Unlike most of the costumes, he usually cooperated with the cops, and even testified in court when he helped put someone away.

DeLaHoya walked around to the driver's side. The verb *to walk* was probably not giving what he did enough credit. The Bruiser tended to stomp, on account of he weighed a ton, and O'Malley was just waiting for the day that the pavement gave out under him and he fell into the sewer.

"Officers, how you two doin'?" the Bruiser said. He was bending over and staring into the window at O'Malley, getting so close that he could smell the cheap coffee on the costume's breath. DeLaHoya kept his dark hair close cropped, and it just accentuated that his head looked like a trapezoid, with no noticeable neck—just went straight from the jaw line to the shoulders.

"Whaddaya want?" O'Malley asked.

"Got somethin' you two'll wanna see."

O'Malley looked at Fiorello. "You believe this?" He turned back to the costume. "Look, DeLaHoya—"

"It's *serious*." With that, the Bruiser stood upright and stomped toward an alley between two apartment buildings.

Fiorello got out of the car.

"Hey, Paulie, what the hell?" O'Malley asked, but his partner was already crossing in front of the blue-and-white to follow the costume.

Shaking his head, O'Malley said, "Fine." He turned off the ignition and got out, pulling his ballcap out of his back pocket and putting it on his head. Technically, the plain black ballcap wasn't proper uniform, but O'Malley had always hated the blue department-issue hat. Fiorello, of course, wore his, with the SCPD logo on the front and the word CENTRAL under it—and it never messed up his hair. O'Malley really had no idea how he did it.

Adjusting the bill of the cap as he walked toward the alley, O'Malley asked, "You wanna give us a hint, DeLaHoya?"

"I got a tip that some of Turk's boys were dealin' outta here."

This was starting to annoy O'Malley as he followed his partner and the Bruiser, pulling out his flashlight so he could see. "Turk's boys been dealin' outta here forever." His nose started to wrinkle, as the alley smelled like half a dozen homeless guys had taken a shit and then all croaked. O'Malley started breathing through his mouth.

"Not the last six months, they ain't," the Bruiser said, and O'Malley could hear the pride in his voice. "So I was checkin' it out, and I found this."

The Bruiser and Fiorello had stopped walking, the costume pointing between two Dumpsters. O'Malley shined his flashlight where the Bruiser's meaty finger was aimed, and Fiorello did likewise.

Barely, O'Malley could tell that it was the body of a man—and then only because the face was more or less intact. The rest

6

of the body, though, had been torn apart. Organs and bones were sticking up through ripped flesh and torn clothes, and blood was all over everything. The limbs, what he could see of them, were all pointed in different directions than legs and arms usually went.

Something was stuck on the man's forehead.

The light got dimmer, and O'Malley turned to see Fiorello run across to the other side of the alley to throw up. He almost made it. His retching echoed off the brick walls of the two buildings. Uncharitably, O'Malley wondered what all those women who ignored him and chased Fiorello would think if they saw the two of them right now.

O'Malley shined his flashlight directly on the victim's forehead. It was a yellow Post-It with a pen-and-ink drawing of an eagle's talon on it.

The Bruiser said, "That's what I think it is, right?"

Nodding, O'Malley said, "Yeah." He turned and flashed his light on Fiorello, who was still doubled over, and was now dry heaving. His regurgitated dinner was doing nothing to make the alley smell better. "Guess *I'm* callin' this in."

"Look, I still gotta find Turk's boys. Can you just say this was an anonymous tip or something?"

"You didn't touch nothin', right?"

The Bruiser sighed. "Look, I'm sorry about what happened. That was a mistake, and I already apologized to Detective MacAvoy—twice. I didn't touch *anything*, okay?"

O'Malley was about to argue some more, but there wasn't any point. Besides, he now had bigger problems. "Yeah, fine, go beat the shit outta Turk's boys. Oh, and hey—Mrs. Tavares, from the pawn shop? She says thanks."

At that, the Bruiser actually broke into a big grin, which made his ugly face even uglier. "Tell her she's welcome." And then he stomped back out of the alley.

Fiorello was now standing with his hands on his knees, still dry heaving. O'Malley grabbed the radio that was clipped to his right shoulder. "PCD, this is Unit 2202 with a signal 85. We got a dead body in the alley on the 400 block of Ayers. Need crime scene and Homicide."

"PCD roger."

"And hey, PCD?" O'Malley looked down at the mangled corpse and the distinctive Post-It. "Tell Homicide that the Claw's back."

PART ONE
MONDAY

6am

"Good morning Super City! And welcome to News 6 at 6. I'm Mindy Ling."

"And I'm Chuck Ortiz. Later on, we'll tell you how you can win a date with a real-live superhero, give you the latest on the reconstruction of Kirby Park's south lawn, and reveal new secrets to sleeping better straight from the Terrific Trio—plus, Spectacular Man is gonna be on Broadway! We'll also have Ian Michaelson with sports, Debra Fine with weather, and Donna Brodsky with traffic. But first our top story. Mindy?"

"It's not good news, Chuck. The Claw is back in town. The mutated spree killer, who has never been captured or identified by his real name, has come back to Super City and claimed four victims—two in Simon Valley and two in Leesfield. We go now to Matt Barnett. Matt?"

"The corner of Kanigher Avenue and 38th Street is a quiet residential block in the Leesfield neighborhood of Super City. That quiet was shattered late last night when a mutilated body was discovered in a garbage can cubbyhole in front of a three-story apartment building. This is one of four sites where bodies were found, each horribly mutilated, and each with the distinctive eagle talon trademark of the Claw on a Post-It affixed to the victims' foreheads. I was able to talk to Erik Golden, who found one of the bodies, and he had this to say…"

"I gotta tell you, man, I lost my freakin' dinner on 'at one. I was just takin' out the trash, y'know? Garbage trucks come first thing Monday mornin', so I was takin' it out, y'know? An' bam! There's this body all messed up and covered in blood an' stuff. And it had that eagle mark, an' I remember from a couple years back, that's the Claw. So I called 911 right away, an' the cops, they came faster'n I ever saw, an' I been livin' here all my life, yknow?"

"At first, police were unwilling to confirm that all four bodies were the handiwork of the Claw, but in a brief conference call with the press, SCPD spokeswoman Regina Dent confirmed that they are proceeding on the assumption that the Claw is responsible, pending final examination of the bodies. The identification of the four victims is being withheld until their families are notified, and Ms. Dent said that Mayor Sittler will be holding a press conference at eleven o'clock this morning. In the meantime, the Superior Six has already released a statement saying that they are investigating the Claw's return and hope to capture him once and for all. For *News 6 at 6*, I'm Matt Barnett."

"Thanks, Matt. The Claw is a half man, half bird who first appeared in Super City six years ago. He killed five people with his bare hands—or, rather, bare claws—including Officer John Mulroney of the SCPD. The Claw has returned to Super City twice since then. On his first return four years ago, one of his victims was the superhero known as Herakles. A founding member of the Superior Six, Herakles had recently left the group due to undisclosed differences with his teammates. At the Claw's second return two years ago, his third kill was interrupted by the Bengal, who only managed to drive him off. Counting last night, his death toll has now gone up to fifteen. Chuck?"

"The Claw's return comes at a time when the federal government is considering tougher laws regulating superheroes—or, 'costumed loonies,' as Congressman F. Richard Wert refers to them. The congressman, from the first district in Montana, has authored legislation that will compel anyone who has enhanced abilities to report them to the federal government. At a press conference last night, Congressman Wert had this to say…"

"I know that this isn't the first time a bill like that has gone to the House floor, but I think *this* time it has a good chance of passing.

The situation has gotten out of control, and we need to do something about it before it irretrievably damages the very fabric of our great nation."

"Critics of Congressman Wert's bill point out that it would be difficult to enforce, especially given the limited resources legitimate law-enforcement has to combat enhanced abilities. In addition, Super City would be one of the locales that would bear the brunt of this new legislation, should it pass into law, due to the high concentration of enhanced people in this metropolis and its outlying areas. Mindy?"

"*It's Spectacular, Man!* is a go! The new Broadway musical loosely based on the life and career of Spectacular Man, is finally set to open at the Schubert Theatre in New York City next week. The production has been beset by legal difficulties, as well as last-minute financing problems that almost closed the curtain before it could be raised. Because so little is known about Spectacular Man's life, the playwrights have taken numerous liberties, and that has been the source of the legal problems. While Spectacular Man himself has made no comment, several other people who are portrayed in the play, including wealthy Super City philanthropist Marc McLean, have attempted to get the play stopped. The McLean Foundation owns the trademark to the Superior Six, and also provides financing and marketing for the group. The play stars Tony Award winners Hugh Jackman as Spectacular Man and Terrence Mann as McLean. Chuck?"

"There's still more to come, including Donna Brodsky telling you how to avoid the inter-dimensional portal that opened up on the Goodwin Expressway during the Superior Six's battle with the Pantheon yesterday."

"But first, a commercial break."

6.45am

As soon as Captain Javier Garcia walked up the large brick staircase that led to the front entrance of Super City Police Department Headquarters, the headache started. It never hit him until he approached the door that led to the chaos of the squadroom, and it only occasionally went away when he walked out.

His right hand held a plastic bag with his lunch; in his left was his ZP500 phone, held against his ear as he pretended to listen to his mother. The ZP500—or "Zap," as the ads called it—was the latest model in mobile phones developed by Ms. Terrific. It was a combination phone, PDA, music player, television, radio, eBook reader, Internet browser, GPS, e-mail reader, and personal computer, all at twice the processing speed (and half the price) of anything produced by Apple or Motorola. Garcia mostly only used it for a phone and purposefully ignored the rest of it.

"Yeah, I know all about the Claw, *mami*."

"Well, you be careful, Javy, okay? I worry."

"I know you worry, and I *will* be careful, I promise." He nodded to two uniforms who passed him as he entered. For the life of him, Garcia couldn't remember their names, even though he'd just stared at their name badges as he walked past.

After placing the plastic bag in the refrigerator in the kitchen, which involved cradling the Zap against his shoulder as he shoved other people's brown bags and Tupperware out of the way to clear space, then he squared his shoulders and entered the squadroom. Immediately, *mami*'s words were drowned out by the cacophony of indistinct voices belonging to officers, complainants, perps, lawyers, and whoever-all-else was parading through.

Garcia's goal was to go straight to his office at the other end. However, that way was blocked by the stout form of Sergeant Paula Taylor. Her arms were folded over her expansive chest; glasses, attached to a chain around her neck, were perched menacingly on the bridge of her nose as she peered over them like an elementary school teacher admonishing a recalcitrant student. Taylor wasn't very tall, but she made up for it in breadth. She kept her curly dark hair cut short, giving her the air of someone who didn't take any shit—which, in fact, she didn't. It was a skill she had honed as the single mother of four children, the youngest of whom was now away at college, and which served her very well as the day-shift desk sergeant at SCPD HQ.

When Javier Garcia started feeling stress, he undid the top button of his shirt and loosened his tie. Today, he'd worn a maroon shirt and a dark green tie, and he unbuttoned the former and loosened the latter the minute he saw the look on Taylor's face. Rare was the day he made it all the way to his office with the button fastened.

"*Mami*, I gotta go, I'm at work now, I'll call you later." He ended the call before his mother could tell him "one more thing, Javy!" and stuck the ZP500 in his jacket pocket.

"Y'know," Taylor said, arms still folded, "I think it's cute that you call her Mommy."

"*Mami*—it's Spanish. What's wrong?"

"Why do you think something's wrong?"

"Because you don't stand there with your arms folded like that unless something's wrong."

Taylor nodded. "Yeah. We got a problem in holding."

Garcia closed his eyes and counted to ten in Spanish. "Let's see it," he said after opening them again.

He followed Taylor to the back stairs that led to the basement, where they kept the holding areas. Garcia knew something was odd when he felt a breeze stirring his thinning dark hair—this whole floor was sealed off from the outside.

14

Then he saw the big hole in the wall.

They had a total of four wire-mesh-fenced holding areas down here, all against one of the thick outer walls of the building. Each cell's maximum capacity was about seventy-five people—a hundred if they wanted to give them the rush-hour-on-the-subway feeling. Normally, they didn't have more than twenty per, unless there was a raid or some such.

Each of the other three holding areas had people in them, most of whom looked like they'd been woken out of a sound sleep. Many were grumbling, but at least they weren't directing any invective at Garcia or Taylor. The presence of two uniforms probably had something to do with that, especially since they both had their clubs out and were tapping them into their palms: universal cop language for, "Don't fuck with me."

Garcia counted to ten again. "That ain't gonna be holding much, is it? What happened?"

"Fontaine and Baptiste brought in a DUI. Guy was weaving around on Nantier and running red lights, they pulled him over, and he practically melted the breathalyzer. He had no ID and apparently couldn't remember his name. So they brought him in to sleep it off. I swear, I was actually *reading* Fontaine's report on it when I heard the boom."

Rubbing the bridge of his nose between his thumb and forefinger, Garcia said, "He was a costume."

"Well, either that or he was hidin' a cannon up his ass." Taylor shook her head, and took her glasses off her nose, letting them dangle over her chest by the chain. "According to these other fine, upstanding citizens, he shot a ray-beam of some kind out of his hands, blew the hole in the wall, and walked out. Followed by six other people. I already got their sheets together, and I'll put the word out at roll call for the day shift."

Before Garcia could compliment Taylor on her efficiency, a uniform handed the sergeant several pieces of paper that looked like they'd just been spit out by one of their departmental printers—Garcia knew the smell of their color laser jet anywhere.

Taylor glanced at the papers, then handed them to Garcia, who looked down to see a bald white guy. No, it was more than that—he had no eyebrows, either, and no facial hair. The top of the page read, HIRAM DONEWITZ, A.K.A. THE BOLT.

"According to this," Garcia said as he read over the sheet, "he can fire some kind of coherent light beam out of any pore of his body. Explains why he doesn't have any hair." He looked up at Taylor. "This our guy?"

She nodded.

"Why the hell didn't they use the damps?"

Taylor put her hands on her hips, and Garcia realized she was going to go all mama-bear on him with regards to the uniforms. "It ain't like the fool had any ID on him. He wasn't even wearing his damn costume, what the hell were Fontaine and Baptiste *supposed* to do? All they knew was they got a drunk bald guy."

"Yeah, okay." Garcia sighed. The Enhanced Ability Dampening Restraints, or "damps," were designed by Ms. Terrific to prevent people with enhanced abilities from accessing those abilities. They weren't a hundred percent, but anytime a costume got booked, policy was to put the damps on.

But that policy could only be enacted if the officer in question *knew* the person had enhanced abilities.

Letting that go, Garcia asked, "So we got, what—six half-processed drunks?"

"Seven if you count *him*," Taylor said, indicating the file on the Bolt with her head. "We'll take care of it. What do I do about our new window?"

"Get the usual guy in—y'know, the one with the hair on his nose."

"You know he's gonna overcharge again, right?"

"That's 'cause he does it fast and right. I'm perfectly willing to pay for that with the city's hard-earned money."

"We ain't even halfway through the fiscal year yet, and we're already breakin' the damn budget."

This time Garcia counted backward from ten to one. "Look, Paula, the Claw's back in town. That means we've got half the department chasing his feathers down, plus the other assholes decide to get cocky 'cause they figure we're too busy chasing the Claw, plus there's the copycats. We're gonna need four working holding areas, not three of them and a room with a view. Call Hairy Nose."

Now Taylor put her hands on her hips, which meant she was displeased. "Whatever you say, you're the captain."

Staring at his sergeant, he said, "Any time you want the job, Paula, it's yours."

"*Hell*, no. I wouldn't last a week in your job—dealin' with Dellamonica and the mayor and all that other garbage. I'd tell them all to kiss my ass, and then we'd need another captain."

"It'd be worth it just to have someone say that to them. Some days…" Garcia sighed and turned toward the staircase. "I'm going to my office. Oh, and I'm gonna need a minute during roll call."

"What for?"

Looking over his shoulder as he started upstairs, he called back, "The Claw, what else?"

When Garcia got to the top of the stairs, he braced himself for the onslaught, then pushed open the swinging doors.

Straight ahead of him was the small reception area, which included the big desk that was Taylor's domain—currently it was occupied by her assistant. To the right was the bullpen, where the officers and special units had their desks. To the left was the staircase to the detectives on the second floor. And ahead was a long corridor that eventually ended with Garcia's office.

When he got to the end of that corridor, Garcia saw Merkle sitting at the desk outside his office, a phone at his ear. Merkle was given a uniform even though he was pretty much just a glorified secretary, and was also the living embodiment of *mousy*. Garcia always expected him to be nibbling on cheese and scampering out from under the file cabinets.

As Garcia tried to walk past Merkle, he said, "Uh, hold on, Commissioner."

Great. Garcia gave Merkle a pleading expression, which the officer typically either missed entirely or ignored.

"It's Commissioner Dellamonica on three, sir."

"Of course it is," Garcia said, not knowing or caring if Enzo Dellamonica could hear him. He turned the knob of the door that had the words CAPTAIN JAVIER GARCIA stenciled on the frosted glass window, but the door wouldn't budge. After he forced it open by slamming his shoulder into the door, causing a rattle throughout the corridor and soreness in his shoulder, he added, "And get someone to fix the damn door."

Merkle said, "Maintenance said the door's fine."

"Maintenance can kiss my ass." Shrugging out of his jacket and tossing it on the guest chair, Garcia shoved aside the various papers on his desk and unearthed his phone, touching the button labeled "3" next to the blinking light while picking up the receiver. "Yes, Enzo?"

"Javier, you're killin' me, you know that, right?"

Garcia sighed. Enzo Dellamonica was married to the sister of Giancarlo LaManna, the mob boss, who was now in jail serving consecutive life sentences. The arresting officer of record was Giancarlo's brother-in-law Enzo, and it got him into the commissioner's seat. The fact that the Bengal had dedicated himself to bringing LaManna down and had put the biggest dent into LaManna's activities—one of those life sentences was for the death of a woman the Bengal had sworn to protect—conveniently was left off of the commissioner's press releases.

"How, exactly, am I killing you, Enzo?"

"Don't kid a kidder, Javier. I got the city comptroller crawlin' up my butt. You're already over budget, and the fiscal ain't half over yet. I'm gonna need to cut back on OT, you keep this up."

"Uhm..." Garcia almost dropped the phone. "Enzo, you *do* know the Claw's back, right? I'm gonna need *more* OT, not less."

"Oh, please. The Six'll take care of it. Don't worry about it."

"Don't *worry* about it? Enzo, we've got four bodies that we *know* of, and all the physical evidence and the witnesses are telling us that it's the Claw—which we kinda already knew. We gotta find him, and we need bodies on the street. And it isn't like the Six has caught him any of the other times."

"Don't overdo it, okay? I need to keep the budget down, 'cause once the comptroller's done crawlin' up *my* butt, he's gonna crawl up the mayor's, and then we're both gonna be hip-deep, you know what I'm sayin'?"

With that lovely image, the commissioner hung up. Garcia was torn between anger at being hung up on without getting a chance to get in the last word and relief that he didn't have to talk to him anymore.

Garcia told Merkle to let him know when roll call started, and also to catch any calls. Then he closed the door to his office and sat down, turning his brain off by signing off on some paperwork that needed his initials. He had no idea what he was going to say during roll call, but with the Claw back in town, he had to say *something*.

The phone beeped. "Sir, it's your mother on four."

Great. This time he closed his eyes and counted from eleven to twenty in Spanish. Then he tapped the button labeled "4." "Hi, *mami.*"

8am

Lieutenant Therese Zimmerman had been looking forward to a quiet week.

It had been fairly calm lately. No major blowups, no big murders, no crime sprees beyond the usual. The costumes had more or less been behaving themselves, and things were fairly routine. Of course, "routine" generally meant a ton of work for the detectives she supervised, but it wasn't anything out of the ordinary, or anything they couldn't handle. She'd even managed to get a full night's sleep without the assistance of pharmaceuticals a couple of times.

That all ended when she woke up this morning to see that *News 6 at 6*'s top story was that the Claw was back.

The first thing she had done was call the sergeant in charge of the overnight shift and tear him a new one for not calling her right away. Then she put on her dark red suit, the one that looked good on camera, on the theory that she might be called upon to talk to the press. Javier Garcia was a great police captain, but he gave the world's worst press conferences, so whenever Regina wanted to put a cop on the podium, they usually went to her.

And even if she wasn't going to be on TV, she also had a date tonight, and she hated changing clothes at the office.

She was currently sitting in that office, located on the second floor right over Garcia's on the first. She faced Detectives Peter MacAvoy and Kristin Milewski, who'd caught the Claw case, sitting in the two guest chairs on the other side of her immaculate desk.

MacAvoy, a twenty-nine-year veteran who was counting the milliseconds until he reached his thirty and longed-for retirement, looked haggard. The bags under his eyes had bags under them, his salt-and-pepper hair was all over the place, his rimless glasses were askew on his nose, and he sported a five-o'clock shadow on his craggy cheeks to go with his dark mustache. His suit looked like he'd slept in it. By contrast, Milewski, the newest addition to the Homicide Unit and the only woman, looked perky and ready to run a marathon. Her brown hair was neatly tied back in a ponytail, her blue eyes were bright and alert, and her navy blue pantsuit looked cleanly pressed. They'd spent the entire night at the four crime scenes.

"So," Therese said, "tell me about our victims. Anything in common?"

"Besides being ripped to pieces?" MacAvoy asked. "Not a goddamn thing."

Consulting her notebook, Milewski said, "The two in Simon Valley were Pablo Martinez and Dr. Sophie Ashlyn. Martinez was the one in the alley that O'Malley and Fiorello called in. He's the manager of Paperbacks and Things at 222 Ayers, and he lives four blocks away, so he usually walks home."

Therese blinked. "In that neighborhood?"

MacAvoy shook his head. "The amazing thing is he stayed alive this long."

Peering down at her notebook, Milewski went on: "Last person to see him was one of the clerks when they locked up. She drove home, and offered him a lift, but he said he was okay to walk."

"She was tearin' herself up about not insisting," MacAvoy said. "Also said he didn't have any enemies that she knew about."

"What about Ashlyn?" Therese asked.

"Gynecologist," Milewski said after flipping pages in her notebook. "Was doing a shift at the Severin Free Clinic on 12th and Gaines. She was walking to her car."

"That clinic does abortions," Therese said, recalling several calls there over the years, "so she's probably got a longer list of enemies."

Milewski nodded, and MacAvoy added, "Lady we talked to at the clinic who found the body said she figured it was one of the pro-life thugs that've been harassing them until they saw the Post-It."

Therese scratched her chin. "Check the thugs out. It's probably nothing, but let's be sure."

"No problem," Milewski said.

MacAvoy, though, frowned. "What the hell for, Zim? We *know* this was the Claw. Why waste time with side shit?"

While Therese could have tried to justify her desire to make the lives miserable of people who claimed to be pro-life while harassing and injuring doctors, she had no reason to do so, instead simply saying, "Remind me, Mac, when did detectives start outranking lieutenants?"

"We'll get right on it," Milewski said quickly. "The bodies in Leesfield were Soon-Li Han and Monte Barker. Han was co-owner of a deli on 35th with her husband, Tomo—she was taking out the garbage when she was attacked. Barker was a student at Drake High who was walking up the stoop to his home."

"Tomo Han's in three," MacAvoy said, referring to Interrogation Room #3. "We're waiting on a translator. One of the customers we talked to said *she* was the one who spoke English."

"As for Barker," Milewski said, "his mother was a wreck. We'll talk to her again once she stops screaming."

"Which, at the rate she was going, will be next Christmas," MacAvoy said. "We'll go to the high school in a bit and talk to the kids, too—if nothing else, no teenager's out that late on a Sunday unless he's hanging around with *someone*."

"And they've got nothing in common?" Therese asked, though she realized it was a dumb question—how much crossover would there be among a high school student, a gynecologist, a bookstore manager, and a deli owner?

"Not that we've noticed," Milewski said, "but we'll keep digging. Also—"

"No!" MacAvoy said suddenly, standing up.

"What?" Therese asked.

"I told you," MacAvoy said, "we ain't—"

Milewski ignored him and looked at Therese. "I think we should check with the Superior Six and the Terrific Trio. They've all faced the Claw before, and maybe if we pool our resources—"

"They ain't gonna 'pool' anything," MacAvoy said. "Besides, they don't know shit. It's a waste of time, which is what I told you an hour ago when I told you not to ask *her* about it." That last was with a point of his finger at Therese.

"And he was right," Therese said. "The Six have never cooperated, even when it would do us all some good, and as long as they've got Marc backing them, they have the political clout to stay above it all."

MacAvoy muttered, "And you'd know," which Therese ignored. She'd been dating Marc McLean, one of Super City's wealthiest citizens and the money behind the Superior Six, for months now. It was mostly a good relationship, except for when they argued about this very subject.

"The Trio never shares that kind of intel, either, and with all the toys they've given us, the commissioner and the mayor get cranky when we bother them." Therese looked at Milewski, who was obviously crestfallen. "It's a good idea in theory, but it'll just be a waste of time."

"But, Lieutenant—"

Not wanting Milewski to get fixated on this, Therese changed the subject. "Is there any pattern to the crime scenes? Layout, significant locations, anything?"

MacAvoy shook his head. "The crime-scene geeks are playing with their laptops to be sure, but there's nothing obvious—just like all the other times. Doesn't help that we still don't know *who* the Claw actually *is*."

"No pattern," Milewski said, "no commonalities among the victims, no nothing, Lieutenant, just torn-up bodies."

"Speakin'a which," MacAvoy said, "Soohoo's supervisin' the autopsies his own self."

Therese rolled her eyes. Chief Medical Examiner Ryan Soohoo only roused himself to actually be involved in something so mundane as an autopsy when headlines might be involved. "And what does his royal highness say?"

"Nothin' yet. Did talk to the lab geeks, though. There were feathers on the bodies, like last time, which match the others. They ran the DNA from the feathers through the fancy-ass scanner again, but it *still* doesn't match anybody in the system."

One of the toys that the Terrific Trio had donated to the SCPD was a DNA scanner that was faster and more efficient than that of any other crime lab, which enabled them to process their DNA requests far faster than most other cities.

Shaking her head, Therese said, "So the Claw isn't someone who's been added to the database in the last two years."

"Nope."

A voice from the door said, "You mean we still don't know anything?"

Therese looked up to see Javier Garcia standing in the door.

Milewski rose, standing ramrod straight. "Captain."

MacAvoy just rolled his eyes. "Christ, rook, it's just Javy."

"Thanks for the testimonial, Mac," Garcia said with a smirk. Then he grew serious again. "Kristin, get the pole outta your ass. I need you two working this case, and working it hard. Cover any

angle, no matter how stupid—and close it, 'cause if you don't..."
Garcia trailed off and shook his head.

Wincing, Therese said, "The feds?"

Garcia nodded. "I just got a call from the local field office.
They're calling in an expert profiler and offered up whatever
resources we need."

"Fuck," MacAvoy muttered.

"I don't see the problem," Milewski said. "We can use all the
help we can get."

"Shit," MacAvoy said, "how long you been police? Fibbies
can't find their asses with both hands, and they step in, we lose
the collar."

Milewski shrugged. "When I was in Narcotics, we worked
with the DEA all the time. They were a big help."

"Well, the FBI won't be a help here," Garcia said. "The next
profiler I meet who actually knows what he's talking about will be
the first."

"'Sides," MacAvoy said, "it's bad enough everyone thinks the
costumes do all the police work in this town, last thing we need is
the fibbies comin' in."

"Well, the Claw hasn't crossed state lines that we're aware of,"
Garcia said, tugging on his tie, which Therese knew he only did
when he was angry but didn't want to show it, "so technically, they
can't get involved unless we ask them to. And that isn't happening.
Hell, I'd rather get the costumes involved than the feds."

Milewski perked up. "Sir, actually, I had an idea about that."

Therese felt her cheeks get warm. She said, "Detective, I don't
think—" at the same time that MacAvoy said, "Rook, don't—"

But Milewski barreled forward, ignoring them both. "I think we
should consult the Superior Six and the Terrific Trio. They've already
said they're looking into it, and maybe we can pool our resources."

To Therese's annoyance, Garcia nodded. "It's not a bad idea, actually. Normally, I'd say don't bother, but in about ten minutes, the mayor's gonna call my office, and he's gonna wanna know what progress we've made. I assume that you two just got finished telling Therese that there's nothing at any of the crime scenes that'll help us locate the Claw?"

"Yes, sir," Milewski said. Therese just glared at her.

"Then if I can tell him that we're consulting with the costumes, he'll be able to spin the press conference at eleven. I'll have Erica make appointments for you two to go up to the Six's blimp and Triad Tower. Mind you, it'll be a total waste of time, but at least it'll keep people off our backs for a while." He turned to leave. "Therese, let 'em have anyone you can spare from the squadroom. Don't empty the pantry, but give 'em as many bodies as you can. Feel free to go crazy with OT."

That got MacAvoy's attention. "Really?"

"Yeah. Enjoy it while you can, 'cause Dellamonica's gonna cut the budget to ribbons soon enough, but we gotta get this guy this time." As he stepped over the threshold, he stopped, turned around, and looked right at Milewski, who had an annoyingly self-satisfied look on her face. "Oh, and Kristin?"

"Yes, sir?" she asked eagerly.

Garcia smiled pleasantly as he said, "You do an end-run around Therese like that again, you'll be doing solo foot patrol in Simon Valley at night, understood?"

It was actually worth the little twerp getting her way just so Therese could watch her deflate like a balloon. Therese had championed Milewski being moved up to Homicide after the Pusher's arrest, and she didn't appreciate being repaid this way.

Milewski turned to Therese after Garcia left. "Lieutenant, I'm sorry, but—"

Therese spoke in a tight voice. "Get out of my office now, before I say something *you'll* regret, Detective."

"Yes, ma'am," Milewski said quickly, and she bolted.

MacAvoy hung back. "Sorry 'bout that, Zim, she—"

Shaking her head, Therese waved a hand, her anger already burned to ashes. "Forget it. She's young and stupid. Time'll solve one and being murder police'll solve the other." She grinned. "Why do you think I teamed her up with your cynical ass, Mac?"

Snorting, MacAvoy said, "You just wanted to make retirement look more attractive."

"Is it working?"

Another snort, and MacAvoy left without another word.

Her phone chirped, and she glanced at the caller ID: Marc's office. Smiling, she picked it up. "Hi, Beth," she said, knowing that it would be Marc's assistant. *Heaven forfend the great Marc McLean dial his own damn phone.*

"Hello, Therese. Hold for Mr. McLean, please?"

"Sure." Therese chuckled at the fact that Beth called her by her first name, but still went formal for Marc.

A click and then: "Hello, sweetness."

"Hi, Marc." She had never been able to come up with a nickname for him. Lots of people called him "Mac," but that, to Therese, was the detective who'd just left. "What's up? You're not cancelling dinner, are you?" One of the many stumbling blocks in their relationship—besides the fights over the Superior Six's relationship with law-enforcement—was Marc's tendency to postpone dates. He always made up for it eventually—especially in bed, the man had *amazing* stamina—but it was frustrating.

However, that wasn't a problem this time. "No, we're still good. I wanted to make sure *you* were still on—I heard about the Claw."

"Yeah," Therese said with a sigh of relief, "but I get the feeling I'm gonna *need* the break, the way this day's gonna go. Emmanuelli's at five-thirty, right?"

"The reservations are already made. See you—" Then she heard an all-too-familiar beeping noise. "Darn, I've got to get that. See you tonight, sweetness!"

With that, he hung up, without even waiting for her to reply. That damn ZP500 of his pretty much ruled Marc McLean's life. It drove her crazy.

On the other hand, he said "Darn." Marc *never* used any kind of profanity which, after spending all day being surrounded by cops—arguably the most foul-mouthed subset of humanity—was incredibly endearing.

Therese shrugged, hung up the phone, then looked at the overnight shift's run sheets. That was the one thing about being promoted—the paperwork just metastasized as you went up in rank…

11am

In all the ten years that Charlie Duffy had been covering the mayor's office, he had yet to sit in a comfortable chair.

When he first was given the beat by his editor at the *Super City Gazette*, he'd complained about the flimsiness of the folding chairs to the mayor's press officer, who didn't quite laugh in his face, but came close.

Two mayors and four press officers later, the chairs hadn't gotten any better. Oh, when Aaron Sittler was elected, he put in newer chairs with blue things that were called cushions on them, but they were hard as rocks.

Eventually, though, he came to understand the reality: the reporters weren't wanted. The politicians had to put up with the reporters, of course, because the alternative was that the journalists would all make stuff up, and if it was fiction to be printed or spoken anyhow, it was going to be the mayor's *official* fiction, dammit. But they weren't about to let the reporters actually enjoy the experience of facilitating the first amendment.

Charlie almost liked Sittler. The reporter had never fully liked *any* successful politician, which made a certain sense. You couldn't survive in that world if you weren't an unlikeable asshole, so all the non-assholes tended to wash out pretty quickly. A bunch of years back, Charlie covered the City Council campaign of wealthy philanthropist Marc McLean. McLean was genuinely optimistic and earnest, and really wanted to make the city a better place. His opponents tore him to shreds, of course, and he wound up with only one percent of the vote. After that McLean stuck to the private sector. Charlie was of the considered opinion that McLean did more good throwing money at things like the capes and various charities than he ever would have managed amidst the bribe-takers and mendicants of the City Council.

But Sittler wasn't bad. Unlike the previous two mayors, who seemed to be spending half their time apologizing for the capes, Sittler embraced them. Instead of focusing on the property damage and the insurance claims, he focused on the lives saved and the celebrity that the capes brought to Super City. Plus, Sittler had allowed Charlie to follow his campaign around, giving him full access on the proviso that he not print anything until after the election. That series of articles knocked the *Gazette*'s circulation up ten points and got Charlie several awards. (Though not the Pulitzer, as that went to that hack Branker for his crap piece for the *SC Post* on the Terrific Trio that didn't tell anybody anything about the three capes that they didn't already know. Charlie already had two Pulitzers—one for his exposé on the aliens who had taken over the McLean Foundation, and one for his interview with the last man to call himself Old Glory—but he really wanted the hat trick before he retired.)

As Charlie wiggled uncomfortably in his folding chair, he once again checked his Zap to make sure that everything was working right. For years after his colleagues went over to tape recording, Charlie had continued to jot down his notes, having seen too many tapes get chewed, damaged, or swallowed by recorders and players and just the reality of daily life. He'd seen countless stories ruined by spilled cups of coffee, for crying out loud.

But the digital revolution changed everything. Now he could record everything digitally on his Zap, which could also e-mail the audio file straight to the computer on his desk at the *Gazette*. Charlie's arthritis was such that gripping a pen was increasingly painful, so this new toy pretty much saved his career.

Just as he finished checking the Zap over, the door behind the podium opened, and four people entered: the mayor's press officer, two members of the mayor's security detail, and then finally the perfectly combed blond hair and aquiline nose of Mayor Aaron Sittler.

The press officer walked up to the podium. The press room in City Hall had had the same podium since this place was built in the 1950s, replacing the old City Hall that had been destroyed by the Red Menace. The podium had belonged to the beloved Mayor Vincenzo Colletta, and every mayor since had also used it.

"Ladies and gentlemen, if you'll please be seated."

Everyone took a seat, and shifted around as the chairs went to work on their lower backs. Charlie knew they were all avoiding sitting in the chairs any more than they had to, but Charlie knew it was better to sit early and adjust to the spine-chewing nightmare *before* the press conference started, so you could concentrate.

Even with that, his lower back felt like it was being turned into a pretzel. Charlie wondered how bad it would have been without the aspirin he'd popped an hour ago.

"Thank you. Mayor Aaron Sittler would like to provide a statement, and then he will take a few questions. Mayor Sittler?"

The press officer stepped aside, and Sittler stepped up. The microphone was omnidirectional, so he didn't need to adjust it for his greater height. "Good morning."

Charlie winced. Sittler's tone was much more subdued than usual. Generally, the mayor spoke boisterously, his voice projecting to the cheap seats, as it were. If it weren't required for television, radio, and online recording, Charlie doubted he would have bothered with the microphone.

Today, though, he was much quieter. Charlie supposed he couldn't really blame him.

"As you all know, the Claw has returned to Super City and is once again wreaking havoc on our citizenry. Last night, he claimed his twelfth, thirteenth, fourteenth, and fifteenth victims: Sophie

Ashlyn, Monte Barker, Soon-Li Han, and Pablo Martinez."

Finally, names. Even as the phone's microphone captured the mayor's words, Charlie made a note in a file on the Zap to look up those four. Probably some intern back at the paper was watching the press conference and had already started, but he made the note anyhow. Besides, the first of the names sounded familiar.

When he was done with that, he called up the quote he'd gotten half an hour ago. He was real curious to hear Sittler's reaction to *that.*

Sittler continued. "At the present time, the police are not prepared to announce any arrests. However, our forensic technicians are going over each scene with the proverbial fine-tooth comb. In addition, the case is being handled by two of SCPD's top detectives, Peter MacAvoy, a thirty-year veteran of the department, and Kristin Milewski, whom some of you may recall from the arrest of the drug dealer known as the Pusher last year."

Charlie knew both names. MacAvoy was a pain in the neck who hated reporters. He'd actually decked someone from the *Post* once, which Charlie had always viewed as just good sense. As for Milewski, she had indeed made a name for herself with the Pusher arrest, although from what he'd heard from the reporter who covered the story for the *Gazette*, it was the Bruiser who did most of the work. Charlie hadn't heard that she'd been bumped up to Homicide.

"I'm told that Detectives MacAvoy and Milewski will be consulting extensively with the Superior Six and the Terrific Trio and that they anticipate a quick end to this investigation."

That'll be a first, Charlie thought. The capes didn't "consult" with anyone. Hell, from what he'd heard, the Superior Six barely consulted with each other. They'd kicked out two members over the years, and two had left in very public disputes. One of those last two was Herakles, who soon thereafter became a victim of the Claw. Charlie missed the Justiciars—now *those* were *real* heroes…

"I would only like to add that my heart goes out to the families of all four victims, as well as my promise that we will do everything in our power to bring their killer to justice. Now, then, I'll take a few questions."

Charlie smiled as everyone raised their hands. Only four people were asking questions today, which had already been worked out ahead of time. Charlie knew he would the last of the four—that election piece had made him a favorite of Sittler's, and Charlie had known how to cash in that coin.

Sittler first looked at *News 6 at 6*'s Adriana Berardi, a tall woman with long, dark hair and a nice voice. Scuttlebutt had it she was next in line for an anchor seat. "Adriana?"

"Mr. Mayor, I've been told by a source that the FBI will be involved. Is this true?"

"The Super City field office has opened their doors to us, and also provided a profiler, but we're confident that we can solve this case in-house, as it were."

"So you're saying you don't need the FBI?"

"I don't know that I'd go that far, but I'm confident in the resources that this city can bring to bear on the case."

Charlie smirked. The Claw hadn't crossed state lines, so the feds had no actual jurisdiction. They would have to be asked in, and Charlie couldn't imagine a circumstance under which Enzo Dellamonica would make that request.

Next was John Knoll, whose "Knoll-age" political blog was getting hit rates in the millions. "John?"

"Mr. Mayor, this is the fourth time the Claw has gone on a rampage in Super City. What makes you think this city will be able to handle it better this time?"

"Experience, John. This city has dealt with threats ranging from having the entire city east of the Thomas being encased in a force field and sent into orbit to the coming of Ragnarok in Kirby Park. The Claw isn't our first serial killer—or spree killer, as I'm sure the FBI's profiler would wish correct me. We will be *fine*."

Knoll looked like he wanted to follow up, but the mayor had already moved on to Charlie's biggest competitor, Yvonne Hoffman from the *Post*. "Yvonne?"

"By 'we,' are you referring to the SCPD, or are you referring to Super City's superhero population?"

Ye flipping gods, what a stupid question. And, since she was riffing on the answer to Knoll's question, it meant that Hoffman had either gotten a question spot without having an actual query prepared, or she did have one, and she dropped it for that nonsense.

"I'm referring to the considerable resources of this city, Yvonne. That includes everyone who has chosen to call this city home, whether they be deputized officers of the law or costumed heroes—all of whom put their lives on the line every day to make our city safer. And that will include getting the Claw off the streets once and for all."

Now that he knew his number was up, Charlie actually raised his hand along with everyone else. "One more. Charlie?"

Charlie stood up and held his Zap in front of him for easy reading. "Mr. Mayor, a source on Congressman Wert's staff has said, and I'm quoting here, 'The Claw's continued freedom proves that we need to pass the congressman's registration bill, and quickly, before more people are killed.' Do you have a comment on that?"

Sittler gripped both sides of the podium and looked down for a second, then looked up, shaking his head. "I've never met Mr. Wert, Charlie, but I can't believe that he'd actually use this tragedy to further his own agenda. I hope that source of yours is fired from the congressman's staff posthaste."

Not much chance of that, Charlie thought, since the call he'd gotten had been from Wert himself. He would only give the quote if Charlie attributed it to a staff source.

"As for the quote itself, I'm sure that the congressman's bill makes sense in Montana, which hasn't had any significant super-powered activity in fifty years. But in New York, in Los Angeles, in Chicago, in New Orleans, in Houston, in Atlanta, and especially right here in Super City, I don't see how its passage could possibly help matters. The Claw thinks nothing of murdering innocent people without rhyme or reason, in defiance of our harshest laws. What makes this source of yours think that, should the bill pass, he'd be *more* likely to obey *that* law and register himself?"

Not bad. Charlie hadn't expected that clever an answer. It still avoided the meat of the question, something Charlie fully intended to point out for the op-ed piece that would appear in tomorrow's *Gazette.* After all, a big part of Wert's registration bill included officially deputizing certain cape groups into local police forces. In cases like this, the SCPD wouldn't have to "consult" with the Six or the Trio, they would already *be* an official part of the investigation.

Several more people raised their hands, but Sittler had already headed for the door. "No more questions, ladies and gentlemen," the press officer said. "Thanks!"

Charlie hoisted himself up from the folding chair, feeling the snap-crackle-pop of his spine and knees as he did so. He definitely had plenty of fodder for tomorrow's column.

I just hope that somewhere in all this crap they actually, y'know, catch the guy...

3pm

`Kristin Milewski tried not` to shift uncomfortably in the old wooden chair at the Barker kitchen table. If she did, the chair would creak, and draw attention to her squirming.

But this was agony. She had known intellectually that being murder police meant dealing with grieving relatives on a regular basis, but she hadn't realized how stomach-twisting the process would actually be. When she was in Narcotics, she had to have regular conversations with junkies, which tended to bounce from topic to topic, and it took a certain amount of patience and verbal dexterity to stay even in the same county as the topic. Milewski had figured going from that to the occasional crying mother would be a walk in the park.

Not so much. She and Peter MacAvoy had been sitting with Aimee Barker for half an hour now, and most of what had come out of the latter's mouth had been sobs, punctuated by the occasional platitude regarding what a good boy Monte was.

"I remember last year," she said after blowing her nose for the thousandth time, "he said there were some people comin' 'round the block—they was lookin' for what they called 'street muscle.'"

This was something Milewski knew about. "Henchmen."

MacAvoy looked at her. "You gotta be kidding me."

"Where do you think the bad guys get flunkies to help them out? I saw that in Narcotics all the time. I can't begin to tell you how many CIs I lost 'cause Apollo or the Clone Master or the Pantheon or one of them went on a recruiting drive."

Aimee said, "Well, Monte, he didn't go for that. Some of them boys tried to get him to go, but Monte said no. He was a good boy."

This prompted another crying jag. So far, nothing Aimee told them had been in any way useful, mainly because there was really only one question that mattered. Milewski had already asked it twice, but she gamely hoped the third time was the charm. "Ms. Barker, do you know what your son was doing last night?"

"He—he said he was goin' out with his friends. I don't know which ones—he had a lot of friends, and I couldn't ever keep track of 'em, y'know? Such a good boy. He got great grades, too, did you know that?"

Milewski managed to refrain from pointing out that Aimee'd mentioned his grades enough times that she all but had his transcripts memorized—mostly because MacAvoy spoke first: "Were these friends of his from Drake?"

"I think so. I think he said something about studying, so it was probably some of his classmates."

Another crying jag later, they excused themselves. MacAvoy gave her a business card in case she remembered anything.

As soon as they were outside her apartment door, Milewski let out a long breath. "That was a nightmare."

"Get used to it. Half this job is standing there while women cry their eyes out for two hours."

Milewski looked at MacAvoy with something like disgust. "And back in the real world, men cry, too."

"Sure, sometimes." MacAvoy shrugged. "Mostly, though, it's the chicks who cry in front of you. Men, they wait till you're gone. See, you gotta budget your time—if you're giving a death notice to a woman, make sure you got at least an hour. On the other hand, if it's just a man, you'll be in and out in five minutes. Once you've left, *then* he'll bawl his eyes out."

"That's ridiculous," Milewski said. In her experience, death didn't have any predictable results.

Shrugging, MacAvoy reached into his denim jacket pocket and took out a pack of cigarettes and a lighter. "Fine, don't believe my years of experience. You don't wanna learn, you'll be back in

Narcotics before you know it." MacAvoy stuck a cigarette in his mouth, cupped the front with one hand while lighting it with the other.

They got to their department-issue Chevrolet Malibu, which was parked in front of a hydrant, with their SCPD credentials in the dashboard to avoid towing. Milewski headed to the driver's side, but MacAvoy said, "You're *not* driving. We talked about this."

"What, don't like women drivers?"

MacAvoy puffed smoke out of his mouth. "Spare me the feminista bullshit, okay? The fact that you're a woman is of very little interest to me. Talk to anybody in the squadroom, I always drive. I get in the passenger seat, I get seasick."

"Uh huh." Milewski had been a cop too long to believe that. For her entire career, she'd been listening to the snide remarks. She walked back around to the passenger side. "You think I can't cut it 'cause I'm just a *girrrrl*, right? I only got into Homicide because I blew Dellamonica."

"Actually, the story I heard was that you and Zim had a thing." MacAvoy grinned as he got into the car.

Milewski climbed into the passenger seat, trying to keep the bile down. She'd heard that story, too. "She's not my type."

"Glad to hear it. 'Sides, if you and Zim *did* have a thing, you'd be honor bound to share any pictures with your partner." MacAvoy actually waggled his eyebrows as he said that. "Seriously, though, you could do worse for a rabbi than Zim. I knew her back when she got her gold shield. Not great police, but she knows how to play the game." MacAvoy put down the window—Milewski was willing to put up with him smoking in the car as long as he kept the windows down, though it was right on the edge of it being too chilly to do so—and then pulled out into the traffic on Giacoia Street.

"What's that supposed to mean?" Milewski didn't really know much about Zimmerman, indeed hadn't had any significant encounters with her until she offered Milewski the job in Homicide.

"She caught a call back about ten years ago—the Bruiser brought in a heroin dealer. Problem was, this dealer was the commissioner's nephew."

Milewski's eyes widened. "Dellamonica's nephew's a dealer?"

Shaking his head, MacAvoy said, "No, the commissioner before him. Anyhow, it was made abundantly clear to Zim that it would be good for her career if she buried the case. The nephew was sent to rehab in another state, the press never got wind of it, and Zim kept everything on the down-low. And now she's the youngest lieutenant on the job, and the only woman."

"Well, I didn't blow anybody or suck up to the bosses or anything like that. I'm good police. I worked my *ass* off getting the Pusher busted. I *earned* the promotion."

"Yeah, but you ain't earned the stay yet. And it's got nothin' to do with where your plumbing is. Know who the best murder police I ever worked with was? Missy Howard. Only person in the history of SCPD Homicide to have a hundred percent clearance rate in one year, and she did it twice."

Milewski had been reaching into the glove compartment, where she'd stashed some protein bars. She knew she could easily forget to eat when she was on a case, and her hypoglycemia made that dangerous, so she always stashed some in the glove of whatever Malibu she signed out to forestall that. She never heard of this Missy Howard woman, and said so with her mouth full.

"Before your time. She was me to her you."

Somehow, Milewski parsed that. "She partnered with you when you came up into Homicide?"

"Yeah, and I was as wide-eyed and stupid as you. Thought I

was hot shit, right up until the Jane Williams case."

That Milewski remembered. Jane Williams was a ten-year-old girl who was vaporized in the middle of Nantier Boulevard in front of a dozen witnesses in 1992. There was no noticeable cause, no costume activity in the area. Plenty of theories flew back and forth. Milewski remembered reading that it was on the same spot where the Red Menace killed the first Old Glory back in the 1950s, and also where Amelia Van Helsing had her final battle against Dracula in the 1980s. "That was your case?"

"Howard was the primary, I just backed her up. That was the one that broke her first streak, actually."

"So, if it's not that I'm a woman, what, exactly, is your problem with me, Mac?"

"You're a rookie. You don't know shit. Worse, you *think* you know shit. Right now, you're in the only part of police work where you can't interview the victim. You can't just be a good cop anymore, you have to be a great cop. And the only way to be a great cop is to realize that you're a lousy cop."

Swallowing some more of the depressingly dry protein bar, Milewski said, "That doesn't even make sense."

"Which proves you don't know shit." Cigarette dangling from his mouth, MacAvoy turned onto 40th Street. Drake High was located at the end of the next block. "When that *does* make sense, then you'll be real murder police. Till then, you're just someone with frizzy hair who looks good in a pantsuit."

Unconsciously, Milewski's hand went up to her ponytail. "My hair isn't frizzy."

"Believe what you want." MacAvoy turned the Malibu into the high school parking lot. Milewski noticed that there was already a shrine up for Monte Barker against the chain link fence on the north side of the lot. It consisted of soda bottles full of flowers, a few crosses and rosaries, and a big picture of Monte that looked a lot better than the grisly crime-scene photos she'd been looking at that morning. It was probably a blowup of his yearbook photo.

"This just feels like a waste of time," Milewski said, blowing out a breath as she walked toward the front door, pulling her linen jacket tight. It had gotten colder since they left the squadroom, and she wished she'd brought her leather coat. She also hoped that the school had soda machines or something, as the combination of the protein bar and MacAvoy's smoking had completely dried up her mouth. "It's not like there was a *reason* why this poor kid was targeted. He was just unlucky enough to be the latest victim."

"Prob'ly, but maybe somebody saw something." MacAvoy took one final drag on his cigarette, then dropped it to the pavement, stepping on it. "And it's not like we got anything else to go on. That's the other problem with not getting to interview the victim, you gotta sort through a metric ton of chaff to get to the wheat."

"That's always true," Milewski said as they approached the big metal door.

"Yeah, but it's worse here." MacAvoy grabbed the metal handle and yanked open the door. A security guard directed them down a hallway with a linoleum floor and walls lined with green metal lockers to the principal's office, where they were supposedly expected. To Milewski's relief, there was also a set of vending machines on the way, and she slid a dollar bill in and got a Superior Cola.

"And what if somebody did see something?" Milewski asked after sipping the soda, and suppressing a belch. "All that'll tell us is what we already know: it's the Claw."

"Maybe, but we do what we do."

Milewski snorted. "That's either very Zen or very cliché."

"No reason it can't be both." MacAvoy used his finger to push his glasses further up his nose as they entered the reception area outside the principal's office.

About seven kids, all either African American or Latino, sat there on metal cushioned chairs. They looked uncomfortable and unhappy, which was to be expected, though how much of it was due to the death of a classmate and how much was because they were seated outside the principal's office was an open question.

A hefty Hispanic woman said in a harsh tone, "Can I *help* you?"

Stepping forward Milewski pulled her jacket aside to reveal her gold badge, clipped to her belt. "I'm Detective Milewski, here with Detective MacAvoy. We're supposed to see Principal Pettitte."

The woman's face softened at the sight of their shields. "Just a minute." She picked up the phone on her desk, pushed one button, then said, "The police are here. Okay." She hung up. "He'll be right out."

A moment later, a very short man—Milewski was actually a couple of inches taller—came out from between the large double doors behind the Hispanic woman. Also African American, his face looked ashen, his eyes haunted.

Somehow, Milewski managed not to laugh. She knew Pettitte's name from talking to him on the phone earlier, but it was a great deal funnier now, since that name derived from the French word *petit*, meaning *small*.

"You must be Detective Lovsky," Pettitte said.

"It's 'mah-LOV-skee,'" she said, slowly pronouncing her name as she had been for most of her life, especially to people who insisted on Anglicizing it. "This is my partner, Detective MacAvoy."

Shaking each of their hands in turn, he said, "Thanks for coming. It's such an awful tragedy."

Milewski wondered what the point was of modifying the word *tragedy* with *awful*. Was there really another kind?

Indicating the kids in the chairs, Pettitte said, "These are the people who saw Monte last, Detectives."

MacAvoy glanced at them, then looked at Pettitte. "There somewhere we can talk to each of them in private?"

Pettitte nodded. "Dean Gevlin's out sick all week. You can use her office."

The dean in question had a small office with a big wooden desk that was piled high and deep with papers and a desktop computer that looked like it was at least ten years old, and three guest chairs. MacAvoy quickly arranged the guest chairs so that two of them faced the third, bypassing the dean's desk altogether, which Milewski silently agreed was the wisest course. Meanwhile, Milewski finished off her soda, and tossed the can into the metal garbage can under the dean's desk.

The first kid they talked to was a young man named Alberto Gonzalez, who shrugged a lot. "We just be studyin' over at Frieda's, 'cause her Moms ain't never home. We a study group. We was studyin' for our history test on World War II, and Monte was helpin' us 'member who got hit with them A-bombs, tellin' us it's super-Hiroshima, and that kinda thing, y'know?"

"When did you last see Monte?" MacAvoy asked.

"We was done studyin' around eleven, and Monte just walked home. Didn't see nothin'."

"Where does Frieda live?"

"She at that big building on 37th and Roth."

Next was another boy, Jay Bond, who wouldn't stop looking at the floor.

"What were you doing last night?" Milewski asked.

"Studyin'."

"For what?"

"Hist'ry."

"Where were you studying?"

"Frieda's."

"What was the test on?"

"Second World War. Monte showed us how to 'member Hiroshima."

"You see anything when Monte went back home?"

"Nah."

After that was a girl, LaWanda Jones. "We was studyin', you know, over at Frieda's. Her Moms works all'a time, so we got the whole place to ourselves, you know. Better'n my place, that's for *damn* sure, my Moms is always up in my face."

"What were you studying?"

"History, you know, Mr. Costello's class, which is just crazy, you know. He a kooky man, you know, givin' us weird tests all'a time. We doin' World War II, you know, and Monte was tellin' us how to remember Hiroshima with one'a them demonic devices."

Milewski smiled. "Mnemonic devices, you mean."

"Whatever, you know, helpin' us remember. Worked, too."

"What happened when Monte left?"

"He left, you know, went straight home from Frieda's. I last saw him walkin' down 38th toward Giacoia, and that was it."

Before the next kid came in, Milewski looked at MacAvoy. "So what do you think they were really doing last night?"

Sarcasm dripping from his tone, MacAvoy said, "Studying World War II, obviously."

Then the next one, a girl named Ashanté Till, came in. She gave the same answers as the others, down to Monte's mnemonic device. When she got up to leave, MacAvoy said, "Have Principal Pettitte come in, will you please, Ashanté?"

Nodding, the girl left. The principal came in a minute later. "Yes?"

"Who's left out there?" Milewski asked.

"Frieda Jackson and Corey Robinson."

"Before you send Frieda in, can we see her school records?"

Pettitte nodded. "Sure, I guess. Why, is something wrong?"

Milewski was about to say yes, when MacAvoy cut her off. "No, we just want to verify some things. Procedure stuff."

"Of course." Pettitte walked out.

Turning to MacAvoy, Milewski asked, "What the hell?"

"What the hell what?"

"These kids are *lying*. They're not even lying *well*. And this is a *murder* investigation."

"And these are *kids*," MacAvoy said. "They were probably doing something they weren't supposed to do, using Frieda's mother's neglectful tendencies as a cover. If it was just guys, I'd guess they went to a strip club, but since girls are involved, I'm guessing they were smoking or drinking or shooting something they shouldn't have been."

Milewski blinked several times. MacAvoy seemed to be making her point for her. "And we don't tell the principal this, why, exactly?"

"Because we don't know for sure that what they were doing is any of his business, because this is a murder investigation that's under eight thousand kinds of scrutiny from on high, which means we can't afford to get distracted by side stuff, because school principals always assume the worst, and I'd rather not tell him anything until we know for sure, and because I *said* so, rook."

"If these kids did something illegal, we need to know about it, and so does the principal."

"C'mon, they're just being kids. Experimenting—it's what

being a teenager's all about."

Unable to believe what she was hearing, Milewski said, "Jesus, Mac, you just said they might be going to *strip clubs?* This is *normal?*"

Giving her a pitying look that Milewski just wanted to punch, MacAvoy said, "God, you were one of those uptight girls we always hated in high school, weren't you? Lemme guess, National Honors Society? In the running for valedictorian? On the yearbook?"

Turning away, hoping she wasn't flushing with embarrassment, Milewski said, "So what?"

"I knew it." MacAvoy barked a laugh. "Explains *so* much."

Right at that moment, Milewski wished she hadn't pissed Zimmerman off, because now there was no way she was going to be able to ask to be reassigned a new partner. Whether or not MacAvoy treated her like shit because she was a woman or because she was a rookie or just because he was a flaming asshole, it still boiled down to her being treated like shit, and she was sick and tired of it.

Pettitte came in, then, with a manila folder, which he handed to Milewski. She considered that a minor moral victory.

Opening the file, the first thing she saw was her address, 1220 Roth Street, which would put it right at the corner of 37th Street, just like Alberto said.

"Well, they got the address right." Milewski scanned the file. "Her father's dead—apparently he was in the Conway Building." That got a shudder out of Milewski. The Conway Building had been destroyed by the Brute Squad while it was filled with office workers. Hundreds had died, and the process of identifying all of them was *still* going on. "Mother works two jobs, one of which is at a diner, which explains her not being home on a Sunday night."

MacAvoy frowned, and grabbed the folder out of Milewski's hands.

47

"Hey!"

"Roth and 37th," MacAvoy muttered. "That doesn't make sense. The Jones girl, she said that she saw Monte going down 38th toward Giacoia."

"So what?" Then Milewski thought it through. "Wait, Monte's apartment's on Giacoia and 34th. Why would he go up to 38th first?" She regarded MacAvoy. "Any strip clubs on 38th?"

"How the hell should I know?"

"Well, you're the expert."

"Please." MacAvoy peered at her over the top of his glasses. "When I'm hungry, I don't watch someone cook a steak. If I'm gonna pay for tits, I wanna touch 'em."

Charming. Milewski didn't say that out loud, though, because something was nagging her in the back of the head. "Hang on, remember when we were checking the scenes last night, there was a radio call for CSU for a scene at 38th and Siegel, where that condemned building is?"

"No," MacAvoy said. "And anyhow, that call would've been way after these kids left."

"It was for a costume fight—the Bengal against somebody. That fight started around ten."

Shrugging, MacAvoy said, "If it's about costumes, I'll take your word for it." He grinned, showing teeth gone yellow from smoking. "You're the expert."

"Very funny." She got up and opened the door. Pettitte was sitting outside with two other children; she assumed the girl to be Frieda Jackson. "Frieda, you can come in now."

The girl, who was smaller than any of the others who'd come in, sat down in the chair facing the two detectives. Like Jay Bond, she kept looking at the floor.

Putting on the voice she used with her eight-year-old niece, even though Frieda was a teenager, Milewski asked, "Frieda, what were you and your friends doing last night?"

Frieda looked up for a second and said, "Studying for our history test." Then she looked back down.

"World War II, right?"

Without looking up, Frieda nodded.

"I'm curious, Frieda, did you hear about the fight the Bengal had last night?"

She looked up again. "What?"

"It was right in your neighborhood—that condemned building on Siegel."

In a much quieter voice, Frieda said, "I don't know nothin' about that fight Bengal had with Arachnos."

One of MacAvoy's eyebrows raised. Milewski had to keep from smiling as he asked, "How'd you know he fought Arachnos?"

Defensively, Frieda replied, "You just *said.*"

"No, Frieda, we didn't," Milewski said, thinking, *Sometimes it's too easy.* "Why don't you tell me what you guys really did, okay?"

MacAvoy added, "You won't get in trouble. Whatever you tell us stays between the three of us."

"Among," Frieda said, looking back down at the floor.

"What?" MacAvoy asked, sounding as confused as Milewski felt.

Frieda looked back up at MacAvoy. "If it's three people, it's among, not between."

Now Milewski did smile.

"Fine," MacAvoy said tightly, "it'll stay *among* the three of us."

Frieda looked back down again for several seconds. Just when Milewski feared she had fallen asleep or something, she looked back up, and there was terror in her eyes. "We didn't mean nothin'—we heard the Bengal and Arachnos was throwin' down and we wanted to see! We knew we'd get in trouble if we went to that building—some kids got arrested when they went in there last month—so we all promised we'd say we was studyin'. Monte was the one who came up with that Hiroshima thing, so if anybody asked, that's what we'd say. We said we was at my house, 'cause my Mom's never home. We ain't gonna get in trouble, are we?"

Amazingly, Frieda said all that without taking a breath. Her expression had gotten more terrified as she went on.

"It's okay, Frieda," MacAvoy said. "We're just trying to find out who killed Monte."

"I don't *know*! We didn't see nothin'! I mean, we saw the Bengal, and we saw Arachnos go after him with all those extra arms he got, but then it was gettin' late and LaWanda and Jody had to be gettin' home, so we left. Monte went off home, and that was the last time I saw him, honest!"

MacAvoy and Milewski both assured Frieda several times that they wouldn't tell Pettitte what they'd done. They then brought Corey in, who told the same bullshit story.

"What do you think?" Milewski asked.

"Oh, *now* you care what I think?"

Rolling her eyes, Milewski said, "Come off it, Mac, just tell me what you thought."

"That's rich—you telling *me* to come off it. Real funny." He took off his glasses and wiped them with his tie. "Anyhow, I think this was a waste of time. Doesn't matter if these kids studied, saw two costumes beat each other down, or shot up on heroin, they didn't see anything we give a damn about. So we go to the M.E.'s and see if Soohoo finished the autopsies yet."

"Yeah." Milewski sighed. "Woulda been nice if somebody saw something."

"They didn't," MacAvoy said. "I knew this was a dead end

from the moment the first kid started talking. These are Monte's friends, they weren't about to leave out anything that might find his killer."

Milewski was aghast. "So why'd you keep going?"

He shrugged, putting his glasses back on. "In case I was wrong. 'Sides, I knew they were lying about the studying thing, and I was curious." He walked toward the door. "C'mon, let's get outta this dump. Reminds me too much of when I was a pimply faced kid."

Shaking her head, Milewski followed MacAvoy out, wishing there was some way to get a new partner.

3.45pm

"So she comes up to me, and she's wearing this white tube top that's barely holding in cleavage you could lose a horse in. Hip-hugger jeans that were as far as they could go without giving me cause to arrest her for exposure. And her hair—oh, man, the *hair*."

Detective Bart Billinghurst of the Homicide Unit had the drawer to his desk open. He had been resting his feet on it while leaning back in his creaky metal chair and listening to his partner, Detective Marty "King" Fischer, go on—and on and on—about his sexual exploits. By the time he got to her hair, he had put his feet down, and was now contemplating the department-issue Beretta nine-millimeter pistol inside the drawer.

Looking up at Fischer, Billinghurst said, "Y'know, King, I'm looking down here at my weapon, and I'm trying to figure out what's the best way to use it to put me out of my misery—by shooting myself or shooting you."

"Gimme a break, Bart." Fischer smiled, showing his perfect teeth. It had always driven Billinghurst crazy, seeing Fischer's straight, white, magnificent smile every day while Billinghurst himself had strained the department's dental plan to the limit with a series of gum surgeries, root canals, and fillings.

Fischer went on: "I've literally got *nothing* to do. I'm caught up on paperwork—for, I might add, the first time in my career—and Zim wants us on the phones in case a body falls."

"Yeah." Billinghurst looked around the Homicide section of the detectives' squadroom on the second floor, and it was unusually quiet. Most of the Homicide Unit was out working the Claw case. Having just closed the triple in Leesfield, Fischer and Billinghurst were next up in the rotation.

They had asked Lieutenant Zimmerman what they needed to do—since they figured that MacAvoy and Milewski would need all the help they could get on this red-ball case—but the lieutenant surprised them by telling them to stay on the phones. "I don't want a citizen bitching us out for not closing their loved one's murder because they were unlucky enough to die when we were Claw chasing."

Fischer's main complaint was that it meant they wouldn't be getting the overtime that everyone else was reaping the benefits of. At this point, it didn't matter—in fifteen minutes it would be four o'clock, and they could both go home. Billinghurst planned to pick up the kids from Thelma's. Billinghurst's sister-in-law was house-bound ever since a brick wall fell on her back during a fight between the Terrific Trio and some aliens or other. The Trio's settlement money meant Thelma could afford to stay home (and refurbish her house to make it wheelchair accessible), and she took care of the kids while their parents were at work.

"So anyhow, we talked for a while—she's a dental hygienist. I say to myself, 'what a time to have good teeth.' If I just had crap molars like you, I'd've been in like Flynn."

Billinghurst leaned back, his chair squeaking. "Okay, first of all? Nobody, and I mean *nobody*, says 'in like Flynn' anymore. And secondly, I don't care if this woman was the second coming of Halle Berry, there is no amount of sex in the universe that's worth my dental problems."

"That, my friend, is a sad commentary on your sex life." Again, the perfect smile, which went naturally with his blond hair and blue eyes. When they were first partnered up, Billinghurst had pegged Fischer as *Aryan bastard*, but he was actually good police, and he was only an asshole when pretty women were around.

And even then it was only certain pretty women. He'd learned the hard way that Zim wasn't someone he should be hitting on under any circumstances. Which was why he sat up straighter when she walked over to the desk. Billinghurst leaned forward, straightening his back and making the chair squeak again. He actually had smelled Zimmerman coming before he heard or saw her—she was wearing the Chanel perfume she always put on when she had a date with her socialite boyfriend.

Zimmerman was holding a Post-It in her hand. "Got something for you guys."

Fischer looked at his watch. "It's almost quittin' time, boss. Can't you give it to the next shift?"

"Yeah," Billinghurst said, "I promised Ida I'd pick up the kids today. Besides, she's workin' late, and I don't want Thelma to have to take them half the night."

"Sorry, Bart. This is Super City. I need two detectives on the evening shift doing what you've been doing for the *next* body that falls, with everyone else on the Claw. So you guys gotta get this one."

Billinghurst was about to renew his objection, but Fischer talked first. "We get OT?"

Smiling, Zimmerman said, "*Yes*, you get OT."

Thinking about that trip to Florida that they'd been promising Mikey and Kendra for months, Billinghurst relented. "Yeah, okay, fine."

"Good. Someone called in Amethyst tangling with the Clone Master, and unis just reported a body."

Billinghurst's face fell. "No."

"Yup. It's the Clone Master."

"C'mon, Zim, not *again*, we got him last time."

"Actually, no, Mac and Milewski got him last time—that was Kristin's first case."

Billinghurst put his head in his hands. "Yeah, great way to break her into Homicide, with the nightmare. You can't do this to us, Zim."

"I can and I will. You know the law, boys—a body falls in Super City, Homicide investigates."

Taking the Post-It from Zimmerman, Fischer said, "We're on it, boss, don't worry."

"I knew I could count on you two to follow my direct order," Zimmerman said with a grin. "Now if you'll excuse me, I have to get ready for my date."

Fischer had a grin of his own. "Ah, another hot date with Mr. Clean?" Billinghurst derived a certain satisfaction from the fact that he'd deduced Zimmerman's date with Marc McLean while his partner had had to have it spoon-fed to him.

"Go solve your case, Detective," Zimmerman said coldly, turning on her high heels and heading back to her office.

"You know what I don't get?" Fischer asked.

Billinghurst still had his head in his hands. Zimmerman's perfume continued to linger in the air like rainclouds before a storm. "Probably."

"I don't get why she tries to be so secretive about her love life when she's dating Super City's answer to Donald Trump. She's the only cop who appears on the society pages." Fischer walked over to his desk, which was perpendicular across the aisle from Billinghurst's. "And I don't get why you're pissin' and moanin' about getting OT on a dunker."

"It's not a dunker, King. Dunkers are when somebody's standing over the body holding a smoking gun or a bloody knife. Dunkers are when somebody walks in and says, 'I killed my wife and stuck her in the basement freezer and I'm just sick about it, could you arrest me, please?' Dunkers are when the Bolt fries somebody right under a traffic camera. But when a guy who has about a hundred clones of himself all mind-linked to him, and the one that's currently floating around dies, it's not a dunker, it's just us doing paperwork for no good reason until the next clone shows up to exact revenge for his own murder, and then we wind up with an open case under our names."

Shrugging into his suit jacket, Fischer said, "Yeah, and starting in seven minutes—which is about as long as it should take us to pry a Malibu out of the motor pool—we're getting paid extra to do it. I ain't seein' the downside here."

Billinghurst opened his mouth as if to say something, then closed it again. *Life's too damn short*, he decided. "Forget it." He stood, put on his own suit jacket, then pulled his cell phone out of the inner pocket. "I gotta let Ida and Thelma know what's goin' down."

5.45pm

Emmanuelli's reminded Therese Zimmerman of Florence. She'd first visited that Italian city when she was a teenager, and had been utterly charmed by it, enough to go back four times. Emmanuelli's had the same exposed brick, beautiful landscape paintings, and general continental charm.

She was almost finished with one glass of red wine—a Chianti classico—and was trying to get the waiter's attention to order another when Marc McLean *finally* arrived.

The last trip to Florence a year ago was with Marc. It was over a long weekend, and it was glorious. He'd never been, so she got to show him her favorite places. They'd gone shopping on the Ponte Vecchio, they'd spent all of Sunday at the Uffizi Gallery, and they'd had some amazing dinners.

"Sorry I'm late." He shrugged out of his charcoal pinstriped jacket. He draped it neatly across the back of his chair, then leaned over to kiss Therese. As always, his lips were warm and salty, and the touch of them against hers never failed to calm her.

"Couldn't get a cab?" she asked with a warm smile.

"No, just got held up at the office. Some documents had to go out tonight, and they needed my signature, and—well, call me crazy, but I like to *read* things before I sign my name to them." He seated his six-foot-eight-inch frame, adjusting his glasses and running a hand through his straight dark brown hair. He was wearing an immaculately pressed white shirt and a dark blue tie. Even though he'd run breathlessly into the restaurant, there was no sign of sweat on his person or on the white shirt. His pants, which matched the jacket, were held up by a pair of suspenders the same color as the tie, and he had a clip on one belt loop of his pants that held a Zap.

"You could've called," she said, swallowing the rest of her

wine. "Honestly, every second I'm out of the office right now, I get nervous."

"The Claw?"

"Among other things. We had to kick a guy today that the Cowboy brought in. He was the only witness, and without him, we didn't have—have anything to hold the guy on." She was going to say "we didn't have shit," but even though Marc never objected when other people cursed, she felt funny doing so around him. It was like he had an air of purity around him or something. "The deputy prosecutor had us let him go."

"I'm sure the Cowboy didn't mean any harm," Marc said. "He was just bringing in a criminal."

How did I know he was going to defend the costume? Before she could point out that bringing in a criminal wasn't enough all by itself, there needed to be actual evidence of a crime, the waiter came over, and spoke with an Italian accent. That was another thing Therese liked about this place, all the staff were first- or second-generation Italian. "May I get the gentleman something to drink?"

"Just water," Marc said.

"A bottle of mineral water for the table, perhaps?"

"That'll be fine, yes, please. And I know what I'm going to order."

"Me, too," Therese said, having memorized the menu and heard all the specials long before Marc finally got here. "I'll have *insalata verde* to start, and the salmon special. And another glass of Chianti, please."

"*Si.* And for the gentleman?"

"The same salad, and spaghetti *al pomodoro*," Marc said. Therese smiled, as he always ordered that.

"*Bene. Grazie, signor, signora.*"

The waiter took the menus away, and once he was out of earshot, Therese picked up right where they left off. "The problem, Marc, is that we can't just take the Cowboy's second-hand word for it that the perp did anything. There's some due process involved here. I mean, I *know* this guy's dirty, but the DP needs to be able to *prove* that he's dirty."

"Well, it's too bad, but the Cowboy has done a lot of good for this city. I think that, in the final analysis, that outweighs the occasional problems he might cause."

"What good? Two unis wasted half a day processing this guy, and then the DP wasted an hour of his life deciding that he couldn't bring him to the grand jury, all because your friend can't be bothered to follow procedure."

"He's hardly my friend, Therese. I've only met the man a couple of times."

She was surprised they'd ever met at all. "Really? When?"

"After Herakles left the Six, they had a recruiting drive, and they considered him for membership. But he turned it down. In any case, Therese, it's a dangerous world out there. Sometimes procedure won't work."

"Look," she said, "I get that when aliens invade or the Pantheon holds the city hostage or the Osmium Obliterator blows through town, my guys are overmatched. But this is street-level stuff. We—"

Marc suddenly reached out and grabbed Therese's hand. His fingers were warm and comforting, and suddenly the temper tantrum that she was building to in her rant collapsed like a house of cards. He said, "The Claw's really getting to you, isn't he, sweetness?"

Therese closed her eyes and let out a long breath. "I guess so. I just feel so helpless, you know? I mean, this is the fourth time he's shown up. My guys can't stop him, and neither can the people in tights. There's no kind of pattern to what he does, he just—he just *kills*. Usually sprees and serials have *some* kind of logic—even if it's twisted logic—but this?"

He stared at her with those perfect blue eyes of his and said, "I know."

Suddenly, Therese had a tremendous need to get this dinner over with so she could take him home.

The salads arrived. They ate in companionable silence. Therese found her heart rate slowing down for the first time since she woke up this morning to the *News 6 at 6* report about the Claw.

Then Marc's Zap beeped at the same time that Therese's Zap rang.

They exchanged glances and guilty smiles as each answered. Marc's was a text message. Therese looked at the display and saw that it was one of HQ's trunk lines. She put the rectangular device to her ear. "Zimmerman."

"Lieutenant, it's Sergeant Strange. Milewski and MacAvoy just checked in and said you approved them doing OT. Just wanted to make sure you really approved it."

Zimmerman sighed, feeling her heart rate speed back up. While she appreciated the evening-shift sergeant's attention to detail, interrupting her dinner was going a little overboard. "Darius, they're on the Claw case. There's no more important case anywhere in the city right now."

"That doesn't always mean OT's approved, Lieutenant."

She had to concede that particular point. "Well, it is in this case."

"Thanks, Lieutenant. Sorry to interrupt your dinner."

Not sorry enough, she thought as she disconnected and put the phone back in her purse.

Marc shot her a look. "Uh, Therese—"

"No!" she said a little too loudly, recognizing the pained expression on his face. Several people at surrounding tables whirled to look at her. She smiled sheepishly, then said again more quietly, "No. C'mon, Marc, it's—"

"I'm sorry, but it turns out that some of those documents were printed improperly. I need to go back to the office now and sign them. They *have* to go out tonight, so I have to sign them before the FedEx place closes. I'm *so* sorry."

Therese was about to complain, but it died on her lips. How many dates had he broken or ended early? Florence had been the exception, not the rule, as it was the only time they'd been together for more than twelve hours at a time. He was the head of a huge corporation, responsible for dozens of businesses that the McLean Foundation owned, and that meant he couldn't have much of a social life.

To be fair, her own schedule wasn't exactly full of free time, and there were plenty of occasions when he was available and she was stuck at the office.

But tonight—dammit, she had really wanted a night alone with him, both in and out of bed. Given the day she'd had and the day she was likely to have tomorrow, she needed his calming influence, his surety, his strength. Plus, the out-of-this-world sex would've been *really* beneficial.

However, she just said, "Go. We'll pick this up tomorrow?"

"I can't tomorrow, but definitely Wednesday, okay?"

"Okay," she said, knowing full well that he was likely to break Wednesday's date, too.

He yanked his jacket off the back of the chair and dashed for the door.

She finished her green salad, wondering if it was worth

keeping this relationship up. They got together so rarely, and half the time when they did, they wound up having some variation on the argument they'd just had.

The other half, though, he was sweet and generous and wonderful and solicitous. He was very very good to her when he was able to focus his attention. The four days in Florence were some of the happiest days of her life.

She sighed, and looked over at the window, which was one table away from where she was sitting. Emmanuelli's was located on the second floor of an office building downtown, and she had a view of several other buildings, as well as cars, buses, and taxis slowly moving by on 12th Street. She also saw a streak bisect the night sky—one of the costumes flying through the air. She wondered which one it was, what he or she was up to tonight, and if it was more exciting than eating a green salad alone—or signing misprinted documents before FedEx closed.

7.15pm

`Fatigue hung on Javier` Garcia like a shroud as he initialed the run sheets and the 24-hour reports from his detectives. It was his last duty of the day, a mere twelve hours after his eight-hour shift began. It was the final act he would perform before going home and trying and failing to sleep because he'd be sitting up waiting for the phone to ring. Either he'd get a call telling him that the Claw had been caught, which wasn't very likely, and he didn't expect it, or he'd get one saying that there were several new victims.

The phone on his desk beeped and the tinny sound of Merkle's voice came through the small speaker. "Commissioner on line two, sir."

Garcia sighed and again ran his hands through his hair. He should've known better than to think he'd get away without a final call from one of the bosses.

Letting out a long breath, he picked up the phone, stabbed the pad labeled "2" sharply, and said, "Yes, Enzo?"

"Catch the Claw yet?"

"No."

"What the fuck, Javier?"

Garcia came up short. Back in the day, Dellamonica was as foul-mouthed as any police, but since being elevated to the top cop position, he'd made an effort to, as he put it, "sound like a schoolboy." Of course, most schoolboys Garcia knew cursed like sailors, but the point was, Dellamonica was strictly PG these days.

So this f-bomb was unexpected. "Commissioner?"

"You bitch at me that you need OT, you get the costumes on your side, and it's past the end of the shift, and I have yet to get a call telling me the Claw has been captured."

Clenching his teeth, Garcia said, "I don't have *anything* from the costumes. My secretary left a message with both the Six and the Trio, but we ain't heard back yet."

"Regardless, *Captain*, if you want me to give overtime, I need results."

"Can't get the results without the OT."

"Fuck you, Javier."

With that, the commissioner hung up. Again, Garcia stared at the phone. *Two fucks in one conversation. That may be a record.* The mayor had probably reamed Dellamonica out, so naturally the commissioner kicked it down the line.

After hanging up, the captain rose, yanking his jacket off the back of the guest chair. He always put it there, since if he put it on his own chair, it would fall off. There was a hook on the back of the door, but every time he hung it there he forgot he did, and spent half an hour searching the office for his jacket.

Of course, he'd have noticed it today, since the door was closed. He didn't normally do so, but with the Claw case, the ambient noise in HQ was unusually loud, so Garcia had kept the door shut.

He grabbed the knob and pulled, nearly yanking his arm out of its socket as the door didn't move. Snarling, he pulled again, and this time it opened, allowing him to see Merkle at his desk, reading the sports section of today's *Gazette*. One of the things Garcia admired about Merkle was that he never left until after Garcia did.

"Merkle," he said as he put the jacket on, "call maintenance and tell them that if they don't fix the door, I'm going to send Singh and the EATers to their offices with tear gas."

"Uhm—" Merkle hesitated, no doubt wondering if Garcia really would send the Emergency Action Team to gas the maintenance department.

"Just get them up here to fix my door."

"They say it isn't broken."

"And the mayor says the Superior Six and the Terrific Trio are cooperating with the SCPD on the Claw case. Yet here we are, getting no cooperation from the costumes and with a busted door."

"Yes, sir. I'll call them now. Anything else?"

"Has anyone caught the Claw?"

"Er, no, sir."

"Then I'm going home."

"Good night, sir," Merkle said as he picked up the phone to call maintenance.

"Night," Garcia said as he walked down the hall. As he went through the gauntlet of interrogation rooms, praying that no prosecutors would spring out like jacks-in-the-box to talk about plea bargains, his Zap rang. Fishing it out of his jacket pocket, the display informed him that it was his mother. Sighing, he hit TALK and put the phone to his ear. "Hi, *mami*."

"Have you gone home yet, Javy?"

"I'm actually about to go into the subway, *mami*," he lied, "so I need to cut this short, okay?"

"Why do you leave work so late?"

"There's a serial killer on the loose, *mami*," Garcia said, nodding to a couple of unis. "There's a lot of work."

"You always work late, Javy. You need to keep regular hours. This is why Maria left you."

"*Mami*, Maria left me because she had an affair with a firefighter and he got her pregnant." Garcia regretted the words as soon as he said them, and did not elaborate further, as he was still at HQ. That wasn't something he wanted to broadcast to the cops who worked for him.

"And the only reason she saw this fireman is because you were never home!"

As he walked outside, the cool evening breeze wafting over him, he said, "*Mami*, I'm standing at the top of the subway stairs—I need to go down and get home, okay? I'll talk to you later."

"Okay, Javy."

Dropping the Zap back in his pocket, Garcia nodded to the various unis and detectives he saw as he headed down the brick staircase to the sidewalk of 61st Street. He stopped at the base of the stairs and gazed across the street at the door to Manny's. The urge to have a drink was suddenly *very* powerful. He didn't keep much alcohol in the house—a bottle of Jack Daniel's, a bottle of red wine, a beer or two in the fridge—as he hated to drink alone. Generally, though, he only went into Manny's as part of a large group to celebrate: a birthday, a retirement, a big case going down, something like that.

A sonic boom sounded overhead. Looking up, Garcia saw a blue-and-red streaked afterimage. *There goes Spectacular Man, off to get a cat out of a tree.* Or maybe he had a lead on the Claw.

God knew *somebody* should. Most of Homicide had been pounding the pavement since last night, the lab was working furiously (and, so far, futilely) to try to find a useful piece of physical evidence, politicians were making excuses on the air, and none of the costumes were saying a goddamn thing.

That was the worst part. Usually when there was a crisis on this scale, either you could *see* the costumes in action—the Superior Six fighting the Pantheon over the Thomas River, the Terrific Trio battling the Brute Squad in Kirby Park, the Bruiser beating up the Clone Master on Ayers Street, and so on—or they had their publicity people making statements right, left, and center. The ones that *had* publicity people, anyhow. The Superior Six usually went through four press agents a year, all fresh-faced pretty young women right out of college who used working for costumes as a stepping stone.

Garcia had long since given up keeping track of them.

But today, there was nothing. A vague statement from the Six, nothing from the Terrific Trio or any of the other public heroes.

And it's only a matter of time before the Claw kills someone else. Or he blows town and leaves us holding the bag again.

Deciding that he was going to be an unpleasant drunk, he turned away from Manny's and joined the dozens of other people who were all walking down 61st toward Nantier Boulevard, intending to catch the Silver Line. Garcia had a battered old Toyota Corolla that was comfortable, sturdy, and screamed *middle-aged man's reliable car*—which wasn't great, but it was better than a midlife-crisismobile, which he couldn't afford anyhow.

However, he preferred not to drive into and out of the heart of Super City during the week. Taking a Super Transit Train was faster and easier. Besides, after a long shift (and they were all long shifts, it seemed), driving was more work than he was willing to do to get home.

No, to my apartment. "Home" is the place Maria's living in with her son out in Fingerville. That's the home I bought. The firefighter had left the picture before the third trimester. That had been the worst part of it for Garcia. Maria had destroyed their marriage for a fling with a guy with whom she couldn't manage a long-term relationship.

Since the divorce, he was living in a studio apartment in Woodcrest. It was a decent enough neighborhood, but the rents were low due to it being a popular spot for the Dread Gang to hit. And the building had a basement garage where he could keep his car.

He turned onto Nantier. A wide street, with a tree-lined divider between the westbound and eastbound sides, Garcia always looked up when he reached it, allowing him to see the night sky. It was supposed to be a crescent moon tonight, and Garcia always liked crescent moons.

But the view was blocked by the Superior Six's blimp headquarters, which circled the city. And the other pedestrians kept jostling him and muttering curses as they maneuvered around his standing form.

His shoulders slumped, Garcia continued north on the Nantier Boulevard sidewalk, catching up to and passing the people who jostled him, eventually coming to the stone staircase that led to the STT's 63rd Street station. As he walked down the steps, his eyes passed over four billboards: One encouraging kids to apply for the Terrific Trio Scholarship, designed to help "economically disadvantaged children"—poor kids—go to college. Another for FOX's Monday night television lineup. Then an ad for Sliney and Shalvey, Attorneys-at-Law, who specialized in injury lawsuits against costumes, complete with web site and toll-free number for information about a free consultation. And finally a reminder that there was a Dunkin Donuts in the station.

When he arrived at the station, he approached the turnstile, taking out his ZP500. The turnstile scanned it for his fare. Each Zap had a unique signature—like a barcode, but which Ms. Terrific had insisted in the press release was "more unique," whatever that meant—that linked to the owner's personal information. Among the options was to start an STT account linked to the phone that deducted the fare every time you had your Zap scanned.

One time at Manny's, for Lieutenant Modzeliewski's retirement shindig, Detective MacAvoy went on a lengthy rant about how the Terrific Trio was using the Zaps to gather information about everyone and were planning to use it to take over the world. Someone else—Garcia couldn't remember who, as both he and Mac were pretty drunk at that point—said that that was crazy, the

Trio *stopped* people from taking over the world. Mac just said they were keeping other folks from getting at it ahead of them.

The next morning, Mac denied ever saying that, but Garcia always thought of it whenever he used the Zap.

But he kept using it anyhow.

One advantage of staying late at work was that the worst of the rush-hour crush was past, and so the platform for the Silver Line wasn't packed like sardines, the way it would be at 5.30 or so. Sixty-third Street was a transfer point for the Gold Line, so it was never completely empty.

To his amazement, a Silver Line train pulled in only seconds after he went through the turnstile. He joined the masses lingering near where the doors would be when the train came to a complete stop. Once the train screeched to a halt and the doors whistled open, a surge of humanity poured out, about half heading for the exit, the other half heading to the down escalator that would take them to the Gold Line.

As usual, Garcia felt as if he could just go limp and let the crowd carry him, but instead he shuffled forward with everybody else.

There were no seats available—the people who'd gotten up from them to get off had had their seats taken by the folks remaining in the train—so Garcia immediately did an inventory of the people sitting on the long benches against the walls of the car between the doors. The Silver Line ran under Nantier through Eisnerville, an upscale neighborhood, and Leesfield before reaching Woodcrest and going on to Heckton.

Latino male in battered work clothes. The soonest this guy was getting off was Woodcrest, and more likely in Heckton.

African American teenager wearing Funkmaster T-shirt and jeans with holes in them. Definitely Heckton. Funkmaster came from that neighborhood, and his merchandise had only increased in sales since he was killed by the Hippo four years ago.

Middle-aged Latina woman in an off-the-rack suit, reading the Gazette. Probably getting off with (or near) Garcia in Woodcrest.

Irish American teenagers wearing knockoff Superior Six T-shirts and jewelry, sharing earbuds for their Zap. Almost certainly Woodcrest, which still had a heavy Irish population.

Caucasian male wearing pinstriped suit, listening to music on his Zap, fancy briefcase at his feet. This guy had to be Eisnerville, which began only two stops away.

Garcia stood in front of him.

Sure enough, as the train pulled into the 85th Street station, the man in the pinstriped suit got up, and Garcia easily slid into his seat. Looking up, he saw that every piece of ad space in the car—the long rectangular ads above the windows and the square ones on the walls—was taken up with ads for Superior Soda. There were, naturally, six types—cola, diet cola, cherry cola, root beer, lemon/lime, and orange—each with a different member of the Superior Six holding up a bottle of a different beverage. Each costume was surrounded by a different group of pre-teen kids painstakingly chosen for their ethnic diversity. The images were all taken in Kirby Park, with the very same blimp that had obstructed Garcia's view of the crescent moon in the background.

Garcia was particularly amused to see that one of the six ads had Mercury holding a bottle of Superior Root Beer. Mercury had left the team late last year after retiring due to chronic back issues. He'd been replaced by Suricata. Idly, Garcia wondered how Suricata felt about the fact that she wasn't represented in these ads. He also wondered if Mercury was still getting residuals.

Then he wondered why he cared.

Forty minutes later, he arrived at the Robbins Avenue stop

and got up to leave. To his amusement, the Latina woman and the teenagers sharing the earbuds got off with him.

Climbing the stairs that would bring him to the Nantier Boulevard sidewalk, Garcia felt drained. Usually, when he got home, he decompressed while watching television and eating dinner. If it was Friday or Saturday, he'd have a beer as well. But tonight, he wasn't at all hungry, and he knew if he watched TV he'd just gravitate to the news channels, and they'd all be talking about the Claw and how ineffectual the SCPD had been in capturing him.

No, Garcia decided, *I'm just gonna go to bed. I could use a quiet night, especially since tomorrow will probably be worse than today.*

Walking down Nantier, which was just a simple two-way street without a divider now, he looked up.

Here, he could see the crescent moon.

7.55pm

Kristin Milewski hated coming to the morgue.

It had actually gotten better since she came over to Homicide. When she was in Narcotics, trips to the morgue usually meant the end of a case—someone they were trying to track down would wind up dead, usually because of something only tangentially related to her own case. Her former partner, now retired, had always said that calls to the morgue were the death knell of good drug cases.

Now, though, the morgue visit was when things were getting rolling. True, the real beginning of the case was the crime scene, but it was a medical examiner's declaration that the manner of death was homicide that made it an official case for her.

She still hated coming here, though, because the O'Neil Building that housed the Super City branch of the County Medical Examiner's office was so bland and sterile. Milewski much preferred the brick and wood and glass of police HQ—they gave the structure some character. The O'Neil Building, by contrast, was all plaster and metal and plastic. All the worst elements of your average hospital without any of the redeeming features. She supposed it was a byproduct of their patients all being dead, but it still did nothing to make her want to come back here.

However, in all the times she'd been to the O'Neil Building, she had never once met the Chief Medical Examiner, Ryan Soohoo. Were it not for his frequent television appearances, she wouldn't even know what the man looked like. Of all the autopsy reports she'd read, not a single one contained his signature. On a whim, she'd once done a computer search, and discovered that Soohoo had only performed a dozen autopsies in his fifteen years as chief, all high-profile cases that had a ton of press coverage, and, more often than not, involved the costumes. In fact, his first autopsy was of Gold Star when she was found dead on a rooftop

72

in Woodcrest. As Milewski recalled, they never did find out who killed the heroine.

Seeing Soohoo in person as he walked through the metal swinging doors of the autopsy room into the drab hallway, the first thing Milewski noticed was how *short* he was. On TV, he was always sitting down, and he had excellent posture, so he came across as tall. Now she realized that it was due to his having short legs for his height, that height not exactly being all that. Five-six at the most.

Yanking his latex gloves off with a snap, Soohoo regarded the detective through his slightly slanted brown eyes. "Detectives, what can I do for you?"

"What the hell do you think?" MacAvoy asked before Milewski could give a polite answer—which was pretty much the story of their partnership.

"My autopsy report will be filed by morning. You'll see it when it's routed—"

MacAvoy rolled his eyes to the ceiling. "Seriously, Doc? You're pulling this? We're the primaries in charge of this case."

Soohoo made a clucking noise as he walked down the hallway. "There's a procedure to be followed, Detectives. My report will be filed—"

"Yeah, we *know* that," MacAvoy said, following him. Reluctantly, Milewski did likewise.

"So why are you here bothering me?"

"Same reason detectives are *always* coming down here—to get prelim from the M.E. You'd know that if you actually ever *did* autopsies."

Soohoo turned and regarded MacAvoy with the same look one might give to a bowl of soup in which one had discovered a dead cockroach. "I consider that unlikely, Detective, since *my* medical examiners are trained to never provide information to

SCPD until the *full* report is done."

Again, MacAvoy rolled his eyes. "On what planet—"

Milewski stepped in, unable to bear this any longer. "Doctor Soohoo, I'm sorry, but this is a very important case—"

"Which is the only reason *your* sorry ass is even involved," MacAvoy muttered.

Ignoring him, Milewski continued: "—and we're under considerable pressure to solve it quickly. If you could at least give us *something*."

"Well, I can safely tell you that the manner of death is likely to be homicide, so you will still *have* a case."

With that, Soohoo turned a corner and opened a metal door with a nameplate affixed to the wall next to it that read DR. RYAN SOOHOO, CHIEF MEDICAL EXAMINER. Soohoo opened it, went through, and then slammed it in the detectives' face.

"Good approach, rook."

Milewski whirled on her partner. "Oh, right, 'cause *your* method of insulting him and berating him was really getting good results."

"There are plenty of M.E.s down here I respect. He ain't one of 'em. Five'll getcha ten that the autopsy'll be leaked to *News 6 at 6* or the *Gazette* before it ever makes it to the second floor of HQ."

"If you were so sure of that, why did we even come down here?"

MacAvoy shrugged. "Thought maybe, with four people being dead, including a kid, Soohoo might not've been such a jackass."

Shooting MacAvoy an incredulous look, Milewski asked, "What happened to the whole cynical, pessimistic act?"

Another shrug. "I have my moments of cockeyed optimism. They usually get cured pretty quick, though. Either someone acts like Soohoo or I just drink a lot. Or I talk to you for three seconds. C'mon, let's blow this pop stand."

As soon as they exited into the cool evening air, Milewski's Zap rang. The display indicated that it was HQ.

"Milewski," she said as she put the phone to her ear after pressing TALK.

"Can I speak to Detective Milewski please?" It was Zoey, the evening-shift secretary, and she pronounced it "mill-EW-skee." After all these years, Zoey still didn't recognize Milewski's voice on the phone, and still couldn't pronounce her last name right. She wasn't sure which annoyed her more.

"It's 'ma-LOV-skee.' What is it, Zoey?"

"Oh." Zoey sounded confused for a moment. "You received calls back from both the Superior Six and the Terrific Trio."

"Great."

"Not a hundred percent great. The Trio is off Earth right now, and their receptionist didn't really know when they'd be back on the planet."

Milewski couldn't believe that, with the Claw on the loose, the Terrific Trio thought this was a good time to go to outer space, but she supposed there was a good reason. "And the Six?"

"They've agreed to meet with you and Detective MacAvoy at eight a.m. tomorrow morning."

"As opposed to eight a.m. tomorrow evening?" Milewski asked, slightly snidely.

"Huh?"

MacAvoy cracked a smile. Milewski waved her hand back and forth across her face. "Never mind. Where's the meet?"

"You're to go to the Schwartz Building at 1915 75th Street, fourth floor."

"Got it," Milewski said. "Thanks, Zoey." She ended the call, then looked at MacAvoy. "We actually have an appointment with the Six." She passed on the information.

"I can't believe they keep an office in that dump." MacAvoy shook his head. "Whatever. I think we've officially exhausted everything we can do tonight—especially since, as Doctor Soohoo so snidely reminded us, we don't technically have a case until he waves his magic wand and calls this a homicide. Or, rather, four homicides. So since we've already logged in another four hours of OT—"

Milewski's eyes widened, and she glanced at the display of her Zap, which confirmed that it was just after eight p.m., four hours after their second straight shift ended. "Christ."

"Yeah. Gotta love a red-ball. We both need some shut-eye, so let's dump the Malibu back in the motor pool and head home."

Nodding, Milewski said, "Sounds like a plan. I'll let the sarge know."

As she dialed HQ, MacAvoy headed for the car, which was parked in the tiny lot next to the O'Neil Building. "We've already wasted our time with the victims' nearest and dearest, then wasted time with the M.E. Tomorrow morning, the costumes—it'll be a trifecta of useless!"

With an ease the frankly relieved her, Milewski ignored her partner while she talked to HQ, again wondering how long she'd be in Zimmerman's doghouse before the new partner request would even be considered.

PART TWO
TUESDAY

6am

"Good morning Super City! And welcome to *News 6 at 6*. I'm Chuck Ortiz."

"And I'm Mindy Ling. Later on, we'll tell you about some bad news for the residents of Woodcrest and good news for Kirby Park. We'll also have Ian Michaelson with sports with bad news for the Capes, Debra Fine with weather with good news for sun-worshippers, and Donna Brodsky with traffic with bad news for commuters. But first our top story. Chuck?"

"Thank you, Mindy. The Claw remains at large today, having added gynecologist Dr. Sophie Ashlyn, bookstore manager Pablo Martinez, delicatessen owner Soon-Li Han, and Drake High School student Monte Barker to his list of victims Sunday night. According to a statement by the Superior Six, they are devoting every resource into finding the Claw. A statement by SCPD spokeswoman Regina Dent said much the same thing, which was the same statement given by Mayor Sittler. A statement from Chief Medical Examiner Ryan Soohoo this morning confirmed that the four latest victims were killed by the same method as the previous Claw victims. Seems to me, Mindy, that nobody knows much of anything that we didn't know yesterday."

"So it would seem, Chuck, but at least we made it through the night without anyone else being killed. Drake High is closed today with most of its faculty and student body scheduled to attend the funeral of Monte Barker. Meanwhile, the Severin Free Clinic, where Dr. Ashlyn worked, is surrounded by protestors from pro-life groups who are claiming that Dr. Ashlyn got what she deserved. Chuck?"

"Thanks, Mindy. The reconstruction of the south lawn of Kirby Park looks to be finished ahead of schedule, thanks to a special sod provided by the Terrific Trio. The reopening ceremony is currently scheduled for next Friday at three. It'll be hosted by Governor LaSalle, and include performances by the popular local band known as Yellow Spandex, singer Clay Aiken, and comedian Rondell Sheridan, as well as appearances by Kirby Park's architect, Jacob Kurtzberg, and, from the Terrific Trio, the Flame. Originally scheduled to attend was Super City Capes catcher Cornelius Pascoe, but his leg was broken in a collision at home plate with Evan Longoria during last night's game against the Tampa Bay Rays. Ian will have more on that later on during our *News 6 at 6* sports coverage. Mindy?"

"Thanks, Chuck. There's more to come, including Spectacular Man's fight against the Riders of the Purple Wage, plus Donna Brodsky will tell you how traffic in Woodcrest has been snarled by that very fight."

"But first, a commercial break."

8.10am

Peter MacAvoy was of the opinion that if the Superior Six were really such hot shit, they'd have more up-to-date magazines in their waiting room. *This is worse than my dentist's office, and she's got a copy of* Time *that talks about Dewey defeating Truman.* At least one of the periodicals on the wooden coffee table had ceased publication six months ago.

He idly flipped through a three-month-old copy of *SC Magazine*, having grown bored with staring at the six framed photographs of the current roster of the Six in action that took up all the wall space. The room was disappointingly generic. It could have belonged to anyone: simple elevator to the fourth floor, a brief walk down a hardwood-floored hallway to a metal door with the Six's logo on it. He was buzzed in after identifying himself over a standard intercom, and the bored-looking middle-aged woman with the massive head of hair that looked like it'd been shellacked in place, sitting at the metal reception desk, told him in a dull monotone to have a seat on a battered leather couch that leaned up against a wall that was painted a very unfortunate shade of green.

Somehow he expected more from the "World's Premiere Heroic Team!" as intoned on the old clip of Don LaFontaine, speaking in that distinctive voice of his, that the Six had been using in their television and radio commercials for years. At least the Terrific Trio owned Triad Tower, which was a nice building. In fact, they made it look snazzier every time they rebuilt it. And the Justiciars had been set up in a complex on Colan Island back in the day.

The ugly green walls were covered with the aforementioned photos: Spectacular Man flying past the Romita Building at dawn; Komodo Dragon tussling with one of the Brute Squad on a rooftop, the SC Tower visible in the background; Suricata in the midst of a backflip off a tree in Kirby Park (she was the newest member, so hers was the only one with a pristine frame, the others being chipped or worn); Olorun lifting a Mack truck on Nantier; the Bengal delivering a nasty kick to the Osmium Obliterator; and Starling flying between the spires of the Shuster Bridge.

A buzzing sound startled MacAvoy out of his reverie, only then realizing that he'd read the opening paragraph of an article on the wineries in Miller Valley six times, and that he'd dozed. He shook his swimming head in order to clear it.

The receptionist touched a button. "Yes?"

A tinny voice replied. "Detective Kristin Milewski of the SCPD."

"That's my partner," MacAvoy added.

After fixing MacAvoy with a look that indicated that she'd just as soon swat him like a fly, the receptionist buzzed his partner in.

Milewski entered, looking breathless. She yanked out her earbuds; they were attached to her Zap. MacAvoy had one of those also, but only because Zimmerman insisted. MacAvoy considered it a point of pride that he'd never figured out how to make it play music. Besides, digital recordings didn't sound right to MacAvoy, who was raised on vinyl records. One of his goals for retirement next year was to spend his days listening to his entire Moody Blues collection on his old turntable.

To his partner, he said, "You're late."

"Sorry, they had to divert the Platinum Line. Prism was fighti—"

MacAvoy held up a hand. "I don't care." He turned to the receptionist. "Ma'am, now that we're both here—"

"I'm sorry, Detectives, but until I am told you can go back, you have to remain in the—"

"Fine," MacAvoy said, leaning back on the couch, which made

the leather squeak in a manner that sounded way too much like passing gas. He held up the *SC Magazine* to Milewski, who was moving to sit next to him. "Can I interest you in a three-month-old magazine? I particularly recommend the article on the wines of Miller Valley as a sleep aid."

Milewski barked a laugh and took the magazine. "That's the last thing I need. Slept like a rock last night."

"Really? I'd've thought you'd have been tossing and turning all night."

"Why," Milewski snapped, "because I'm just a *girrrrrl?*"

"No, 'cause when I had my first serial killer, *I* was up all night."

"Yeah, well, I'm not you." Then she broke into a grin. "Also, I have an Ambien prescription."

MacAvoy threw his head back and laughed. "Nice, rook, you've learned one of the first rules of Homicide."

Milewski raised an eyebrow. "Oh?"

"Better living through chemistry. Drugs are your friend."

"Hardly. I came out of Narcotics, remember?" She started flipping through the magazine, then closed it to look at the cover. "Jesus, this really *is* three months old." She tossed it to the table and then looked at MacAvoy. "You shaved. Trying to create a good impression for the costumes?"

MacAvoy's hand went to his shaved (but not smooth; teenage acne had done its damage to his face at a young age) cheek. "Yeah, I figured there might be press. It *is* the Stupid Six, after all, and since the whole point of this nonsense is to make the department look good—"

"You didn't want to look like your usual shitty self?"

Chuckling, MacAvoy said, "Exactly. You take your wiseass pills this morning?"

"Bite me entirely, Mac."

"Hey, I ain't complaining. I like you better this way, honestly."

"Yeah, 'cause your approval was keeping me up at night," Milewski muttered, looking up at the photos.

"But you got Ambien for that, so you're okay," MacAvoy said with a grin. Then he added: "Oh, and did I call it, or what? I checked in with Zimmerman, and Soohoo's autopsy report hasn't made it to HQ yet—but the fucker's already sent out a press release. It got mentioned on *News 6 at 6*, and in the *Gazette* and the *Post*. He's a tool, that guy."

However, Milewski was now staring at the picture of Komodo Dragon. "Wow. That's a great shot. I can't imagine how the photographer managed that one."

"What's the big deal?" MacAvoy asked. "Prob'ly took it from the adjoining roof."

Milewski shook her head. "Couldn't have. That's gotta be the Moore Building they're on—it's the only roof that's got that view of the SC Tower with the courthouse to the left like that."

Squinting at the photo from his seated position, MacAvoy said, "Yeah, okay, I see that."

"Only way to get that shot's to hang out a window on the top floor of the office building across the street—and you can't do it from the roof. You can't get up there." She smiled. "We did surveillance on the Moore Building roof in Narcotics a couple times."

MacAvoy had to admit to being impressed. "Not bad, rook. You almost sounded like a detective there."

Whatever Milewski's retort might have been, it was cut off by another buzzing from the desk, but of a slightly different type. This time the receptionist picked up the phone. "Yes? Okay." She hung up. "You two can go back."

Hauling himself up from the couch, MacAvoy said, "About time." He walked to the only door besides the one that led to the hallway, a big metal door to the right of the reception desk. The woman pushed a button, and a low hum came from the door, which presumably unlocked it. MacAvoy opened it and saw only an empty room. No windows, no other doors, just a featureless square room, no more than twenty feet per side, with blank walls.

Turning back before Milewski could follow him through the door into this empty closet, MacAvoy glared at the receptionist. "What the hell, lady?"

"Please go in and close the door, Detectives. You'll be taken to Six Headquarters."

"Mac, go in," Milewski said.

"But—"

"Just do it." Milewski shoved him through the door and then followed. "It'll be fine."

Stumbling forward from his partner's shove, MacAvoy said, "Christ, what're you—?"

"Mac, shut *up*." Milewski closed the door behind her. The room didn't seem to have any light source, yet MacAvoy could see just fine.

Then whatever the light source *was*, it got brighter, as the room became almost blinding. After only a second, it dimmed again, and MacAvoy had to blink spots out of his eyes. "What the *fuck?*"

"Christ, Mac, don't you know about the Six's teleporter?" Milewski asked as she reopened the door.

MacAvoy slowly walked through, only to find himself in a completely different room from the one he was in before. The walls were painted a cheery bright yellow, there were more seats, all of which were in better shape than the leather couch, and there was a big picture window on one wall.

The view out that window was rivaled only by that which you got at the top of the SC Tower. Milewski ran over to it and stared at it like she was five years old. "Will you look at this *view?*"

However, MacAvoy was more interested in how he got here. "Jesus Christ. I didn't feel a *thing.*"

Without turning to look at him, Milewski asked, "What did you expect?"

"I dunno, but I figured I'd feel *something.* I mean, Christ, we just went from 75th Street to a mile over the skyline in an instant. You'd figure there'd be *something.*"

"Whatever. Look at this *view.*"

MacAvoy didn't bother. The first time he went to the SC Tower as a kid, he threw up. That was the old one that had been blown up by Dr. Destruction, not the new one the Justiciars rebuilt before they disbanded. Since then, he tended to avoid anything that reminded him that he was very high off the ground.

Instead, he looked around the reception area. *Now this is more like it.* Instead of a bunch of framed photos, this had a giant flat-screen TV that scrolled through several high-res images of the Six. Some of them were the photos in the street-level office. Others were artist's renderings, including a painting MacAvoy recognized from the cover of *Rolling Stone* last year.

A pleasant synthetic female voice sounded over a speaker. Unlike the intercom in the office, this sounded like it was coming from someone standing next to MacAvoy. "Welcome to the Superior Six's flying headquarters. Someone will be with you shortly. Please make yourself comfortable."

"You know what I don't get?" MacAvoy asked as he went to sit in the couch—which was not only in better shape, but considerably more comfortable than the one down below.

"Would me saying I don't care stop you from telling me?" Milewski still was staring out the window.

"No."

Now she turned around, smirking at him. "Then what don't you get?"

"These guys have a gadget that can transport you instantly from one place to another with *no* side effects. It obviously works pretty good, since they took us up here with it. Their insurance is probably through the roof. But what I don't get is—why the *hell* don't they market this? That's what the Tiresome Trio does. The Six could bankroll their whole operation just by patenting that thing. Wouldn't even need Zim's boyfriend's big wallet."

Milewski opened her mouth to reply, but then her eyes widened, and her mouth stayed open, making her look like a fish.

Before MacAvoy could point this out to her, a deep voice explained her sudden shock. "I'm afraid we can't do that, Detective."

Turning, MacAvoy saw Spectacular Man.

In pictures, MacAvoy had always thought Spec Man's outfit was silly. A skintight outfit—red top and gloves, blue pants—with a blue mask covering the top of his face and a red cape that matched the shirt, it didn't look like anything a sane person would wear.

But standing there looking at the man himself—freakishly tall, shock of wavy blond hair sticking out from above the mask, cape flowing elegantly behind him, muscles bulging through the outfit—MacAvoy realized that it didn't matter what this guy wore, he'd look *incredibly* intimidating. And the advantage of the outfit was that nobody would mistake him for anyone else. Not that there were a whole lot of stupid-tall guys with muscles like *that*, and who didn't so much walk as *stride...*

Milewski was still all goggle-eyed, so MacAvoy got to his feet and held out a hand. "I'm Detective MacAvoy, and the lady doing the piscine impersonation is my partner, Detective Milewski."

The insult shocked Milewski out of it, and she shot a look at

MacAvoy before saying, "It's a pleasure."

Spectacular Man returned MacAvoy's handshake. His grip was firm, but friendly. The gloves were surprisingly thin, and MacAvoy could feel hands that were smooth and un-callused, which was a neat trick for someone who spent most of his time punching things. *Guess it pays to be invulnerable.*

"The pleasure is mine," Spec Man said. He even sounded like he meant it, which was more than MacAvoy expected.

"Why can't you do that?" MacAvoy asked, breaking the handshake.

"Do what? Oh, you mean market the teleporter? It's alien technology."

Milewski said, "So you can't re-create it?"

"Oh, no, we could—but the design's proprietary. This particular teleporter was given to us three years ago as a gift from a grateful planet that we saved called Zagnar. But if we did as Detective MacAvoy here suggests, we'd be breaking Zagnari law." He smiled, and MacAvoy noted that his teeth were, of course, perfect. "We'd each of us be sentenced to three years in a Zagnari prison."

"That doesn't sound too bad," MacAvoy said.

"Zagnar's rotation around its sun takes a hair under a century, Detective. That prison sentence would be two hundred and ninety-six *Earth* years."

MacAvoy found he had nothing to say to that, so instead he said, "We're here to ask about the Claw."

"Are you two the detectives assigned to the case?"

"Yes," Milewski said, "and we'd appreciate you sharing anything you can about him."

"I'm afraid that there's nothing we can share, Detectives. But I can assure you that the Superior Six are devoting every resource to apprehending the Claw. He won't kill again, I can tell you that."

Christ, he's worse than the City Hall flacks. Aloud, MacAvoy said, "Not to put too fine a point on it, chuckles, but you guys haven't done such a hot job catching this guy in the past. In fact, one of his victims was one of your guys."

"And another was one of yours," Spec Man said, now staring down at MacAvoy, a look that was positively scary, despite the fact that MacAvoy couldn't see his eyes through the mask. "He won't escape our clutches this time."

MacAvoy blinked in astonishment that the costume actually used the word "clutches" in a sentence, but before he could comment, Milewski spoke. "Do you at least have an idea where he—?"

She was interrupted by a voice that sounded from the same all-over-the-place speaker that the voice welcoming them to the blimp came from. "Yo, SM, we've got a call."

Turning, MacAvoy saw that the image on the screen had changed to that of the Bengal. He wore a tiger's head helmet that covered his entire face, save for his mouth, which was visible through the open mouth of the tiger.

"What is it, Bengal?"

"The Brute Squad's tearing up the post office." MacAvoy saw a smile between the tiger teeth. "Guess they're pissed about the price of stamps going up again. The other four are en route."

"I'll be right there," Spec Man said. After the Bengal's image faded, to be replaced by the *Rolling Stone* painting, the hero turned to look at Milewski. "I'm sorry, Detectives, duty calls."

"Funny, how you're 'devoting every resource'," MacAvoy said, "yet you're all taking on the Brute Squad."

"The SCPD is still solving other crimes, yes? Well, we're still handling other cases. You can take the teleporter back to the office, Detectives. We'll let you know when we capture the Claw."

With that, Spectacular Man strode out of the room. *It's like he's exiting stage left in a goddamn Shakespeare play.*

MacAvoy turned to look at his partner. "Well, that was a total waste of time."

Milewski looked like a kid who'd accidentally let go of her balloon and was watching it float away from her. "I don't believe it. I mean, okay, I wasn't expecting us to team up or anything, but—"

"Really?"

"Yes, Mac, *really*. I'm not as stupid as you think I am. But—" She sighed. "I wasn't expecting him to be *quite* that much of a flaming asshole."

9.10am

Paul Fiorello tried and failed to stifle a yawn as one of the Superior Six struck Brute #4, the largest of the six-person Brute Squad, in the jaw. His neck cracked as his head lolled back a bit, and pins and needles went up and down his arms. This always happened when he worked a triple, his body cried out for more sleep—and they were still only in the second of three shifts. Wouldn't have been so bad working Monday night through to Tuesday night if he hadn't spent all of Monday afternoon with Sheila—or was it Gia? Something ending in an A, anyhow. There was a reason why Fiorello tended to refer to whatever woman he was with at any given time as "babe." In any case, she called saying she was lonely and Fiorello just couldn't resist.

Brute #4 went crashing into a (thankfully empty) water tower. The hero who threw the punch was probably Olorun. It was a large African-American man, in any case—and since Olorun was named for a Yoruban god from west Africa, the term "African-American" was even more apropos than usual.

O'Malley chuckled as Fiorello put his hand in front of his mouth. "We keepin' you up, Paulie?"

"Sorry." Fiorello rubbed the grit out of his eyes with his right thumb and forefinger. "Ain't been sleepin' much lately."

O'Malley scowled at him, then. Fiorello knew his partner was self-conscious about Fiorello's successes with women, and so he tried not to rub it in.

Well, not *too* much, anyhow.

Brute #6—the only current female member of the Brute Squad—had the one dressed like a meerkat—was it Suricata?—in a headlock, but then the latter did a backflip that broke the hold. She kicked Brute #6 and sent her careening right toward Fiorello.

He flinched as Brute #6 crashed into the force field that was set up about two feet in front of him, creating a massive light show, but stopping Brute #6 as readily as a brick wall might have. The air crackled and started to smell of ozone.

Two weeks ago, Bennett, one of the lab geeks, came into roll call and excitedly demo'd the FF36—a force field generator, which was to be used for crowd control. The generator was a gift from the Terrific Trio, created by Ms. Terrific based on some extra-dimensional technology, or so she said. Bennett had downplayed that, trying to make as if he'd invented it, but everyone knew he had trouble operating the coffee maker in the lab, much less coming up with something like this.

Each cruiser was issued an FF36, and the one belonging to Unit 2202 was on the sidewalk of 12th Street about half a yard from Fiorello's feet. It projected an energy field of some kind that turned the air around the massive edifice of the Super City Post Office an orange color. Baptiste and Fontaine were across the street with their own FF36.

Some days, Fiorello wondered what happened to FF1 through FF35.

Behind Fiorello and O'Malley across 12th was a phalanx of blue-and-whites, which formed a more visible barricade to keep the general public away from the FF36s—which were expensive to maintain and difficult to replace—as well as another step removed from the fighting.

"What," O'Malley said at Fiorello's flinch, "you don't trust the gadget?"

"Says the guy who always gives me shit about using the damps."

"That's 'cause the damps don't always *work*. But this contraption's worked okay every time."

"Hope so," Fiorello said as Brute #6 took two ray-guns out of holsters at her side. He hadn't even noticed the black holsters on the brute's all-black costume. The only way you could tell them all apart was the number stenciled on the foreheads of their face masks. Fiorello would've found them ridiculous if they hadn't proven to be so dangerous over the years.

O'Malley stared at him. "You okay, Paulie?"

Fiorello shook off another yawn. "Yeah, just hate working days. Don't get me wrong, the OT's great, but I really could use some sleep, y'know?"

"Yeah, well, try sleeping alone some time. Might work wonders."

Fiorello just gave him the finger, even as Spectacular Man grabbed Brute #2 by the arm and tossed him right into Brute #6, who—up until having one of her teammates thrown at her—had the hero who looked like a bird lined up in the sights of her ray-guns. The impact spoiled #6's shot, and her ray-beam fired at a metal trash can on the corner of 12th and Kurtzman.

The can glowed and turned into a pile of ash.

The two brutes crashed into the force field, and this time there was a beeping noise and sparks flying from the FF36.

Then the air stopped being orange.

"Oh, that's bad." Fiorello heard a clunking sound behind him—it sounded like something hitting off one of the cruisers. He whirled around, but didn't see anything.

The air near Baptiste and Fontaine across the street was still orange, so it was just their unit. Fiorello was trying to remember what Bennett's instructions were for shoring up the force field, and he was about to call out to Fontaine to ask her.

But then, a second later, the beeping stopped and the air turned orange again. The two brutes got up, shook it off, and ran back into the fray.

"Looks like it's okay," O'Malley said. "We better give this back to Bennett when we get back to the house, though."

"Yeah."

O'Malley frowned. "Hey, the girl—number six."

Fiorello gave him a sidelong glance. "You find dirty pics'a *her* online, too?"

"No, I mean *look* at her. She only has one ray-gun. What happened to the other one?"

"Who the hell knows? And who the hell cares? The Six'll take care of it, and then we can get dinner."

Staring at his partner, O'Malley said, "It's still morning."

Fiorello shrugged. "We been on for ten hours, far as I'm concerned, it's dinner."

"We're still going to need to turn in our FF36."

"Whatever." Right now, he just wanted to head to the diner so they could get some food—and coffee. Lots and lots of coffee.

Looking up, Fiorello saw that Brute #1 was about to get the drop on the guy in the bird suit. "Jesus, fly out of the way!"

"You think he can hear you?" O'Malley asked with a laugh.

Spectacular Man flew in to grab Brute #1 before he could cause any harm.

Fiorello shook his head. "That's the second time one of the Brutes almost took the bird guy out."

"That's Starling," O'Malley said in the long-suffering voice he always used when he corrected Fiorello about the costumes. Fiorello figured that he didn't need to keep track of them, since O'Malley did anyhow, but that didn't stop O'Malley from being an asshole about it.

"Right, him. You think he's off his game or something?"

"Who the hell knows? Whaddaya expect from someone named after a wussy little bird like that?"

"I think that means he's lithe and athletic and stuff. I mean, c'mon, he's not about to call himself 'the Pigeon.' People actually *like* starlings."

Spitting on the pavement, O'Malley said, "All starlings're good for is annoying Puck."

Komodo Dragon took down two of the brutes as Fiorello chuckled at his partner. "I thought your dog was named Scooter."

"That's the mastiff. Puck's the golden retriever."

"Wait, I thought it was a keeshond."

"No, that's Murphy."

"And people wonder why you can't get laid." Fiorello shook his head. "You're like those crazy old cat ladies, except with dogs."

O'Malley glared at his partner. "And I'm a guy."

"Eh." Fiorello made a *mezza-mezza* gesture with his hand, which prompted O'Malley to give *him* the finger.

"Nice to see you two playing nice, still," came a voice from behind Fiorello.

Turning around, Fiorello saw Charlie Duffy, the elderly reporter from the *Gazette*, walking toward them. A protest died on his lips—every uniform on the SCPD knew Duffy, and he could get through any police barricade if he wanted to. The journalist was wearing a beige windbreaker, a shirt that had stopped being in fashion during the Nixon Administration, and khakis. A cigarette dangled from his thin lips.

O'Malley coughed. "Those things will kill you, you know."

Duffy grinned, showing perfect white dentures. "That's what my doctor told me when I went into his office with a cough—in 1987. So what're you two doing back on day-shift?"

"We ain't," Fiorello said, "we're doin' a triple."

"The Claw?"

Fiorello nodded. O'Malley asked, "Since when're you chasin' capes?"

"I'm not. I just came from the mayor's presser, and was headin' back to the office to file." He pointed at the tableau, specifically at the Bengal and the meerkat woman making short work of Brutes #2 and 5. "But the road's blocked."

"Don't you just e-mail the story in?" Fiorello asked.

That elicited a snort from O'Malley. "Duffy here's old-school. Bet he types everything on a Winchester."

"That's a rifle, numbnuts," Duffy said with a snort. "You mean a Remington."

Fiorello laughed. It was nice to see someone correct O'Malley for a change.

"Anyhow, paper ain't payin' for laptops no more—budget cuts—and I can't type on those damn things anyhow, the keys're too small. So I gotta use the desktop in the office." Duffy shook his head. "Assuming I ever get there. Hey, I gotta question for you."

Before Fiorello could say anything, O'Malley asked, "On the record or off?"

Duffy waved his hand dismissively. "Off. This is just personal curiosity. The Six said they were devoting 'every resource' to finding the Claw."

"Yeah?" Fiorello wondered where the reporter was going with this.

"Well, there's only six of 'em. It's in the name and everything. And all six of 'em are beatin' up the Brute Squad, which means 'every resource' is out here on 12th Street punching out folks in numbered black suits."

"What's your question?" O'Malley asked.

"Do they even give a shit about the Claw?"

Fiorello found that he didn't have an answer.

12.15pm

Officer Mara Fontaine stared down at the sad-looking hamburger that had been served on a chipped and cracked plate. The bun was misshapen, bits of the burger were flaking off on the ends, and the one pickle she could see poking out from the bun wasn't really the right shade of green.

Looking across the Formica table at her partner, she asked, "Remind me, why do we keep coming back here?"

Grinning widely, Officer Trevor Baptiste picked up his own burger and said with his slightly accented voice, "Because we both have to save money, and the food here is cheap."

"And we definitely get what we pay for." Fontaine grabbed the plastic ketchup bottle with one hand while she lifted the malformed top bun off with the other. The former action unearthed a giant cockroach, which proceeded to skitter away toward Baptiste's side and then disappeared under the table. At this point, Fontaine felt that it was a show of progress in the diner's pest-control policies that there was just the one roach instead of a colony of them under the ketchup bottle. In fact, she found a new health-code violation every time she walked into this dump, and she only didn't report them because then she and Baptiste would have to find *another* cheap place to have lunch.

And, sadly, Baptiste was correct—both of them needed to pinch their pennies. Fontaine had been married to an architect who couldn't keep it in his pants. Unfortunately, one of the many women he banged was his lawyer, and she got him a great deal in the divorce: no alimony, and minimal child support, which the bastard only occasionally paid. All Fontaine's spare cash went into her daughter Rhonda—either for her current needs or into a savings account for her eventual college tuition.

The burger looked worse without the bun in the way—the one

piece of onion could've been mistaken for a straw wrapper—and she quickly covered it with the condiment.

After chewing and swallowing a bite of his own burger, Baptiste said, "And you are changing the subject."

"I'm not changing the subject," Fontaine said, even though she was, "I'm just tired of the argument." She chewed on the burger, trying to focus on the ketchup over the cardboard-like quality of the bun and burger.

"Ah, so you are conceding it then? That Mercury would lose to Spectacular Man in a foot race?"

Her mouth full of burger, she said, "No, I'm not sayin' that!" She chewed and swallowed, then added: "Mercury's whole thing is speed. Spec Man, he does about twelve different things, and being super-fast isn't even the most important."

"Yes, but, Spectacular Man, he—well, he's *Spectacular Man*."

Fontaine washed down her burger with a Superior Diet Cola that tasted way too syrupy—the fountain was obviously wonky again, and without enough carbonation to cut the syrup, she was worried she'd spend the rest of the shift with a stomach ache. "You can say his name all you want. Mercury, all he *does* is run, which means not only does he have the ability, but also the *practice*. I mean, if Spec Man was flying, then yeah, maybe he beats Merc, but in a foot race? No contest. Spec Man almost never actually runs anywhere."

Before Baptiste could respond, the distinct tones of "Proud Mary" came from his chest, which meant his cell phone was ringing. He pulled the cheap fliptop out of his shirt pocket and stared at the small display.

His usually happy face darkened. "Jesus shit. It's Elaine."

Elaine Florio was a lawyer, representing Baptiste in his attempt to get the insurance money from his wife's death. Sylvia Baptiste had gone to the Conway Building for a job interview when the Brute Squad had destroyed it. Since she wasn't a registered employee, they had no real proof that she was in the building when it was vaporized, since the guest register was disintegrated with the building. The insurance company—which had been hit with dozens of nuisance suits from people who didn't have relatives in the building, but sued on the theory that there was no proof either way and it was worth the risk—had made a blanket decision to offer no settlements on such suits. Unfortunately, that screwed Baptiste.

Elaine had been kind about occasionally letting Baptiste slide on billing her, but she had to make a living, too, and the legal action was very expensive.

Which was why they were eating in Janson's. It was your classic hole-in-the-wall diner, with barely enough space to accommodate the four tables, diner-style counter, and tiny grill.

She regarded her burger with disdain. *Maybe I can brown-bag it for a while.*

Her own cell, a used smartphone she'd gotten off eBay, then rang with the theme song from *Super Scooter's Dog House.* Hosted by a talking, super-powered Golden Retriever who'd protected Leesfield until he turned seven and got too old for it, it was Rhonda's favorite TV show, which was why Fontaine had chosen it for the ringtone when she got a call from her house phone.

"Yes, Yasmin?"

The Trinidadian babysitter said, "I am very sorry, Miss Mara, but Rhonda wants to speak to you. I know you do not like to be bothered while at work, but—"

"Of course, Yasmin."

Rhonda's voice came on. "Hi, Mommy! I wanna have a Six-cicle!"

Fontaine sighed. Rhonda had gotten good grades on her last report card, and Fontaine had rewarded her yesterday with a box of Six-cicles—a half-dozen popsicles in the shapes of the heads of the members of the Superior Six. She had already eaten the Komodo Dragon one, which was her favorite thanks to that heroine's lizard-shaped helmet being the shape of the ice cream bar.

"You know the rules, Rhonda-bear. If you have one now, you can't have one for dessert after supper tonight. It's only one per day."

"I know, Mommy, but I want it now."

Another sigh. "Okay, but I don't want to hear any complaints tonight when you can't have one for dessert."

"I won't, Mommy, I *promise*."

"I'm holding you to that. Now I gotta get back to work, all righty?" That wasn't really true, since they were still at lunch, but she wanted to be off the phone when Baptiste was done with his call. She suspected he'd need the support.

"All righty, Mommy."

"I love you lots."

"I love you more than lots!"

Baptiste was still on his call when she ended hers, so she spent the next few minutes choking down her burger. By the time she polished it off, Baptiste had finally closed his phone. His entire side of the conversation had consisted of the word "Okay."

"Everything all right?" Fontaine asked as Baptiste put his phone back in his shirt pocket. She took another sip of the syrupy soda, then abandoned the cup half-full.

"As well as can be expected." He ate the rest of his burger in one bite. "Shall we?"

They each threw five-dollar bills on the table, which covered their burgers, sodas, and a decent tip for Eunice, their waitress.

"Take care, Officers," Eunice said as they headed to the dirty glass door.

"Bye Eunice," Fontaine said. Then she elbowed Baptiste in the ribs.

"Oh, uh, take care, Eunice," he said after shaking his head a few times, as if coming out of a daze.

Moving to the driver's side, Fontaine asked, "What is it, Trevor?" Between forgetting to say goodbye to Eunice and not even asking about Rhonda—which he always did when she called—she knew that the news from Elaine hadn't been good.

"Nothing." At Fontaine's dubious look, he added, "Nothing new, in any event. The expert witness Elaine had secured has withdrawn. Apparently, he's taken a job working for the Terrific Trio, and part of his employment contract is that he cannot testify in cases involving supers."

Fontaine frowned as she climbed into the blue-and-white. "But your case doesn't involve them, it's against the insurance company."

"Apparently, it's close enough. So we need to find another expert to testify." Baptiste sighed as he squeezed into the passenger side.

Sighing, Fontaine turned the ignition on and pulled out into the sparse traffic on 19th Street. Her stomach felt like it had a rock in it, and she made a mental note to make sure the fountain was fixed *before* ordering a soda tomorrow. Or maybe switching to iced tea.

"You wanna let PCD know we're back on?" Fontaine asked.

Again shaking his head, Baptiste said, "Yes, of course." He grabbed the radio. "PCD, this is Unit 2205, signal 2. Our signal 63 is done."

"PCD roger. Hope the meal didn't suck too badly."

Fontaine chuckled. Joe was on dispatch duty again, it seemed.

Baptiste also smiled, though it was more subdued than his usual. "It was edible, PCD—2205 out."

As Fontaine proceeded down 19th, she said, "Look, you gonna be okay with the bills? 'Cause I've got some money saved up, and I can—"

"No chance, Mara. You need that money for Rhonda's college."

"She's not going to college for another eleven years, and it'll just be a loan."

"What if I cannot pay it back? No, Mara, I will not do tha—"

"All units, all units, signal 10, signal 10—the Claw has been sighted by Unit 2202 in the alley of the 4400 block of Esposito, between 21st and 22nd. Any units in the vicinity, please respond immediately."

Esposito was the next block over. Fontaine immediately stabbed the button that would activate their siren while Baptiste spoke into the radio. "Unit 2205, signal 4, proceeding west on 19th toward Esposito."

"Roger, 2205—move your asses."

Fontaine weaved around the cars on the road, only some of whom had the brains to get out of their way, then made a hard right onto Esposito, the tires squealing. As she blew through the red light on 20th, she could hear another siren growing closer, figuring that to be O'Malley and Fiorello, who had unit 2202. The two of them had only just gone back on the street after taking their defective FF36 back to HQ about ten minutes ago, based on their reporting in to PCD. *They must've seen him as soon as they hit the road.*

Once she crossed the intersection at 21st, she saw a cruiser with both doors open, sirens wailing, but no occupants, parked diagonally in front of the mouth of the alley. Fontaine yanked their cruiser to the right, forming a V with 2202.

Baptiste leapt out of the car while Fontaine un-holstered her weapon and waited a second for Baptiste to say, "Clear."

Then she climbed out of the car, ignoring the stabbing pain in her belly from the damn soda, pointing her Beretta straight ahead, trying not to think about what would happen to Rhonda if she caught a bullet. Every time she un-holstered her weapon, she had that thought; every time, she convinced herself that her ex would take care of her.

Sometimes, she even believed it.

She couldn't see anything in the mouth of the alley, but it stretched all the way to Simonson, and she could only see about ten feet in. The alley was covered about ten feet off the ground with a horizontal chicken-wire fence, no doubt put there to protect the alley's contents from the many things that tended to fall out of the Super City sky.

She couldn't hear anything, but with two cars' worth of sirens blaring, they'd never—

A clanking noise interrupted that thought, followed by a shout that Fontaine was pretty sure was O'Malley's voice. After that was a sound like the air was being sizzled.

"That was a ray-beam," Fontaine said as she and Baptiste slowly approached the mouth of the alley.

"The Claw does not use ray-beams."

"Thank you, Captain Obvious." Fontaine kept her eyes on the alley, but she still couldn't see anything. "Maybe it's a super trying to help."

Slowly, they moved down the alley, weapons pointed straight ahead. Baptiste took the lead, Fontaine staying a few feet behind him, covering him. The alley smelled of day-old garbage and urine. Fontaine noticed a cardboard box with a torn, ratty sleeping bag on top of it. This probably was some homeless guy's hangout, and either he was off panhandling, or had been scared off by whatever was going on up ahead.

As they got closer, she heard O'Malley's voice more distinctly this time. "Watch out, you stupid fuck!"

"Worry not, Officers, I will handle this miscreant!" said another voice that sounded filtered through metal.

Oh, crap. The pain in her stomach worsened, but it had nothing to do with bad diet soda.

Stepping around a Dumpster, Fontaine saw the tableau that had unfolded at the far end of the alley: Fiorello down on the ground, looking stunned (though his hair *still* wasn't mussed), O'Malley standing with his weapon pointed ahead at a figure wearing a rust-covered suit of blue-and-silver armor that covered him head to toe. The latter figure was also carrying a metal lance that glowed at the tip. The wall of the building that made up the alley's north side had scorched brick in a perfect circle.

This was Knight Dude, a self-proclaimed super who was in actuality a second-rate inventor named Englebert Valentine. He dressed in faux-medieval armor and attempted to be a hero. His lance did indeed fire a ray-beam, and it usually resulted in a scorch mark like the one on the brick wall.

Cowering in a corner was a figure that walked upright like a human, but had the wings and head of a bird—and was also covered in feathers. The wings ran from his arms to his back, and his face formed a beak rather than a nose and mouth. The fingers of his hand curled into sharp talons.

In and of itself, the Claw didn't look like all that. Fontaine had seen dozens of stranger looking sights than a half-human, half-bird.

But then she saw the eyes. The crazy, watery, yellow eyes.

Fontaine was very grateful for the chicken-wire "ceiling" of the alley, as it kept the Claw from making an aerial escape.

After his rather unorthodox use of the word *miscreant* in a sentence, Knight Dude raised his lance to point it at the Claw, only to lose his grip on it, catch it halfway down the haft instead of at the handle, struggle with it, and allow the hilt to smack O'Malley in the chin.

If it wasn't for the blood that flew out of O'Malley's mouth, Fontaine might have found it humorous. Besides, Fiorello was likely put down in much the same way.

"Englebert," she said, "drop the lance *now!*"

"What?" Knight Dude turned around in surprise, did so too fast and lost his balance, and fell to the ground in a clanking heap, his lance clattering to the pavement as well.

When the hilt smacked against the asphalt, the tip glowed and Fontaine again heard the air-sizzling sound. A beam of light shot out of the tip, this time slicing through the chicken wire.

"That wasn't what I meant," Fontaine muttered even as the Claw spread his wings.

"Jesus shit," Baptiste muttered and squeezed the trigger of his weapon.

A second later, Fontaine did likewise, but it was already too late. Before Baptiste could throw his shot, the Claw had swooped upward through the newly made hole.

Both Baptiste and Fontaine fired into the sky, but the Claw continued to fly away.

She ran out the other end of the alley onto Simonson, but soon lost him.

"Dammit!"

Turning back, she saw that Baptiste was checking on Fiorello— O'Malley was already on his feet, hand massaging his jaw.

Fontaine grabbed her radio, wincing in her pain as her stomach ache sharpened. "PCD, this is Unit 2205. Signal 89—suspect has fled the scene by air."

"Roger that, Unit 2205. All units, the Claw is now airborne, flying away from the 4400 block of Esposito between 21st and 22nd. Unit 2205, you need a signal 54?"

Baptiste looked over at her as he helped Fiorello to his feet and shook his head. They didn't need an ambulance.

"Negative, PCD," she said. "We do have a signal 12, though—*not* the suspect." She stared daggers at Knight Dude, who was trying and failing to get to his feet, and making a horrible racket as he did so. "A—a *citizen* who got in our fucking way."

"So let me get this straight. There were *four* cops in an *enclosed* alley, and precisely *none* of you were able to slap the bracelets on our suspect?"

Kristin Milewski hadn't known Peter MacAvoy all that long, but there were several things she had learned in their short acquaintance. He was an unpleasant, foul-mouthed, boorish ass. He smoked too much on duty and drank too much off it. He was, much as she hated to admit it, good police and knew what he was doing. He also *knew* he was good police and liked to rub her nose in it as much as he possibly could.

And he also never, ever chewed out other cops. That just wasn't done.

So to see him ripping into Paulie Fiorello right now had her very confused.

They were sitting in the video room. Anybody who'd ever watched a TV show knew about the one-way glass that acted as a mirror in interrogation rooms. SCPD, therefore, like many other metropolitan police forces, dispensed with the subterfuge and just installed video cameras. All five of them fed to a monitor in the video room, which had a battered leather couch, two easy chairs that were scratched and ripped, and a rocking chair that squeaked loud enough to wake the dead.

Fiorello and his perfect hair were seated in one of the easy chairs, with Milewski on one of the couches. MacAvoy, though, was pacing back and forth, gesticulating like crazy. It was a side of MacAvoy she'd never seen, and—like most of his sides, truth be known—one she would've been just as happy never to have seen.

"Mac," she started, "maybe—"

"Shut up, rook," he snapped, not even doing her the courtesy of looking at her. "Paul, you know what I've been doing the past day and a half?"

"Uh—" Fiorello started, but MacAvoy was on a roll.

"I've been gathering evidence. My partner and I—"

Gee, how nice of him to acknowledge me, Milewski thought, annoyed.

"—we've been pounding the pavement, talking to people, checking over lab reports, and gathering a fuck-ton of evidence. All of it tells us something that the Post-It on the victims' foreheads told us in the first place, that the Claw's the one who killed these people. But everything I've been doing has been to build a case so that the Claw can be properly tried by one of the suits in the chief prosecutor's office. There's just one thing we don't have. You know what that is?"

"Uh—" Fiorello looked helplessly at Milewski, who just shook her head.

"We need the fucking *Claw*, Fiorello! And you had him! There were four of you in an enclosed alley! And then *that* fucknut shows up, and you lose him!"

MacAvoy was pointing at the monitor, which had the rather nebbishy form of Englebert Valentine—sans Knight Dude armor—sitting alone clutching a can of Superior Orange Soda for dear life.

Fiorello blurted out, "The guy was a *menace*, Mac! He—"

"I don't wanna hear it!" MacAvoy took his glasses off and rubbed his eyes. "Get the hell outta here."

Leaping up from the ripped easy chair, Fiorello bolted.

Milewski regarded her partner. "What the hell was that?"

"What the hell was what?" MacAvoy asked as he replaced his glasses.

"You think those four didn't feel bad enough as it is? No, you have to call each one in here and read them the riot act? Well, three of them anyhow. Please for Christ's sake tell me you're not gonna bring Trevor in here next and tell *him* about how he fucked up dealing with costumes."

Letting out a long, raspy breath, MacAvoy said, "No." Even *he* wasn't so much of an asshole that he'd do that to Baptiste.

Milewski wasn't entirely sure that letting Baptiste stay on the street was such a hot idea, either, given what he was going through with his lawsuit, but that was Sergeant Taylor's call.

MacAvoy continued: "But I needed to get that off my chest, and those three needed to get yelled at."

Every time Milewski thought her respect for her partner couldn't bottom out any further, he went and lowered the bar. "Seriously?"

"You got a problem?"

Several, but talking to you won't help. "So what now? Do we question Bert?"

Now, finally, MacAvoy looked at her, and it was a goggle-eyed expression. "'Bert'? You're actually on a first-name basis with that hump?"

Shuddering, Milewski said, "Not willingly. When he first showed up in that ridiculous suit of armor, he was trying to clean up Bester Park. I must've brought him in a dozen times when I was in Narcotics."

"Lucky you." MacAvoy shook his head. "I don't much see the point. From what the unis said—"

"On those rare occasions when you let them get a word in."

MacAvoy ignored the dig. "—shit-for-brains in there barreled in from the other side of the alley saying he heard their call for help."

Milewski nodded. "He's got a police radio."

"Of *course* he does. So he heard the signal 10 and tried to 'help.' Probably got the signal codes off the Internet." He sighed. "Let

Schiazza and Bannon talk to him just in case he saw something the other four missed. We've got better things to do."

"Like yell at unis?"

"To use your favorite phrase, rook, bite me entirely." With that, MacAvoy left the video room.

With a sigh of her own, she rose from the couch—and almost fell right back onto it as a wave of dizziness washed over her.

Reaching out to the wall with her left hand to steady herself, Milewski tried to remember the last time she ate anything. The fact that she couldn't clearly recall such a time was in itself a danger sign, as was her swimming brain.

She followed MacAvoy out the door—and almost crashed into him, as he hadn't moved past the threshold.

Standing on her tip-toes, she glanced over his shoulder to see what he was staring at rather than moving down the hall: Lieutenant Zimmerman.

Great, now I get a chewing out of my very own. Milewski had been studiously avoiding Zimmerman all day, but there was no way that was going to last forever with her on the red-ball.

"Y'know, Mac," the lieutenant said, not even looking at Milewski, which came to the detective as something of a relief, "I seem to recall you going to the Superior Six blimp with the express purpose of getting their files on the Claw, and instead I find you in the video room yelling at unis."

"The unis needed to get yelled at, and the Six still aren't playing well with others."

Zimmerman's face hardened. "What?"

MacAvoy lowered his voice to an approximation of Spectacular Man's stentorian tones. "'I'm afraid that there's nothing we can share, Detectives.' That's a direct quote from Spectacular Douche. Aside from being able to tell the grandkids I'll never have that I rode in a teleporter once, the trip was a total waste of time."

Shaking her head, Zimmerman said, "I'll put a call in to Marc. This is ridiculous."

With that, Zimmerman stormed off and Milewski finally let out the breath she hadn't even realized she was holding.

MacAvoy turned to grin at her. "Expecting her to tear you a new one?"

"Something like that." She closed her eyes. Her head started to swim again. "I'm headed to the vending machines, you want anything?"

"A break in the case?"

Milewski smirked. "Gonna need more change…"

Therese Zimmerman wasn't sure *why* she was so aggravated at the fact that the Superior Six were stonewalling them. It was precisely the response she'd expected, what she and Javier and MacAvoy all believed would be the end result of Mac and Milewski's trip up to their dirigible of doom.

Yet actually *hearing* Mac tell her that the expected result was the same as the actual result, she grew livid. Maybe it was because of the abortive argument she and Marc had had at Emmanuelli's last night; maybe it was because they had to kick two more suspects this morning because they were brought in by costumes with no other witnesses around; maybe it was the fact that their best shot at bringing the Claw in was ruined by a lame-ass wannabe.

So it was with high dudgeon that she strode into her office, sat at her desk, and poked angrily the SPEED DIAL button and then hit "3."

Recalling that her boyfriend didn't answer his own phone, she tamped the aggravation down just in time for Beth to answer.

"Marc McLean's office."

"Hi, Beth, it's Therese—is he there?"

"He's in a meeting—"

Therese let out a breath through her teeth in frustration.

"—but it's one of those meetings he *wants* an excuse to get out of." Beth's voice indicated a conspiratorial smile. "Hang on."

Knowing it would take a minute or two for Marc to make his excuses before coming on the line, she hit the SPEAKER button and placed the phone on her desk. A Muzak rendition of a Beatles song wafted tinnily over the phone's small speaker. *And heaven forfend the McLean Foundation use hold music that doesn't make my teeth hurt.*

She shuffled through the papers on her desk, trying to figure out which of the thousands of bits of paperwork she hadn't gotten to yet was most urgent, when she saw Billinghurst walk by.

Bart Billinghurst had always impressed Therese with his near-perfect posture. Sometimes, during interrogations, he would sit next to the suspect, pretending to be friendly but towering over them even while seated, thanks to that posture.

Now, though, the detective was slump-shouldered as he trudged past her open office door. That was never a good sign.

"Hey, Bart!"

Billinghurst turned and gave Therese a haunted look.

Therese gave him a half-smile. "I'd ask how the Clone Master case is going, but the look on your face pretty much answers it."

"Oh no." Billinghurst held up a hand. "You don't know the half of it. See, *not only* have we gone through the usual crime-scene nonsense, *not only* have the crime scene nerds gathered up a ton of evidence for a trial that will never happen because the victim's gonna turn up alive again, *not only* is there a scheduled autopsy—which, given the backlog at the morgue, won't happen until a month after the new clone turns up—but King and I just finished interviewing our star witness!"

Therese's eyes widened. "There was a witness?" Amethyst had a tendency to use the gem that he took his name from to fuzz out the visuals of his fights. He never gave a reason for this—some assumed it was to protect innocent bystanders, others to protect himself—but there were rarely useful observations of his fights.

Billinghurst went on, now standing in Therese's doorway. "It was an old lady who was standing in the lobby of the building next to where they fought. She was down getting the mail, because today was when her settlement check was supposed to come, except it didn't. Apparently, her husband worked in the Conway Building. That got her going for ten minutes about the insurance company and what *schmucks* they are before she finally got around to telling us that she was staring out the little window in the front door to see the fight. I dunno, maybe Amethyst's gem was on the fritz, or maybe he just didn't know she was there, but she provided a detailed, blow-by-blow account of the fight."

"Really?"

"Yup. Second by second, she told us *every fucking detail* of the fight. And whenever we interrupted her for a clarification, she got all confused, and had to start *all over again.*" Billinghurst's eyes widened. "Oh! And she took pictures with her Zap, and she promised to e-mail them to us as soon as she gets her grand-daughter to tell her how to do that, because she never used the camera function *or* the e-mail function on the Zap before. We offered to download them for her, but the battery died, and she left the charger at her friend Zelda's apartment, and she was going there tomorrow night for movie night, and then she'd get it back and charge it right up and get it to her grand-daughter."

"Uh-huh." Therese was trying very hard not to giggle.

"But then the fight took them around the corner, and she couldn't see anything anymore. So she can't tell us anything useful about the part of the fight that *mattered*, which was Clone-Master dying." The detective stepped forward and put his hands flat on her desk, his eyes wide and slightly crazy. "I'm begging you, Zim, *please*. Let us just drop this. It's gonna be an open case under our names anyhow, so why put us through this?"

Before she could respond, the desecration of Lennon and McCartney ceased and Marc's filtered voice sounded through the phone. "Hello, sweetness."

Hastily, Therese grabbed the phone and stabbed a finger at the SPEAKER button to deactivate it. "Hi, Marc."

Looking up at Billinghurst, she saw that he was now standing straight, smiling, and mouthing, *Sweetness?*

With a mild snarl, she shoo'd him out of the office with a gesture. Billinghurst just grinned and even was kind enough to close the door behind him.

But even through the closed door, she could hear a rejuvenated Billinghurst cry out, "Hey, King, you gotta hear this!"

"Sweetness, you there?"

Therese shook her head, and said, "Yeah, Marc, sorry—I've got a bunch of things going on here."

"I understand. Look, I'm sorry, but I have to cancel tomorrow night."

Big surprise.

But before she could comment, Marc went on: "Tonight's stockholder meeting had to be pushed a day."

That brightened Therese. "Great—so we can go out tonight, then?"

"Afraid not, I'm sorry—see, the reason I put off the stockholders is because I've got to meet with the Superior Six's legal team. Apparently, the manufacturers of Superior Soda don't want to keep paying Mercury because he isn't part of the group anymore, but they're still using his likeness to sell the root beer. It's a big mess, and they're talking lawsuit."

Therese should have known better than to get her hopes up, but at least this presented her an opportunity to bring up the reason for her call. "That's actually handy, Marc, because I've got another item you can put on the agenda for that meeting tonight."

"Oh?" Marc sounded genuinely confused.

"Ask them how it would look when the SCPD serves the Six with a subpoena for whatever files they might have relating to the Claw—the very files my detectives politely asked for, and were rudely refused by your pal Spectacular Man."

"I doubt he was rude, Therese."

Ignoring the comment, Therese continued: "In particular, ask your crack legal team how it would look when the mayor and the chief of police hold a press conference talking about how, if the Six doesn't accede to that subpoena, they'll get an arrest warrant for all half-dozen of your buddies for obstruction of justice."

There was a pause before Marc said incredulously, "You're not serious."

Therese was feeling pretty incredulous herself. She had started the conversation fully intending to ask Marc to see if the lawyers could convince the Six to actually cooperate with the SCPD. Somehow, between her brain and her mouth, it modulated into a threat. A wholly empty threat at that, since she had no idea if Sittler and Dellamonica would even consider giving such a press conference, and the likelihood of such an arrest warrant being served was somewhere between slim and none.

"There's an easy way to find out—fail to convince the Six to actually share some fucking intel with us."

With that, she hung up the phone.

Idly, she wondered if she'd just ended a perfectly good relationship.

Letting out a long breath, she realized that she *probably* hadn't. They'd had nastier arguments than this. Not that they were *really* arguments—it was always Therese ranting and Marc being maddeningly calm, totally confused as to why she was so upset, and understanding and sympathetic to her viewpoint. The phone calls ended like this one had. The ones in person either ended with him being called away for something or, if Therese was very very lucky, a passionate roll in the hay.

The regular sex was great. The make-up sex was cosmically magnificent.

She stared at the paperwork, and all the words on the pages started to meld into a mishmash of disjointed letters that made no sense.

Another sigh, and she got up from her desk. She needed a drink. Failing that, she needed coffee.

3.15pm

"I swear to Christ, I'm going to kill him and then I'm going to resurrect him so I can kill him again."

Trevor Baptiste had nothing to say to Mara Fontaine's outburst, too concerned as he was with holding onto the dashboard. While ranting and raving about Detective MacAvoy, Fontaine was also driving down 13th Street at a pace that could kindly be called brisk.

"Where the fuck does he get off ripping into us like that? He's *not* our boss, and it's not like our sole purpose in life is to make it easier for him to close *his* cases."

"Uh, Mara," Baptiste started as he noticed their cruiser accelerating directly toward a Honda Civic that was double-parked in their lane.

At the last second, Fontaine swerved the blue-and-white to the left to get around it. Baptiste felt his awful lunch lurch in his stomach.

"And I'm telling you," Fontaine continued as if she hadn't just treated the cruiser like they were in a NASCAR race, "if he'd pulled that shit on *you*, I *would've* kicked his ass."

"Well, he didn't, so could you perhaps focus on the road?"

"I'm fine," she said.

Baptiste was about to object strenuously to that particular characterization when the radio squawked.

"Unit 2205, we have a signal 52 at 2547 Giacoia, 3D. Neighbors complained of strange noises."

That caused Baptiste to wince. Every uni who'd patrolled Simon Valley had taken at least one domestic call at that particular address.

Grabbing the radio, Baptiste said, "Unit 2205, signal 4." Then he turned to Fontaine, who drove through Siegel. "So, you think Mrs. Bajrami will press charges *this* time?"

116

Sounding much more subdued than when she was complaining about MacAvoy, Fontaine replied: "I'm gonna go out on a limb and say no."

Every call to Apartment 3D in 2547 Giacoia was Edon Bajrami slapping around his wife Zamira. And every time, Zamira refused to press charges. Even on those rare occasions when they could justify slapping the bracelets on Edon and bringing him in, he was always back on the street within twenty-four hours, headed home to once again use Zamira as a punching bag.

"I can never understand that."

"Really?" Fontaine briefly glanced over at Baptiste. "C'mon, you see violence every day in this job. How can you not understand it?"

"Yes, but your *wife*?" He shook his head. "Sylvia and I argued all the time—about everything, from cooking to remembering laundry to having kids."

Turning right onto Giacoia, Fontaine asked, "You were talking about having kids?"

"No, we were arguing about it. And after what happened, I'm just glad I lost those arguments…"

"Yeah. Trust me, you do *not* want to have to deal with raising a kid alone in this town." Fontaine pulled the car in front of the fire hydrant situated between the two identical brown-brick apartment buildings that were located at 2547 and 2549. Baptiste was just grateful that she finally decelerated.

They approached the dirty glass door to 2547. The familiar face of the building superintendant, Mr. Krasnicki, stood just inside, and he opened the door for them on arrival. Like ninety percent of the residents within a two-block radius, including the Bajramis, Krasnicki was an Albanian immigrant.

"How do you do, Officer Baptiste, Officer Fontaine," Krasnicki said in an accented voice as he held the door long enough for them to pass into the hallway.

Fontaine asked, "Did you make the 911 call?"

Krasnicki nodded, leading them up the creaky wooden stairs. "But this time, is different."

Baptiste frowned. "Different, how?" As they walked upstairs he smelled lemon and olive oil and garlic.

"Mr. Bajrami comes home early from the work—he comes home *with* Mrs. Bajrami."

"That is odd." Baptiste wasn't surprised that Edon Bajrami came home early—he worked at the post office, so he probably got off early after the Brute Squad's attack—but what would his wife be doing with him?

"This time I hear strange noise like something is shorted out, then I hear scream. But I never hear scream like this. Nobody answer the door, and they never give me key to deadbolt lock. In violation of lease, but what can you do? So I call you."

They arrived at the third floor. Baptiste noticed that the linoleum was just as old and cracked as ever, but it was clean. When he was here last, Baptiste had made an off-hand comment about the state of the floor, and he was glad to see that Krasnicki had taken it to heart. It wasn't much, but maybe a man was less likely to hit his wife if his hall floor was cleaned.

Okay, that is ridiculously stupid. Baptiste shook his head and knocked on the door with a tarnished brass "3D" on it. "Mr. and Mrs. Bajrami, this is the police! Please open the door!"

Silence for several seconds. Baptiste could hear Fontaine breathing.

Another knock. "Mr. and Mrs. Bajrami, please open up!"

Fontaine put in, "It's Officers Fontaine and Baptiste—we know you're home, *please* open the door!"

For whatever reason, that did the trick. Baptiste heard footsteps shuffling toward the door and the distinctive clacking sound of deadbolts being moved aside. Then the big metal door creaked open to reveal the diminutive form of Zamira Bajrami. The middle-aged woman was dressed in a worn blue dress and had the same hangdog expression on her face that she always had. Baptiste could see the faded remains of a facial bruise that was poorly covered by makeup, and her right eye still had a bit of swelling, though it was barely noticeable now.

"I am sorry," she muttered. "He was drinking again, and…"

She started to cry for a brief second, then stopped herself, wiping her eyes with the sleeve of her dress.

"May we come in, please, Mrs. Bajrami?" Baptiste asked gently.

"Of course." She stepped aside to allow them entry into their modest one-bedroom apartment.

There was a small kitchenette on the left as they entered. The sink was empty, a dry-rack filled neatly with clean dishes next to it. Beyond that was the living room, which had entirely brown furniture: couch, easy chair, end tables, coffee table, dining-room table that took up one corner, chairs, and the sideboard where Edon's many bottles of alcohol were stored. It was all the same dull shade of brown. Even the television was brown, as was the carpet. The only thing that broke the monotony of color was the silver cable box on top of the TV. To the right was a small hallway that led to the bedroom and bathroom.

The brown carpet was immaculate—except for a weirdly familiar pile of ashes in the middle of the floor.

"Oh hell," Fontaine said.

"What?" Baptiste asked. But Fontaine was just staring at the coffee table for some reason. When his partner didn't answer, he turned to Zamira. "Mrs. Bajrami, where is your husband?"

Tears welled up in her eyes again, but she said nothing.

"Is he in the bedroom?" Baptiste prompted.

Still she was silent, and now shaking a bit. Baptiste started to move toward the hallway, but Fontaine was now standing over the coffee table.

"Trevor, I don't—I don't think he's there." Fontaine grabbed a tissue from a box on one of the end tables, then picked up a familiar-looking object off the coffee table with the tissue.

Baptiste squinted at it. It looked like a toy gun, at first.

Then he remembered the last time he saw a pile of ashes like the one on the floor: on the corner of 12th and Kurtzman after a trash can had been hit by one of the Brute Squad's ray-guns.

A ray-gun that looked a lot like what Fontaine was holding in her hand.

"Jesus shit," Baptiste muttered.

Fontaine regarded him. "Remember when Sean and Paulie's FF36 fritzed? I *thought* that one of the Brutes was missing her ray-gun after that."

Baptiste turned to Zamira. "What happened, Mrs. Bajrami?"

Again, Zamira wiped her eyes with a now-very-damp sleeve. "I was shopping for food. Edon ask me for coffee for coffee maker for office. I bring it by to give him on way home. When I get there, the *kopuks* arrive at post office."

While Baptiste's knowledge of Albanian was severely limited, he did know that the community hereabouts generally referred to the costumed bad guys as *kopuks*. "Go on, please."

"After Superior Six arrive, and you put up orange light, I feel safe. But then orange light go away for a minute—and then that lands at my feet." She pointed at the gun in Fontaine's hand.

Zamira shook her head, tears running down her cheeks. "I do

not know why I took. I just *did*. And then Edon meets me saying he went home early and everything fine, I make him lunch and we eat and all is good."

She sniffled once. Fontaine grabbed another tissue out of the box on the end table and handed it to her.

"Thank you." She dabbed her eyes and blew her nose quickly, then crumpled the tissue in her fist. "After lunch, he has a drink. Then he starts to yell and scream. And then he raises his hand to hit me and for the first time I think that he does not have to hit me if I point gun at him." Her mouth opened as if to scream or cry, but no sound came out for a second. "He *laugh* at me! He asks me what toy store I bought kids' gun from so he can return it. Or perhaps give to kids in playground for games."

Baptiste shuddered at the fact that both he and Edon mistook a deadly weapon for a toy at first.

"And then he walk up to me and tell me to give him toy and I say it is not toy and he *laugh* at me again! Big laugh, like hyena. And then... then..."

Zamira put her head in her hands and sobbed.

At first Baptiste wanted to comfort her, but he found that he couldn't. Instead, he looked helplessly at Fontaine.

She sounded just as helpless when she said, "Yeah. I guess we have to arrest her, huh?"

"We should award her with a medal—but yes, I'm afraid that this is what we must do." With a heavy sigh, he took out his handcuffs. "Zamira Bajrami, you are under arrest for the murder of Edon Bajrami. You have the right to remain silent…"

11.45pm

"This really really sucks."

Paul Fiorello took a sip of his fifth—or maybe sixth—cup of coffee since they'd started the stakeout hours ago. Their blue-and-white was parked in front of an abandoned building on Jaffee Avenue. "Not that I disagree, Sean, but I'm wondering something."

Sean O'Malley stopped drumming on the steering wheel for a moment to look at Fiorello. "Whatcha wondering, Paulie?"

"What's the difference between it really really sucking now, as opposed to an hour ago when it just really sucked? I mean, what's the cutoff between sucking, really sucking, and really really sucking?"

"What really really sucks is that we volunteered for the fucking triple, right? And what happens? We get our asses kicked by a dork in a suit of *armor*, f'Chrissakes, we lose the Claw, we get yelled at by Old Man MacAvoy and that bitch from Narcotics, and then Sarge sticks us with this shit."

"Hey, c'mon," Fiorello said, "the Claw was seen on this block. He may live near here. Or maybe there'll be a victim here. We gotta try."

"I guess, but I still don't think we deserve to hump a cruiser in Simon Valley all night."

"After our FF36 went on the fritz, I'm surprised Paula didn't give us an even shittier detail." They'd heard about the Bajramis, and both Fiorello and his partner wondered whether or not that would have happened if their FF36 hadn't malfunctioned.

On the other hand, Edon might have killed Zamira, so maybe it was for the best...

Not wanting to dwell on that, Fiorello added, "And Krissie's not a bitch."

O'Malley shot Fiorello a look. "'Krissie'? Really?"

"Yeah. She's not that bad. I was glad she got bumped to Homicide."

Shaking his head, O'Malley said, "Sorry, Paulie, but I never got nothin' but attitude from her. I don't put up with that shit from MacAvoy, and he's almost got his thirty, I sure as hell ain't takin' it from *her*." He turned to look at Fiorello. "Seriously, though—'Krissie'? She ain't a 'Krissie,' she's a 'Kristin.' Or 'your royal highness bitch Milewski.'"

Fiorello shrugged. "We had a thing a while back. I was a rookie, she'd just gotten her gold shield."

"Figures. You really will stick your dick in anything, won'tcha?"

"I ain't never fucked a costume."

Snorting, O'Malley said, "You ain't never had the *chance*."

"Wanna bet?"

Now O'Malley was grinning, showing off his crooked teeth. "Okay, *this* I gotta hear."

"Remember that PAL charity thing last year?"

"Not really—had an open bar."

Fiorello shook his head. His partner was *such* a lightweight. "Remember who the keynote speaker was?"

"Yeah, that chickie that works at that hero academy out in Fingerville, Magda something."

"Firestone." Fiorello sucked down some more coffee. "Anyhow, after her speech, she started hitting all over me."

"Just like half the damn women in the city. So you did it with her?"

Staring at O'Malley like he was insane, Fiorello said, "No way! She's a *mind-reader*! You know what that means?"

O'Malley grinned. "Means she still hit on you even though she could read your mind. You shouldn't'a fucked her, you shoulda *married* her."

"No *way* I'm gettin' in the sack with a girl that knows what I'm thinkin'. It'll mess up my whole thing!"

The grin widened. "Right, 'cause when you tell her you'll call her, she'll *know* you're full'a shit."

"Exactly!" Fiorello frowned, realizing he'd been set up, then shook his head.

O'Malley guffawed. "Look, I don't think that even counts."

Now Fiorello was confused. "What doesn't?"

"That mind-reader chickie isn't a *real* costume. I mean, she was a businesswoman, and now she helps run that super academy. She don't never even *wear* a costume."

"Well, how often do we get that close to one of 'em?" Fiorello brightened. "Although, there was this one time, back when I was partnered with Nugent, when Suricata was at a crime scene."

Rubbing his eyes, O'Malley groaned. "Yeah, yeah, I know, Paulie, she had the most athletic legs you ever seen. That's, like, the ninetieth time you told me that story. Me, I'd rather hit up Komodo Dragon. You ever see her without that lizard helmet? Whoosh."

"Asian girls ain't my thing." Fiorello shrugged. "Now Ms. Terrific? *That's* my kinda gal. Gotta find me some *real* pics'a her." He dry-sipped his coffee cup, then crumpled it in one hand. "Anyhow, costume chicks, they're like on another level. I prefer to stick with *normal* girls, y'know?"

Snorting, O'Malley said, "You ever meet a *normal* one, lemme know, 'kay? I'll throw a party. S'like finding a spotted owl." Then O'Malley straightened. "Or the goddamn Bolt."

Fiorello chuckled. "You seriously think that—"

But O'Malley was opening the door to the blue-and-white. Looking out the windshield, Fiorello saw a bald man walking toward the apartment building across the street.

A familiar looking bald man from every roll call since Monday morning: Hiram Donewitz, a.k.a. the Bolt.

"Don't move!" O'Malley bellowed, un-holstering his Beretta and pointing it straight at Donewitz.

"Shit," Fiorello muttered. He thumbed his radio as he clambered out of the cruiser. "PCD, this is Unit 2202 with a signal 10. The Bolt sighted on the 500 block of Jaffee. Requesting backup."

He took out his own weapon and pointed it at Donewitz from behind the vehicle, his arms on the car roof to steady his aim.

Holding his hands in the air, Donewitz said, "Is there a problem, Officers?"

O'Malley was slowly walking toward the perp while Fiorello covered him. "Don't play dumb with us. You're under arrest for escaping police custody and property damage—plus the DUI you got hit with Sunday night."

"I have no idea what you're talking about, Officer. I don't remember damaging any property or being pulled over for a DUI. Look, I just came from an AA meeting, my sponsor can vouch for my whereabouts."

Something was nagging at Fiorello. This was wrong, on more than one level.

"I don't care if Mayor Goddamn Sittler can vouch for your whereabouts, Donewitz. Get down on the ground *now*!"

"I'm telling you," Donewitz said, not moving, "you're making a big mistake."

O'Malley was now almost on top of Donewitz. "I ain't gonna say it again, douchebag—on the ground *now*!"

Then it hit Fiorello. "Sean, don't get any clo—"

A beam of red light shot out from Donewitz's forehead right at O'Malley, which sent the officer flying back through the air right at the cruiser, and at Fiorello, who flinched.

O'Malley crashed into the blue-and-white with a bone-shattering crunch. Fiorello recovered quickly, and aimed his Beretta at Donewitz—

—who was pointing his left hand right at Fiorello.

Shit!

Fiorello squeezed the trigger of his Beretta even as another red beam emitted from Donewitz's left index finger.

The world exploded a second later.

Pain shot through Fiorello's arm. He found himself lying on the sidewalk of Jaffee Avenue, staring up at the night sky, which was blotted out in part by smoke. He felt tremendous heat to his left, and realized that the blue-and-white was on fire.

His primary thought at the moment was that Sergeant Taylor was going to *kill* them for getting a cruiser blown up.

Focus, Paulie, focus. The Bolt blew up the car. You need to move your ass upright and see if you shot him.

Then Hiram Donewitz's hairless head was staring down at him, smiling. There was no sign of blood, so it seemed that Fiorello missed.

"I tried to tell your partner that you were making a mistake. Shoulda listened."

"Unit 2202, this is PCD, requesting signal 4. All units, signal 10 at the 500 block of Jaffee."

Fiorello tried to reach for his radio, but there were two problems. One was that he couldn't really move his arm. The other was Donewitz, who said, "Nuh uh, copper. Don't touch that dial. You and me, we're going somewhere nice and quiet. When your buddies show up, they ain't comin' close to me, or you get a bolt to the head."

Donewitz laughed at his own lousy joke as he grabbed

Fiorello's uniform shirt and hauled him to his feet. Fiorello felt himself being guided forward by Donewitz's right hand while his left was hovering near Fiorello's temple.

"Make one wrong move, pretty boy, and I slice open your head."

Sirens sounded in the distance, getting closer.

Donewitz looked back down Jaffee. "Dammit. All right, let's get inside."

Fiorello felt his head swim as Donewitz dragged him toward the abandoned building they'd been parked in front of. He couldn't get his arms to work right, and even if he could, the Bolt had the equivalent of a gun to his head.

I am so screwed...

PART THREE
WEDNESDAY

6am

"Good morning Super City! And welcome to *News 6 at 6.* I'm Mindy Ling."

"And I'm Chuck Ortiz. Later on, we'll get the inside scoop on the Brute Squad's attack on the post office, find out about a City Hall insider who's on the outside looking in, and a look inside the hottest new restaurant in Eisnerville. We'll also have Ian Michaelson with sports, Jack Magnusson filling for Debra Fine on weather, and Donna Brodsky with traffic. But first our top story. Mindy?"

"Thanks, Chuck. This is a developing story, as an SCPD officer has been taken hostage by the villain known as the Bolt in Simon Valley. We go now to Judi Bari. Judi?"

"I'm here at the corner of Jaffee Avenue and 10th Street, just a block from where the Bolt attacked two uniformed police officers. SCPD has yet to identify the officers in question, but one of them was taken to Kane Memorial Hospital and is in critical condition. The other was taken by the Bolt into the abandoned building two blocks behind me. The Bolt has the officer on the fourth floor, and has refused to speak to police negotiators. The SCPD's Emergency Action Team was summoned, and have been in place, but are currently in what's known as a hold. None of the officers on the scene have been willing to comment for the record, but SCPD spokeswoman Regina Dent has released a statement saying that the EATers will be doing everything they can to minimize risk to innocent bystanders. The Bolt's real name is Hiram Donewitz, and it's not known how he got his ability to fire a beam of coherent light from any pore in his body, but the ability has led to several jail sentences on a variety of charges, ranging from DUI to assault. For *News 6 at 6*, I'm Judi Bari."

"Thanks, Judi. We'll be returning to this story as it develops.

After the commercial break, we'll tell you about some good eats from the hottest spot in Eisnerville, plus Adriana Berardi's exclusive report on the surprise resignation of Mayor Sittler's travel secretary, which has a bit of a super twist."

7.45am

"You look horrible, Javier."

Garcia let out a breath through his teeth as he climbed out of the driver's seat of his car, walking gingerly to keep his pants from touching his groin area as much as possible. He had taken his Corolla out of the garage for this—no way he was going to rely on STT with one of his officers in a life-or-death—and cut across town from Woodcrest to Simon Valley on the Governor Ditko Parkway. He left the car in the middle of Jaffee Avenue just past the blue barricades that the unis had set up on the corner of 10th to keep civilians and especially the press away from the scene. An Emergency Action Team truck was parked just in front of him, and blue-and-whites were all over the two blocks between 10th and 12th.

The comment came from Lieutenant Mike Singh, the commander of the "EATers," as Singh's predecessor had insisted on referring to them. Garcia hated it, Singh hated it, half the force hated it, but the name stuck anyhow.

"Seriously, Javier, are you all right?" Singh, who was only five-foot-five, looked up at Garcia with his dark eyes from under his blue ballcap, which had letters SCPD sewn into the front. He looked concerned.

"I didn't sleep so hot last night. Kept expecting a phone call." He didn't add that this wasn't the one he was expecting.

"Well, I'm sorry this happened." He looked down at Garcia's pants. "Did you have an accident?"

"Spilled my coffee when I turned on the damn 15th Street exit off the Parkway." The impact of hot liquid on his crotch did more to wake him up than drinking the stuff had done, at least, but this pair of pants was pretty much ruined.

Shaking his head, Singh said, "You shouldn't take that turn so fast."

"Mike, stop sounding like my mother and tell me what's happening."

Singh turned and squinted up toward the fourth floor of the apartment building on the corner of Jaffee and 11th. "We were able to evacuate everybody—except, obviously, for the target and Officer Fiorello. 'Everybody,' in this case, consisted of ten homeless people, four women sharing a needle, and a stray cat. I have sharpshooters on the adjoining buildings and across the street, I have eyes in the room, and I have the blueprints for the apartment." He let out a long breath, puffing his cheeks. "What I *don't* have is ears or a clear shot. We couldn't get a bug in there, and he's staying away from the windows."

Garcia nodded. That wasn't surprising. Most buildings in Super City kept the windows small, since those were the first to get shattered when the costumes went at it. Sure, there were luxury high-rises in Eisnerville and office buildings downtown that paid extra for unbreakable glass—though more than one of those got themselves shattered in mid-fight anyhow—but nobody spent that kind of money on construction down in Simon Valley.

The downside, of course, was the fact that Singh's sharpshooters could only get a good shot if the bad guy happened to stand near one of the windows, but Donewitz could avoid those with ease.

"Where are they?"

Pointing at a fourth-floor window, Singh said, "An interior room, one in from where that window opens onto. It's a very good position, actually, because it doesn't have any external walls, so a breach is not really feasible. He's been looking at his Zap the whole time—he's probably keeping up with the news reports on this. Officer Fiorello's been secured to one of the radiators with duct tape."

"Is he okay?"

Singh shrugged. "Well, he's duct-taped to a radiator."

Garcia just glared at him. "Do I look like I'm in the mood for—?"

"Right, right," Singh said quickly, holding up a hand. "He's got a couple of cuts and his uniform's a mess, but he seems to be all right. We've seen a couple of bloodstains, but they haven't grown any larger that we can see. And, for what it's worth, his hair *still* isn't mussed."

As he spoke, a tall, lanky African American with broad shoulders approached. He was wearing a button-down shirt that was too small for him, a pair of khakis that was too big for him, and a tie that had several colors, none of which were found in nature. Not for the first time, Garcia was grateful that most negotiations were conducted over the phone. No hostage taker who could see Detective Khalil Ferguson's ties would take the negotiator in the least bit seriously.

He was also surprised to see Ferguson, since Lake usually had days. Then he recalled that they'd switched shifts the week before.

Ferguson looked at Garcia's pants. "Jesus, Javy, you piss yourself, or what?"

Garcia didn't even bother answering. "Any luck getting through?"

"Not really. First time, he answered the phone, told us to fuck off, and hung up. He hasn't answered since."

That surprised Garcia. "What, no demands?"

Shaking his head, Ferguson said, "Not a damn thing. I don't know what he's waiting for, be honest with you."

Garcia sighed. "Keep at it."

With a nod, Ferguson went back to the truck to take another shot at calling.

A ring emitted from Garcia's jacket pocket. After shoving his hand into it to retrieve the ZP500, he hoped that it was someone from HQ with the news that the Claw had been captured.

Instead, it was his mother.

For half a second, Garcia debated sending it to voicemail, but he just *knew* that *mami* was watching the television, and he just *knew* that if he didn't answer, she'd assume the absolute worst and call the precinct and talk to Taylor. He liked and respected the sergeant too much to do that to her.

Putting the phone to his ear after hitting TALK, he turned away from Singh. "*Mami*, I can't really chat right now."

"I know, Javy, I know, but I wanted to make sure you're okay. I'm watching the television, and it looks very bad."

"It's fine, *mami*. I'm just supervising. And I have to go."

"Well, you be careful, Javy, okay? I worry."

"I know you worry, and I *will* be careful, I promise."

Just as he ended the call, Regina Dent approached him and Singh. Her curly blond hair was perfect, her blue suit immaculate, her makeup perfectly applied.

"What is *wrong* with you?" Garcia asked her.

Showing perfect teeth, Regina smiled her second smile. Her first smile was the artificial one she used for the cameras when she gave statements that no sane person would smile while reading. Not smiling under those circumstances would cost the woman her job as SCPD spokeswoman, but that smile never reached her eyes.

The second one, though, was much more mischievous, and she would only show when nobody had a recording device nearby. "What *ever* do you mean, Javier?"

"You know damn well what I mean. You were woken out of the same sleepless night I was—I know this because *you* told me that when you called me. So how do you look so perfect?"

"If I look like crap, SCPD looks like crap. You guys are doing that enough without my help." That last was added with a twinkle in her eye. Then she looked down at his pants. "Spill coffee?"

"Yeah," Garcia said. "Part of our ongoing campaign to look like crap."

They both chuckled. "Get your guys to solve this already, would you please, Javier? Bad enough you haven't captured the Claw—*again*—but adding this on top of it is gonna be a PR nightmare."

"Y'know, Regina, I was gonna drag my ass on this, but because you asked? I'll get right to it."

"Knew I could count on you." The second smile fell, and she put her game face on. "I'm gonna give the press a statement, can I give them anything useful?"

Garcia shook his head. "Donewitz has his Zap glued to his hands, so I'd rather you didn't say *anything* to the press. It'll just piss him off." The ZP500s were too damned efficient, was the problem. The only way to keep Donewitz from getting a signal would be to black out the entire block, which would screw up Garcia's people's ability to communicate as well.

She clucked sympathetically. "I wish I could do that, Javier, but no way I can just stand here and not say *something*. I'll keep it vague, okay?"

With a heavy sigh, Garcia nodded. Regina turned on her heel and walked toward the gaggle of press that were lined up on the other side of the blue barricades.

Looking to the heavens in supplication, Garcia reminded himself that Regina was very good at her job and had never once said or done anything to compromise a case. She wouldn't today, either.

Then the heavens actually provided supplication—or at least

something resembling it. A blue-and-red streak was heading right for Jaffee Avenue. The streak coalesced into the familiar form of Spectacular Man, who landed with unrealistic grace on the sidewalk, his blue-booted feet touching surprisingly lightly on the pavement.

In a deep, stentorian voice, he declared, "Who's in charge here?" *Christ, why didn't he just say, "Take me to your leader"?* "I'm Captain Garcia."

"I'm Spectacular Man," he said completely unnecessarily. Then he looked down at Garcia's groin. "What happened to your pants?"

"None'a your damn business. Look, I'm sorry, but this is a crime scene, and—"

"And I'm here to help."

Garcia somehow managed to swallow down a laugh. He kept his distance from the hero—Spectacular Man was about a head taller than the captain, and Garcia found himself less intimidated by that frame wrapped in a bright blue and red suit if he stayed a few feet away. "That's very generous, but we have the situation in hand."

"I've been monitoring the 'situation,' Captain," Spectacular Man said in an almost pitying tone, "and it's far from 'in hand.'" He actually used air quotes both times, which forced Garcia to quell another laugh.

Singh walked right up to the hero despite being more than a foot shorter. "With respect, sir, I don't see how adding a gaudily dressed, super-strong man to an already tense situation will make it *better.*"

"In fact, past experience tells us it'll be worse," Garcia added.

Spectacular Man actually winced at that. "With respect, Captain, I'm not the Cowboy. I'm aware of how he complicated that hostage crisis in the Moore Building last year."

"Yeah, I guess 'complicated' is one word for it," Garcia said, bitterly making an air-quotes gesture of his own. "Another is 'reckless'. Thanks to him, the HT put two of my unis in the hospital." The hostage taker at the Moore Building had actually been somewhat calmed by the negotiator—that one was Lake. Then the Cowboy showed up, and all hell broke loose, getting both Amalfitano and Cortez shot. Both had medical'd out, to Garcia's annoyance; they were good police.

"As I said, Captain," Spectacular Man said a bit more gently this time, "I'm not the Cowboy. You have an officer trapped in there. I assume you don't have any way of getting him out or you would have done so by now. You're at an impasse. As long as your officer is in danger, you can't do anything, and as long as your officer is alive, the Bolt is safe."

Singh looked up at him again. "You believe you can break the impasse?"

"Yes. I've faced the Bolt before, I know how he thinks."

"Come on," Garcia said, "he's a skell. Half his sheet is DUIs. I know how he thinks, too, and so do most of the guys here. How he *thinks* isn't gonna get Paul Fiorello out of that apartment alive."

"No, but I *can* get him out, if you'll let me."

Those last four words brought Garcia up short. *As if we can stop him.*

At first, Garcia had been prepared to reject the notion out of hand, as much due to what happened at the Moore Building as anything. But then he remembered Milewski and MacAvoy's trip to the Superior Six's dirigible. And he remembered Fontaine and Baptiste's domestic from yesterday afternoon. And he remembered why Mac and Milewski were going back to the blimp this morning.

"Fine, you want to help, give it a shot."

Singh shot him a look. "Are you serious, Javier?"

Garcia glared down at Singh again. "I'm always serious when I've got hot coffee on my testicles, Mike."

"Javier?"

Turning around, Garcia saw Regina Dent had returned, and she had an expectant look on her face.

"Hello, Ms. Dent," Spectacular Man said, with a nod of his head.

Garcia got a good, if brief, look at the hero's blond hair as he nodded. He also was completely not surprised that the two of them knew each other.

Regina asked, "Are you assisting in this hostage negotiation?"

"Yes, I am."

"Feel free," Garcia put in, "to tell the press that Spectacular Man is collaborating with the EATers on this."

Spectacular Man winced. "I'd prefer 'cooperating.'" This time he didn't use the air quotes.

With a smile, Garcia said, "Well, you can tell *your* spokesperson to say that, but Regina works for us."

Giving Spectacular Man the second smile, Regina said, "Cooperating is fine." With that, she turned and headed right back to the press.

After counting to ten in Spanish, Garcia turned to Spectacular Man. "All right, here's what I want you to do. You need to coordinate with Lieutenant Singh here, as well as Detective Ferguson, and figure out the best approach to…"

Garcia trailed off, as Spectacular Man rose off the ground and flew toward the fourth floor window that Singh had been pointing at earlier.

"Or," Garcia said to nobody in particular, "you could just fly up to the window."

He hoped that this was the right move.

8.30am

The minute Kristin Milewski got a signal after stepping out of the Platinum Line train at the 72nd Street stop, she dialed Mara Fontaine's number.

Before Fontaine could even say, "Hello," Milewski asked, "Any word on Paulie?"

"Not yet. Singh's guys can't get a shot on the Bolt, and the sonofabitch still won't answer Ferguson's calls."

Milewski winced. "Ferguson? Not Lake?"

"They switched shifts last week."

"Great." Milewski jumped up the staircase that led to street level two at a time. "Paulie's life's on the line and it's left to *that* jackass?"

"What's wrong with him?"

"He's totally incompetent! I worked with him in Narcotics, and he had no idea what the hell he was doing." She strode purposefully down Claremont Road toward 75th and the Schwartz Building, landsharking her way around the various people on the street, most of whom were commuters headed to their offices or one of the many delis and coffee shops in the ground floors of the office buildings on Claremont. Milewski was tempted to head for the latter, but she was barely on time as it was, and if she stopped for coffee, she'd never hear the end of it from MacAvoy.

Not that she was *ever* likely to hear the end of it from him.

"Kris, I thought you didn't even *like* Paulie."

"I don't." Milewski bit her lip. "Exactly."

"Uh huh."

"Look, I know we broke up years ago, and I know he's an asshole, but he still…" She trailed off.

Milewski could hear Fontaine's smile. "You don't want so fine a piece of ass to get killed by some lame super?"

140

"I wouldn't have put it *quite* that crudely." Milewski glared at her Zap even though it was lost over the phone. "But yeah, pretty much. I mean, yeah, he's a total jackass, and I wouldn't go out with him again if my life depended on it, but still…"

"I know. Personally, I wouldn't go near him without a can of Lysol and a full-body condom. But he's good police, y'know?"

"Yeah." Milewski's opinion was mostly the opposite. He was fantastic to look at, but not her first choice to have her back when she kicked a door in. "Look, I gotta go meet with the costumes again."

"By yourself?"

Frowning, Milewski realized that she'd used "I" instead of "we." "No, sadly, I'm still saddled with Mac. Unless he woke up this morning and finally choked on his own bile."

"Yeah, he's a piece of work, that one. I almost kicked him in the balls yesterday."

"You should've. I totally would've alibi'd you." Milewski found herself visualizing Fontaine doing so while in the video room yesterday. The image gave her a warm, fuzzy feeling. "I can't wait until he gets his thirty. Just another three months and I'm free of him."

At this point, Milewski was jogging across 74th Street, avoiding being hit by a Lexus zooming through the yellow light before it turned red.

"You're gonna nail them about the Bajramis, right?" Fontaine asked.

"Absolutely. Mac said he'd pick up the zap gun from evidence on his way."

"Which one of the Inferior Six are you talking to?"

"Not sure. Christ, I hope it's not Spectacular Man again." Milewski shuddered. "He was intimidating as all hell."

"They all are," Fontaine said with a big sigh. "In fact—holy *shit*!"

Milewski pulled the phone away at Fontaine's exclamation. "What is it, Mara, what's wrong?"

"Well, you don't have to worry about Spectacular Man being the one you talk to—he just showed up here."

That got Milewski to briefly stop walking—a man in a three-piece suit almost crashed into her, and gave her a dirty look as he walked around her on the sidewalk. "What?"

"He just came in for a landing, and he's talking to Garcia and Singh right now."

"Jesus." She moved through the revolving door at the front of the Schwartz Building, her free hand pushing the tarnished brass handle that got the doors rotating.

"I'd better go, Kris. Don't know *what's* gonna happen now."

"Okay, Mara. My best to Trevor."

"Will do. And you give 'em hell. Bye."

Milewski dropped her Zap into her purse as she came out of the revolving door, showed her badge to the security guard sitting behind the small particle-board desk reading today's *Super City Gazette* (she noted that the fight between the Superior Six and the Brute Squad at the post office made the front page which, if nothing else, had pushed the Claw off it), and went to the elevator bank.

Upon arrival at the dank office the Superior Six maintained on the fourth floor, the receptionist with the hair immediately said, "You officers can go right back."

"Gee, thanks," MacAvoy said from the leather couch, tossing the ratty copy of *Newsweek* with the cover story about the 2008 Presidential election onto the coffee table and picking up an evidence bag off it. As he got up, he glared at Milewski from over the top of his glasses. "Nice of you to show up."

Even though it wasn't the reason for her being late, she said, "I was talking with Mara Fontaine over on Jaffee."

For what may have been the first time since they met, MacAvoy's face softened. "Any word on Paulie?"

She shook her head as they both approached the door to the teleporter. "Nothing new on him, but as we were finishing up, Spectacular Man showed up at the scene."

Again, MacAvoy stared at her from over his glasses. "What the hell is Spectacular Douche doing *there*?"

"Dunno, but look on the bright side—at least that means *we* don't have to deal with him."

"Oh, I know we're not," MacAvoy said as the room's glow increased. Once it dimmed again, he continued: "Iron-hair at the desk who can't tell the difference between officers and detectives said that we'd be talking to Kimono Dragon." He shook his head. "Why would a dragon wear a Japanese bathrobe, anyhow?"

Milewksi opened the door to the blimp's fancier reception area. She noticed that one of the screens had footage of the Six's battle against the Brute Squad at the post office yesterday which, considering the subject of their visit, was kind of ironic. "First of all, a kimono isn't a bathrobe."

MacAvoy shrugged. "It *looks* like a bathrobe."

"Second of all," Milewski went on, letting that pass, "her name's not *Kimono* Dragon, it's *Komodo* Dragon, which is a type of lizard."

"Wait, there's an actual dragon in the world?"

Before Milewski could answer, a harsh, electronically filtered voice came from the other side of the reception area. "No, it is merely *called* a dragon. You might be surprised, Detective, how many misnomers run through the animal kingdom."

Both detectives turned to look at a small woman who wore a greenish-gray, scaly suit of armor, similar in texture to that of the komodo dragons that Milewski had seen in the Super Zoo. It was topped off by a helmet in the shape of that animal's head: beady eyes on the sides, separated by a snout that jutted out with two nostrils and a mouth in a perpetual frown.

Where Spectacular Man looked far more intimidating in person after looking silly in photos and video footage, Komodo Dragon was the opposite. Milewski had always found her lizard-style body armor to look impressive from afar, but standing next to her, she looked somewhat ridiculous.

She put her gloved hands to the sides of her head. A second later, Milewski heard a pneumatic hiss, and then the hero lifted the helmet up, revealing a woman with Asian features and a really unfortunate case of hat hair.

"The blindworm, for example, is neither blind nor a worm." Without the helmet the woman's voice was gentler and softer. "And guinea pigs are not pigs and are not from Guinea."

"Much as I'd love to keep watching Animal Planet," MacAvoy said, holding up the evidence bag, "we need to talk to you about something."

She squinted at the bag while running a hand over her tousled hair in a failed attempt to flatten it. "Is that one of the Brute Squad's AC-50s?"

"Jesus, I didn't realize that ray guns had makes and models." MacAvoy shook his head. "But yeah, it's from the Brute Squad."

Komodo Dragon stared at it with open-mouthed fascination. "We have been attempting to acquire one of those for *years*. I assume that you are donating it?"

MacAvoy actually sputtered at that. Milewski came to his rescue. "I'm sorry, ma'am, but that's an *evidence* bag."

"Oh." Komodo Dragon looked visibly crestfallen. "Well, then, I am afraid I do not comprehend the purpose of your bringing it here."

Milewski stepped forward, interpolating herself between her partner and the costume. "We need confirmation that it *does* belong to the Brute Squad, and that it was used against your team yesterday at the post office."

Nodding, Komodo Dragon said, "I cannot confirm for sure. However, one of the members of the Squad we captured had two AC-50s during the fight, but only one when we brought her in."

"Waitasec," MacAvoy said, "why're you so hot for *this* one if you've got one already?"

"Whenever one of the Brute Squad is captured, he or she always makes sure to activate a self-destruct switch that destroys the interior workings of whatever equipment or armaments they are carrying, rendering it useless—and also impossible to study. Brute #6 did so with her AC-50." She stared at the weapon again. "Was this found at the post office?"

"Not exactly." MacAvoy's tone was even snottier than usual, and again Milewski felt the need to jump in.

"I'm afraid it was found at a crime scene, ma'am. Specifically a murder scene." And then she outlined the Bajrami case.

Komodo Dragon's face went from fascination to horror in very short order.

"That—that is simply awful." She turned away. "I do not understand how this could have happened."

"Really?" MacAvoy asked. "'Cause, honestly? It ain't that hard."

Turning back to MacAvoy, Milewski now saw a fury in Komodo Dragon's eyes. "What is it you wish of the Superior Six, Detective?"

"Two things, actually." MacAvoy started enumerating points

on his fingers. "One you gave us—confirming that this murder weapon was misplaced during a fight you guys had with the Brute Squad. The second is to tell you that we requested all your files on the Claw, and we're here to request them *again*."

"And," Milewski added, "if you actually *talked* to us every once in a while, and *cooperated* with us, we might be able to avoid things like Edon Bajrami in the future. Sharing your files on the Claw would be a good start."

Now Komodo Dragon was looking down at the floor. When she looked back up at the detectives, Milewski could practically feel the guilt oozing out of the scales on her body armor. "I am sorry, but—it is not for me to make such decisions."

"Whaddaya mean?" MacAvoy asked.

She went back to studying the floor. "Only a founding member of the Six may release such files to someone outside the Six, as per our bylaws. Of our current roster, that would be Spectacular Man, the Bengal, or the Starling—and none of them are present." When she looked up at MacAvoy, Milewski noticed tears welling in the hero's eyes. She ran her armored wrist across those eyes as she said, "But rest assured, I will take this up with whichever one of them returns first."

"Thank you," Milewski said with a genuine smile. She didn't want to antagonize the woman.

Of course, her partner had no such compunctions. "You'd better. Look, lady, this is *your* mess, and like usual, *we're* stuck cleaning it up. All's we want is you to share some fucking files with us."

Milewski grabbed MacAvoy's arm and started pulling him toward the door to the teleporter. However, Mac had six inches of height and twenty pounds of weight on her, so he didn't budge. "Mac, come *on*."

"FBI, DEA, ICE—any'a them need files, or we need files from them, we get 'em. And that's for cases with body counts a lot smaller'n this one. For serial cases like this, we usually get cooperation out the ass. Except from you people. We come up here, make a polite request, and you blow us off and play patty-cake with the Brute Squad. End result? We *still* can't find the Claw, and a man's dead with his wife in jail because you can't keep track of your toys."

"Mac…" Milewski was now pulling with all her strength on MacAvoy's arm, but her partner refused to move.

Komodo Dragon's gauntleted fists clenched, and Milewski found herself reminded of the fact that the body armor she wore may have looked silly, but it enhanced both her strength and agility to the point where a particularly strong punch could probably have taken Mac's head off. *That option's looking real good right now, actually*, she thought.

Unfortunately, Mac was on a roll. "But, wait—those are actual *legitimate* law-enforcement agencies. They have rules and regulations and *laws* and all that good stuff. You guys just have some rich bastard bankrolling you, good PR, and not a single goddamn law on your side. Only a matter'a time before something happens you can't fix. Hope you can live with that—'cause Edon Bajrami sure as shit can't, and neither can the Claw's victims."

"Be very careful, Detective," Komodo Dragon said, stepping forward slowly.

"Or what?" Mac asked. "You'll kill us? That'll do *wonders* for your rep."

Having given up on dragging him out, Milewski instead stood in front of her partner. "That's *enough*, Mac! We've ID'd the ray-gun, we've renewed our request. Let's *go*." She put her hands on his chest and started pushing him toward the door.

This time, he got the hint, turning his back on Komodo Dragon. Milewski looked at the hero and said, "Thank you again."

She said nothing in response, simply glowering at MacAvoy as the pair of them entered the closet-sized teleporter.

The door closed, the light brightened, and when it dimmed back down again, Milewski threw the door open.

She stormed toward the exit, MacAvoy walking after her saying, "What the *hell*, rook?"

But she refused to respond on the entire elevator ride down, nor the walk across the lobby. When she went through the revolving door, the morning breeze slicing through her open leather jacket, then she whirled on her partner as he came out behind her. "What is *wrong* with you?"

Holding up one hand in a "who, me?" gesture—he only didn't hold up both because his left hand still had the evidence bag— MacAvoy said, "Nothing's wrong with me, I just needed to tell that little costumed bitch what for."

"Oh, you did, did you? Well, congratulations, Detective, you've managed to completely fuck any chance of us getting any files from these assholes."

"What're you talking about, she said she'd talk to the three founders, so—"

"Yeah, she said that, and *then* you decided to rip her a new one. Did you even *look* at her face? We *had* her as soon as I told her about Bajrami, and then you cheesed her off so much I doubt she'll even *mention* the files to anyone. What, you thought chewing out three armed unis wasn't enough, you had to find someone who can bench press a Mack truck to piss off?"

To Milewski's abject shock, MacAvoy actually looked contrite. He mumbled, "You're right."

Milewski blinked. "What was that?"

MacAvoy's face modulated into a snarl. "I said you were right, okay? The law of averages was bound to catch up." He started stomping off toward 74th Street. "C'mon, I got a car around the corner."

At first, Milewski just watched her partner's form walking down Claremont Road's sidewalk, practically bowling over pedestrians who got in his way.

I guess it beats a poke in the eye with a sharp stick, she though as she jogged to catch up with him, though she suspected that her actually getting him to admit to being wrong once was just going to make her life even more of a living hell than it already was.

"Can we stop and get some breakfast?" she called out to him as she fished her Zap out of her purse so she could get an update from Mara.

8.15am

Several years ago, Paul Fiorello met a woman at Manny's. She was one of many women he met at that particular bar. That was where he'd met Sheila or Gia or whoever it was he spent Monday with. It was a cop hangout, and there were always Blue Birds—women who had the hots for police.

The one Fiorello was thinking about right now as he was well into his eighth hour of being duct-taped to a radiator was named Randi. Or maybe it was Candy? In any case, she had told him that she was drawn to cops because they had handcuffs and she wanted him to secure her to the bedpost.

Unfortunately, when he actually got her up to his apartment and cuffed her to the bed, she started complaining that her arms hurt after only a few minutes.

The night didn't last much longer, and when she and Fiorello saw each other at Manny's, they pretty much ignored each other.

If Fiorello lived through this, and saw her again at Manny's, he would walk right up to her and apologize. Donewitz had taped Fiorello's wrists to the radiator in a very similar position to how he'd cuffed Randi (or Candy) to his bedpost, and he got uncomfortable even more quickly than she did.

He also had a splitting headache, his ribs were throbbing, and his left leg had fallen asleep. It had been eight and a half hours since he finished the cup of coffee in the squad car, and his bladder was about to explode. Only the knowledge that he'd never hear the end of it from the guys if he pissed his pants while held hostage kept him from doing so. For now.

Besides, it gave him something to focus on. His head was pounding mercilessly, and dimly remembered safety lectures he'd received at the Academy were burbling to the surface reminding him that, with a head injury, it was a bad idea to fall asleep. Already exhausted from working two-and-a-half shifts and being bored shitless in the squad car for hours *before* Donewitz blew up the blue-and-white and set the tap-dancing troupe going in his skull, it took all Fiorello's strength *not* to doze off.

At first, he kept his focus by taking in every detail of the apartment in the hopes of figuring a way out, but that only occupied the first five minutes or so. The place was abandoned, so there was no furniture, no wall hangings, not even any interior doors, as the frames just had empty hinges. The interior walls were cheap plaster pockmarked with dents and small holes, the floor was cheap linoleum that was cracked and split, and the only other signs of habitation were the occasional cockroach that wandered through. One of the walls had faded soot stains that indicated a fire sometime in the past—that might have even been why the place was still abandoned.

To make matters worse, he was also starving and dying of thirst. His throat was so raw, he couldn't talk. Not that Donewitz was much of a conversationalist. Mostly he just checked newsfeeds on his fancy-ass phone and cursed a few times. And whenever he did talk to Fiorello, he kept calling him "pretty boy," which started out annoying and moved on to a killing offense.

Of course, at this point, the microsecond Fiorello had a weapon again, he planned to empty it into Donewitz's skull.

Since dawn, the only time Donewitz did talk was several times when the phone rang, and he'd say, "No chance, cop," and tap IGNORE.

When it happened again, Fiorello tried to say something along the lines of, "Answer the damn phone, willya please?" But it just came out as a croak.

Donewitz turned to look at him. "You have something to say, pretty boy? Huh? Do you?"

Fiorello tried to clear his throat, and wound up in a coughing fit that managed to, all at the same time, make his headache worse, graduate the throbbing in his ribs to outright pain, make his throat even more raw, and nearly dislocate his shoulder, as the spasms from coughing caused him to tug against his secured wrists.

Shaking his head, Donewitz laughed. "Nice one, pretty boy."

"Fuck you," Fiorello managed to croak out.

"Sorry, pretty boy, you ain't my type."

Two cockroaches chose that moment to wander out into the middle of the floor.

"Jesus Christ," Donewitz said, looking down at them. "What a dump."

You chose it, asshole, Fiorello thought, trying to hold it in. The coughing fit had almost made him release his bladder.

Suddenly, the crack of shattered glass from one of the front windows echoed throughout the apartment.

Donewitz whirled around and shot out one of his ray-beams from his hand. It flew wide into the ceiling. Bits of plaster dust fell to the floor, frightening the two cockroaches enough for them to skitter into the kitchen.

Then Spectacular Man strode into the room.

Oh man, the captain must be having a shit-fit. After the mess at the Moore Building last year, Garcia had sworn never to let a costume near a hostage situation.

"Stay back, hero!" Donewitz fired another shot from his hand. This one hit its intended target, but Spectacular Man's chest just absorbed it, and the costume didn't even budge.

"You know I can't do that, Bolt. Your powers don't affect me."

Donewitz pointed at Fiorello. "Yeah, but they affect pretty boy here just fine. Take another step, and he's toast."

"Christ," Fiorello croaked, "do it already, just so I don't have to *listen* to this hump."

"Shut up, pretty boy!"

Spectacular Man stood his ground. "Bolt, you know there's no way out of this. Sooner or later you're going to need to eat or sleep. As soon as you let your guard down, the Emergency Action Team will storm this place and put their power-dampening restraints on you, and it'll all be over. The longer this goes on, the worse it will be for you."

"Hah!" Donewitz practically spit the word. "You really think it's gonna be *worse* for me after what I did? They're gonna give me a goddamn lethal injection!"

Fiorello just stared at him. "You don't get the death penalty for a DUI, dickhead." That prompted another coughing fit.

Donewitz stared down at Fiorello as he hacked. "DUI? What're you talking about, pretty boy?"

"What did you do, Bolt?" Spectacular Man asked in a calm tone that was nonetheless very insistent.

"Cut the shit! You *know* what I did!"

"No, I don't." Spectacular Man put a hand to his chest. "I'm not a police officer, Bolt, and I'm not privy to their files."

Under other circumstances, Fiorello would have laughed at that, given what Mac and Krissie had been going through with this costume's team.

"I killed a woman! That's the end of it for me! I am *not* going back inside, and if they try to throw me in again, I'll blow out another goddamn wall!"

"If this is true," Spectacular Man said, and now he did take a step forward, which made it that much harder for Fiorello not to pee his pants, "then you need to answer for those crimes."

"Hell with that!" Donewitz was gesturing like crazy now and shouting at the top of his lungs. "I ain't answerin' for nothin'! I was drunk, okay, it was an accident! Ain't my fault she lived on the other side of my bedroom wall, okay?"

Fiorello swallowed, a painful process that just made him feel worse, but his mouth was actually producing spit again. "Listen to me, Donewitz—you got arrested on a DUI. That's *it*." He deliberately avoided adding that he had just confessed to murder to him. Not only that, but it was probably his next-door neighbor, which would make it easy to figure out who the victim was.

Donewitz looked down at Fiorello. "Seriously? That was why I got popped Sunday night?"

"You ran four red lights on Nantier—*yeah*, that's why you got popped."

"But—"

Before Donewitz could say anything else, Spectacular Man grabbed him. Fiorello didn't even *see* the costume move, but suddenly he was just *there*, grabbing Donewitz in a bear hug.

Donewitz tried to break loose, and he did fire one of ray-beams staight out of the top of his head, which just pulverized more plaster.

Spectacular Man wrapped one arm around Donewitz's head and constricted it. Donewitz started turning read and sputtering before he finally went limp.

"You kill him?" Fiorello asked, then started coughing again.

Waiting for the coughing to stop, Spectacular Man eventually replied, "Of course not. But he does need medical attention."

Fiorello's smartass response about how Donewitz's need for a hospital was of very little interest to him was prevented by another coughing fit.

While he hacked up a lung, Spectacular Man gathered Donewitz up and flew him out of the window. *I don't believe it! That bastard just took off with the bad guy, and left me duct-taped to a goddamned radiator!*

Behind him, Fiorello heard the distinctive sound of a battering ram slamming into a metal door, followed immediately by the metal door's impact against a plaster wall as it was thrown open.

That was followed by booted feet running into the abandoned apartment.

"Thank Christ," Fiorello said as the EATers came running in. They were all dressed in full gear with helmets cover their entire heads, black body armor covering the rest of them.

Four of them moved throughout the apartment, each bellowing, "Clear!" except for the one who came into the room Fiorello was in. The nametag stenciled into his body armor right over his heart read BRYANT. "We got a man down!"

"I ain't down, Harry," Fiorello said in a scratchy voice, "but I'm duct-taped to a fucking radiator. Get me outta here so I can take a piss, already, willya?"

It wasn't until the seventh person offered Garcia a cup of coffee that he finally accepted. After spilling an entire cup on his nether regions, he swore off coffee for the rest of his life. Generally when he did that—as he'd done for chocolate, cigars, porno DVDs, and, yes, coffee in the past—the resolution only lasted a day.

It hadn't even been an hour in this case, but enough was enough. The adrenaline high from the spill and the situation had faded, and he was having trouble keeping his eyes open. So he took the coffee from Officer Fontaine.

A second and a half later, he regretted it. Looking over at Fontaine, he asked, "Christ, Mara, couldn't you get something that was made with *today's* dishwater?"

Fontaine shrugged. "Sorry, Cap. It's the only cup of coffee around here that costs under a buck."

"Sometimes you get what you pay for," Garcia muttered.

Suddenly, he really wanted a cigar.

Garcia looked at his watch, then looked at Singh. "He's been in there for two minutes. Maybe we should—"

Spectacular Man flew out of the window, cradling Donewitz in his arms. He landed right at the back of the ambulance.

Setting down his cup of caffeinated sewage on one of the blue-and-whites, he dashed over to the ambo. Spectacular Man was talking to one of the paramedics as he set Donewitz down on one of the ambulance's gurneys. "He needs to have power-dampening restraints, and then he needs to go to the ER."

"Yeah, but not until Officer Fiorello is down here," Garcia added.

The paramedic, whose nameplate read GUTHRIE, nodded and then looked over Donewitz.

Garcia glared at Spectacular Man. "You couldn't bring the injured uni down here?"

"It was imperative that Bolt have the restraints put on him before he regains consciousness. And I knew that your Emergency Action Team would rescue Officer Fiorello."

"Did you, now?"

"I did. Especially since Bolt here confessed to murder."

Nearby, Fontaine and Baptiste had retrieved the damps from their cruiser. The restraints were two metal tubes linked by a small bar, making them look like a large letter H. They rolled Donewitz's prone form over and slid his arms into the tubes under the watchful eye of Guthrie.

Garcia's eyes widened at the costume's revelation. "He did what?"

"Confessed to the murder of a woman—probably his next-door neighbor."

"That's great!" Garcia's smile was as false as Regina Dent's first smile. "And of course you'll come down to police HQ with us and fill out a witness statement, yes?"

Spectacular Man hesitated, then looked down at Garcia. The captain was amused to realize that the mask he wore over the top half of his face did a great deal to spoil his expressions. "You know I cannot do that, Captain."

"Actually, yeah, you could." Garcia held up both hands before the costume could respond. "But you choose not to, and I respect that."

That took Spectacular Man aback. "You do?"

"No, honestly, I don't, but it's not like I can stop you."

"He also confessed in front of Officer Fiorello," Spectacular Man said, "who *can* make a statement."

Garcia let out a breath through his teeth. "Yeah, because there's nothing defense lawyers like better than witnesses who were hostages testifying against the guy who took 'em hostage. His statement'll be less than worthless."

"Captain—" Spectacular Man started.

"Don't worry about it," Garcia said, "we're kinda used to it with you people by now. Even if Fiorello will suck as a witness, his statement'll give us enough for a proper investigation. We'll probably be able to nail him. And if not, we've still got him on two counts of assaulting an officer, kidnapping, and a bunch of others."

"That's not the same as murder." Spectacular Man had an odd tone to his voice.

Figuring he had nothing to lose by asking, Garcia said, "Wanna make it up to me?"

Spectacular Man frowned. "I'm sorry?"

"We've been requesting your files on the Claw for two days now, and you've been stonewalling us. We've got to find this guy before he kills anyone else, and the more information we have, the better chance we have of doing that."

Specatcular Man rubbed his cleft chin, but said nothing.

Before Garcia could prompt a verbal response, Singh's people came calmly out of the building. Bryant and Johanssen were both supporting Fiorello on either side of him. Garcia wasn't surprised that, after being duct-taped to a radiator for eight hours, Fiorello would have trouble walking on his own.

Fiorello's hair was also, for the first time in Garcia's memory, mussed.

As they approached the ambulance, Garcia asked, "How you doing, Paul?"

"I'll live, sir."

Turning back around, Garcia saw that Spectacular Man was rising into the air. "Captain—I'll think it over."

And then he flew off.

"Hey, Captain!"

Turning, Garcia saw Fontaine jogging toward him while putting her cell phone away.

"No more coffee, please, Mara?"

Fontaine smiled. "No, sir. Actually, I just got off the phone with Detective Milewski. She said no luck on the files, but the murder weapon from the Bajramis' place *did* come from the Brute Squad."

At that, Garcia just sighed and looked back up into the sky, watching the blue-and-red streak disappear over the buildings on Jaffee.

3.45pm

Therese Zimmerman approached the desks assigned to Milewski and MacAvoy. Their desks were abutted in the detectives' bullpen, as were many partners' desks, against the north wall. Both of them were seated, and had been since their return from the Superior Six blimp that morning.

MacAvoy's desk was piled high with red folders—case files, probably the previous Claw murders. He was flipping through one of them, a pencil covered in teeth marks in his mouth, eraser-end first. Therese thought that must have tasted awful, though the pencil end would've been worse. His hair looked like he'd slept on it funny, his glasses were almost at a forty-five degree angle to the rest of his face, and he hadn't shaved since the previous morning.

Milewski's desk was neater, but she had a laptop open and was looking at a web site. Her blue eyes looked bloodshot, her hair escaping its ponytail. Her red pantsuit still looked good, though.

Both desks had mostly empty Chinese food boxes all around. MacAvoy had a slip of white paper on top of the buttons of his desk's phone, but Milewski hadn't yet eaten her fortune cookie, sitting as it was to the left of her laptop.

"How goes it?" she asked.

Looking up, MacAvoy flicked the pencil upward suddenly, causing the pencil to snap in twain, sending the pencil end flying across into the wall.

"Sonofabitch," he muttered, spitting out the eraser end. "Worst day in the history of the universe was when the City Council passed that ordinance about smoking indoors."

"Or as I like to call it," Milewski muttered, "the day I stopped needing to bring my inhaler into the office."

As Mac gave Milewski a dirty look, Therese asked, "How's it going?"

159

"Lousy, whaddaya think?" Mac said while slamming the folder of the case file he was reading shut.

Milewski closed her laptop, prompting Therese to ask, "What were you looking at?"

Grabbing the fortune cookie and breaking it in half, Milewski said, "The last of fifteen pro-life web sites, all on the list that the Severin Free Clinic provided of organizations that have harassed them. Nobody's claimed responsibility for killing Ashlyn, though most of them were okay with her not providing abortions anymore. Interestingly, four of them actually decried the murder."

"Wonders will never cease."

"Yeah." Milewski pulled the white rectangular slip out of the cookie and popped half of it in her mouth while reading aloud. "'You will find friendship in unexpected places.'"

MacAvoy shook his head. "Don't talk with your mouthful, rook."

Therese turned her gaze upon him. "What about you, Mac?"

"Goin' back over the old case files, trying to see if there's *some* kinda pattern that we got now with fifteen bodies that we didn't have when it was only eleven, but I ain't found shit."

"It was worth a shot," Therese said with a shrug.

"Also," Milewski said, rooting through a wireframe in-box, "we got an updated profile on the Claw from the FBI." She finally liberated a sheet of paper that was adorned with FBI letterhead in fuzzy black type that indicated a fax.

"Anything useful?" Therese asked.

That prompted a snort from Mac. "You're kidding, right?"

Reading off the fax, Milewski said, "They say he's a white male, late thirties, raised by a single parent, with a psychosis that's probably triggered by a biennial occurrence."

"Something that happens twice a year is setting him off?" Mac gave Milewski a very confused expression.

Gently, Therese said, "'Biennial' means every two years. And that's how often we see him, so it fits."

Mac frowned. "I thought 'biennial' was every six months."

Milewski shook her head. "That's 'biannual.'"

"You sure?"

"Well, Mac, I majored in English in college and you majored in Intoxication, so yeah, I'm sure."

Pointing a finger at his partner, Mac said, "Hey, you were still sucking your mother's tits when I was getting drunk in the dorms."

Therese put her hands on her hips. "Do I have to put you two in separate corners?"

"The point is," Mac said, still staring daggers at his partner, "that, as I predicted, the fibbie profile's useless."

Milewski tossed the FBI fax aside and leaned back in her chair. "Honestly, Lieutenant, I'm not sure what else we can do. We've got all the evidence, we've got absolutely no clue where he lives, where he came from, nothing. Until we *find* him, there's not much police work we can do at this point."

Mac grabbed one of the other red folders. "There was one thing, but it didn't go anywhere."

"Oh?" Therese regarded Mac expectantly.

"During his second appearance four years back, the detective who caught the case was Blue-Blue."

"Who?" Therese had never understood the tendency of cops to come up with bizarre nicknames for each other. Some made sense, like "Mac" and her own "Zim," and even "King" Fischer. But then there were people like "Bunny" Gamble in the Western District, or "Bank" Masterson.

Regarding her with surprise, MacAvoy said, "Geez, thought everyone knew Blue-Blue."

"Four years ago," Therese said, "I was the sergeant in charge of the check-and-fraud squad. Didn't really talk to too many Homicide cops back then."

"Fair point." MacAvoy pushed his glasses up his nose. "His real name was Jacob Elwood. He wanted us to call him Jake, which just made the nickname inevitable."

"Fine." Therese didn't even like that movie. "What about him?"

"Well, the Claw was his last case before he joined the FBI, believe it or not. Fucking traitor. Anyhow, after the second set of murders, he noticed that the victims were all right near where the Stupid Six had their blimp at the time of the killings. He thought that maybe the Claw was trying to call the Six out by killing people in their backyard."

Therese rubbed her chin. "Interesting theory."

"It doesn't hold up, though," Milewski said, shaking her head. "When he showed up two years ago, the two kills and the one attempt that the Bengal broke up weren't anywhere near the blimp. And we checked—only one of the four newest were anywhere near the blimp, and that was Barker."

"Too bad." Therese put her hands on her hips. "Maybe he gave up trying to call them out. Anyhow, I'm off at four—Marc and I are having drinks." To her abject shock, Marc expressed a desire to see her tonight. It wasn't the makeup dinner date they'd originally planned when Monday at Emmanuelli's was busted (the one he cancelled over the phone yesterday), it was just a twenty-minute drinks date, but Therese would take it at this point. She didn't regret what she'd said to Marc over the phone yesterday, but she felt the need to apologize to him anyhow. It wasn't like *he* had any control over what the Six chose to do with themselves. Sure, as their financier he held influence, but that wasn't the same thing.

She continued: "You two should go home and get some sleep. Kristin's right, there's nothing new to learn at this point, and you both look like hammered shit. We'll get back on this in the morning."

Mac stood up. "I like this plan. For starters, I can get a smoke."

Milewski's phone chirped. Therese was about to tell her not to bother—she wasn't up in the rotation as long as she was on this case, and Therese wanted them both to get some needed rest—but before she could say anything, the detective grabbed the black plastic receiver and said, "Milewski, Homicide."

Therese looked at Mac, who was shrugging into his denim jacket and giving her a *what do you expect from a stupid rookie?* expression.

"Yes, that's me—it's spelled 'mill-EW-skee,' but it's pronounced 'mah-LOV-skee.' Yeah. Okay. Why are you telling *me* this? What? Oh, shit. Gimme the address again?" Milewski started jotting down an address on a Post-It. "Yeah, okay. We'll be right there."

She hung up and looked right at Therese.

The last time Kristin Milewski had so stricken a look on her face, it was Monday morning in Therese's office when Garcia dressed her down for going over the lieutenant's head.

Therese had a sinking feeling that she wasn't going to enjoy the reason for that expression this time.

"We've got another body," she said, "in the Cowan Houses in Heckton. Ripped to shreds, Post-It, the whole bit."

Mac put his head in his hands. "You've got to be fucking kidding me."

"Look on the bright side," Therese said with a sigh, "you'll still get your cigarette." She shook her head. "Go. I'll let Javier know."

As the two detectives headed for the exit, Therese considered cancelling her drinks date and heading to Heckton.

After a moment, she rejected the notion. The last thing MacAvoy and Milewski needed was a boss standing over them at a crime scene. She had her phone in case anyone needed to reach her.

And if the Claw had claimed yet *another* victim, she wasn't sure when she was going to get to see Marc again after this.

6pm

"Good evening! From Super City, I'm John Wang."

"And I'm Victoria Solano, and you're watching the evening edition of *News 6 at 6*."

"Tonight we'll find out why the Terrific Trio's been so quiet, why the Bruiser has been so talkative, and why mum's the word on why Angelina Jolie has come to town. Plus we'll have Daniel McCall with sports, Natasha Whitaker with weather, and Frieda Beck with traffic."

"But first, our top story. Tragedy has once again struck Super City, as the Claw claimed another victim this afternoon in Heckton. Matt Barnett has the story. Matt?"

"Behind me is one of several city-owned buildings originally constructed as low-income housing in the years after World War II. The Cowan State Housing Project first opened its doors in 1957. Home primarily to Hungarian immigrants following the revolution the previous year, it was one of the few structures in this neighborhood that survived the 1968 attack on Heckton by KKKaos, and the community center in the project's ground floor served as a relief center after the Hip Cats and the Groovy Gang teamed up to stop KKKaos's rampage. Most of the residents of the Cowan these days are still immigrants, but from the Dominican Republic.. That population was reduced by one today, as the mutated spree killer known as the Claw claimed another victim: Armando Ramirez. The fifty-five-year-old just last month retired from his job as a janitor at Drake High School, and was on his way home from a bodega on the corner of 125th and Nelson when he was attacked. His body was found by the bodega's owner, Bernabe Arango. I was able to talk to Mr. Arango before he went to police headquarters to make a statement."

"It was very bad. He was just in my store, and he buy groceries

165

for his family. He was a good man to his family, always good to them, providing for them, as a man should, yes? And then I hear screams, and at first I no do nothing. It not always good to do that, yes? But the screams, they no stop, and then they become a kind of weird noise like someone drowning, yes? I never hear no scream like that before. So I run outside, and I see the most horrible... *Madre de Dios, nunca he visto cualquier cosa*—sorry, sorry, my English is no good, but I have never in my life... I move here right before they rebuild the Layton Houses, so I was here when Dread Gang first show up. Even so, nothing like this. Nothing."

"As with the previous fifteen victims of the Claw, Mr. Ramirez's body was found with a Post-It affixed to his forehead, on which was drawn the claw of an eagle in ballpoint pen. SCPD detectives and forensic investigators are still going over the scene and have yet to make a formal statement, but one officer spoke off the record saying that they don't expect to find anything different from the scenes of the other murders. In fact, it's seeming more and more unlikely that the SCPD will be able to solve this case without a significant lucky break. For *News 6 at 6*, I'm Matt Barnett."

"Thank you, Matt. It's worth mentioning that many previous serial killers have been brought down by such lucky breaks—for example, the Son of Sam in New York City was captured thanks to a parking ticket, and here in Super City, the Mad Hungarian was brought down by the Cowboy when the hero accidentally crashed into the villain's apartment window while fighting the Destructon. So maybe the SCPD will get that break, right, Victoria?"

"Let's hope so, John. In related news, the Bruiser has been on a rampage through Simon Valley. Several people, who have been identified by neighbors as known drug dealers, have been turning up badly injured and taken to Kane Memorial Hospital. It's unknown whether or not any arrests have been made. *News 6 at 6* cameras caught up with the Bruiser today, and in an unexpected turn of events, he did provide a brief statement."

"I'm just doing what I can to find the Claw. I saw the body of one of his victims—and *nobody* should die like that. I ain't gonna rest until that *pendejo* is stopped."

"It's good to see that there's *someone* who cares. The streets of Super City are dangerous enough without the Claw roaming the streets. The SCPD really needs to follow the Bruiser's example and do their job."

"Can't argue with that, Victoria. If *you* have an opinion on how the SCPD is handling the Claw crisis, log onto our web site at www. news6at6.com and let us know what you think."

"You can also e-mail John and I directly at the site. Next up after some words from our sponsors, a look at the Terrific Trio's latest mission, which was literally out of this world, and a surprising twist from Montana Congressman F. Richard Wert in his campaign to force superheroes to register."

"We'll be right back."

6.05pm

"Sweet holy motherfucking jumping Jesus cluny frog on a goddamn stick!"

Police Commissioner Enzo Dellamonica's jaw fell open at the mayor's invective. It wasn't that Aaron Sittler made use of words you'd never hear on the *News 6 at 6* broadcast that the pair of them were watching in the mayor's office. In public, Sittler was the picture of decorum, but once the doors closed and the microphones turned off, he could make a sailor cringe.

As someone who came up in the ranks of the SCPD, Dellamonica knew from profanity. There were few subsets of humanity quite as foul-mouthed as your average police. Mayor Sittler would've fit right in at roll call back in the day.

This, however, was an impressive string of swearing even by the mayor's high standards.

Dellamonica had been at a meeting at City Hall when the call came in that the Claw had another victim. After the meeting was over, the commissioner spent an hour on the phone with Javier Garcia, Therese Zimmerman, Regina Dent, and half his staff before he was called into Sittler's office. By that time, *News 6 at 6* was starting, and the ever-image-conscious Sittler wanted to hear what they said.

They were sitting in the mayor's well-appointed third-floor office. City Hall itself was four stories tall, with the top floor used only for storage. The office had a lovely view of the Thomas River out a huge picture window that took up the entirety of the east wall. Sittler sat in his huge leather chair with his back to the north wall, elbows leaning on a magnificent oak desk that he held onto despite fire codes that forbade such large pieces of wood in government buildings. He stared intently at the flat-screen television that was mounted to the south wall, which was showing the news.

After the anchors did their editorializing about the SCPD's competence, Sittler turned his big nose toward Dellamonica. "What the fuck, Enzo? I mean, what the fucking fuck?"

Holding up his hands in a plaintive gesture, Dellamonica asked, "Whaddaya want me to do, Aaron?"

"I want you and your fucking useless piece of shit police force to do your fucking useless piece of shit jobs!"

Running a hand over his bald pate, Dellamonica declined to point out how little sense Sittler's words made. "We're doing the best we can."

"And the fact that *this* bullshit is the *best* the Super City Fucking Police Department can handle, truly scares the motherfucking shit out of me, Enzo."

"Hey, I brought down LaManna, I'll bring down this guy."

Sittler pointed a finger at Dellamonica. "Don't fuck a fucker, fuck-face. You and I both know it was that asshole in the tiger suit who brought LaManna down. And it's becoming more and more fucking obvious that the fuckwads in tights are doing a better job of policing this town than *your* sorry ass."

Dellamonica had had enough of this. "It was *police work* that brought LaManna down. Yeah, sure, the Bengal did some of the legwork, but it was *my* case that got him prosecuted." He leaned back in his chair, tugging on his dark brown mustache, which was annoyingly thicker than any of the hair on his head. "But fine, let's say that the costumes really do all the work. Apart from DeLaHoya, who's *always* helped us out, tell me, *where the hell are they?*"

Just as he said that, *News 6 at 6* came back from their commercial break, and Victoria Solano started talking about the rogue comet that the Terrific Trio stopped from crashing into Europa.

Pointing at the flat screen, Dellamonica said, "See? The Terrific Turkeys are off playing Captain Kirk, the Stupid Six are playing footsie with the Brute Squad at the post office, and—for, I might add, the first time since I became commissioner—we've gone a week without the Cowboy showboating and sticking his nose in things."

Sittler leaned back in his chair, steepling his fingers. "What's your fucking point, Enzo?"

"Whaddaya think's my point?" Dellamonica leaned forward in his. "You know what Europa is? It's one of Jupiter's moons. Or maybe one of Saturn's, I forget. Point is, it's just a lousy moon that's covered in ice. There's a nutjob killing people in Super City, and those three garbanzos are protecting *ice* millions of miles away. At least my cops are *trying*."

"What happened to all that bullshit I spewed about the Six and the Trio 'consulting extensively' with your guys? I mean, shit, yeah, the Trio's been off doing fuck-all in space, but what about the Six?"

Dellamonica sputtered. "You tell me. Two of my detectives went up to that stupid blimp of theirs *twice*. Both times they got blown off. I gotta be honest with you, Aaron, I don't think these guys *want* the Claw caught."

"Don't be an asshole." Sittler grabbed a paperweight off his desk. It was a snow globe, with a really dreadful rendition of the Super City skyline, and a poorly rendered Spectacular Man figure flying past what was probably supposed to be the SC Tower. The old SC Tower. The mayor shook it as he spoke, causing fake snow to fly around Spectacular Man and the buildings. "I see something like that news report, and it's like I'm watching votes drop off like leaves on a tree in fucking autumn."

Frowning, Dellamonica said, "The election's not for another year and a half."

"Yeah, and I gotta start my ass campaigning now. Fucking

Simms already started a goddamn exploratory committee, so you *know* the motherfucker's gonna try to run against me."

Dellamonica nodded. Stephen Simms was on the City Council and had been gunning for the mayor's job since before Sittler was elected.

"This Claw shit is also giving Wert traction on his goddamn bill, and now Simms is starting to talk about how that fucking bill is a *good* idea." Sitter started tossing the paperweight back and forth from one hand to the other. "Christ, this town'll be torn the fuck apart if Simms runs this place."

Patiently, Dellamonica waited. He had his own ambitions to be sitting on the other side of that oak desk some day, and right now, the best way to do that was to stay on Aaron Sittler's good side. He was powerful in the party, and the local businesses loved him because his supers-first initiatives had actually improved tourism. The only way Dellamonica was going to have a chance was to keep his ass firmly attached to Sittler's coattails.

So he let the mayor rant and rave about how today's events would affect an election two years hence—which wasn't something the commissioner could actually help him with.

After a little bit more ranting, Sittler slammed the paperweight down onto the desk. "The Six blew off your detectives?"

"Twice."

Sittler shook his head and scratched his large nose. "Fuck that shit." He grabbed his phone and stabbed at one of the buttons. As soon as he did that, his demeanor softened and his voice went up half an octave. "Jenny, put me through to the Superior Six's PR flack. It's Starkey, right? She left? Too bad, she knew her stuff. Okay, yeah, Parsons. Get her for me. Thanks."

He put the phone back gently into the cradle and then stared at the flat screen. Victoria Solano was doing a puff piece about

Angelina Jolie. There were rumors that she was being cast in *It's Spectacular, Man!* as Southern Belle and had come to Super City in order to talk to Belle at the Ellis Penitentiary, where she was serving her life sentence.

Shaking his head, Sittler's voice deepened again. "Fuckers have the balls to talk about how shit a job SCPD's doing when *this* is their idea of fucking *news*. At least when I catch that shit from Duffy or Hoffman, they stand by it with actual fucking reporting that they actually fucking wrote in an actual fucking newspaper, not some shit they're reading off cue cards."

"You rather they were doing more stories like that shitstorm with Cohen?"

As soon as Dellamonica said the words, he regretted doing so. Jimmy Cohen was the mayor's travelling secretary, and he'd been embezzling by drawing city funds for an "advance person" who didn't actually exist to scout ahead to places the mayor was going. Adriana Berardi of *News 6 at 6* broke the story that his resignation was a cover for his termination. Cohen had minor super-powers, as it turned out, and was able to convince people that a nonexistent person was real.

From what Dellamonica heard, Sittler threw a fit when that particular story aired yesterday that made today's profanity-fest look tame by comparison.

Luckily, Sittler's phone rang just as he was opening his mouth to yell at Dellamonica. He looked down at the phone and wrinkled his face as if it was a dead fish on his desk, then picked it up. "Yeah? Okay, put her through." Only then did the voice go back up an octave. "Hello Ms. Parsons, this is Mayor Sittler. Let me put you on speaker." He hit the SPEAKER button and hung the phone up. "I'm here with Commissioner Dellamonica."

A tinny, perky voice came over the phone's small speaker.

"What can I do you for you gentlemen today?"

"Ms. Parsons, representatives from the Super City Police Department have twice come to the Superior Six's headquarters in order to request that the Six share their files on the Claw. Now I think we can both agree that the Claw is a menace that requires immediate action on the part of law-enforcement *and* the superheroic community before more people die, yes?"

"Absolutely, your honor. And I can assure you that the Six is doing everything in their power to try to apprehend the Claw."

Sittler shook his head. "Well, see, Ms. Parsons, there's where you're wrong."

"I'm sorry?"

Leaning forward, Sittler said, "You're not doing *everything* in your power, because it is within your power to turn over those files, and yet you aren't."

"First of all, your honor, it isn't within *my* power to do anything of the sort."

Dellamonica smiled. Parsons's tone had gone from perky and polite to defensive in very short order.

She continued: "Secondly, the Six feels that those files are sensi—"

"Ms. Parsons, are you headquartered in the Six's blimp?"

There was a brief hesitation. "I have offices in the dirigible, yes, but—"

"And that blimp is permitted to fly over Super City because the Six has been granted permits by the city and by the FAA, yes?"

"I'm not familiar with the particulars of—"

"If Commissioner Dellamonica's people do not have those files in their hands by the end of business tomorrow, those permits will be revoked. And in my experience, the FAA *and* the Department of Homeland Security take a dim view of vehicles that fly over urban areas without authorization. Do I make myself clear, Ms. Parsons?"

A very long pause, then: "I will pass on your message to the Six."

"Do that." With a large smile, Sittler stabbed the END button.

As much as Dellamonica enjoyed that, he was not smiling. "You sure that was such a hot idea?"

"What?"

"Threatening them. I mean—they *are* the Superior Six."

"And I'm the goddamn mayor." Sittler leaned back in his chair, which squeaked slightly. "It's time they remembered that *they* don't run this fucking town."

Dellamonica nodded while he started to think about who else in the party he could suck up to if Sittler found himself on the way out. This kind of crazy-ass maneuver could explode in the mayor's face, and Dellamonica didn't want to catch any of the blowback.

PART FOUR

THURSDAY

11.40am

Trevor Baptiste stared at his flip-top cell phone, playing a tinny version of "Proud Mary" and vibrating in his hand, debating whether or not to open it and answer the call.

Next to him in the blue-and-white, Mara Fontaine was driving. Baptiste only agreed to let her do so if she promised to stay under thirty miles an hour on local streets. She asked, "You gonna answer that, or what?"

He dropped the phone back into his pocket. "Or what. It's the number for Mazur, Randleman, and Levin."

"Uh, okay." Fontaine sounded confused as she turned the cruiser onto Simonson from 25th Street.

Remembering that he hadn't shared every single detail of his lawsuit with Fontaine—the process was tedious enough for him, he wasn't about to bog his partner down in the details, as she had her own problems—he said, "That's the law firm that's representing the insurance company."

Fontaine nodded. "Shouldn't they be talking to Elaine?"

"Yes, which is why I didn't answer the phone. I'll keep the voicemail message—assuming they leave one—and forward it to Elaine. And if they don't, I'll have her pull my cell's records and show that they called. It's a violation of ethics, if nothing else."

"I thought these guys were a fancy-ass insurance firm. Surprised they'd have lawyers dumb enough to do that."

Baptiste shrugged. "Insurance isn't exactly the happiest business in this city."

With a smile, Fontaine said, "True."

"Besides, I was talking with Elaine this morning. Turns out that the same company that owned the Conway Building also owns the building that houses the Super City Post Office."

Fontaine shot Baptiste a look before looking ahead again and slowing down for a red light on 30th. "Doesn't the post office own it?"

"Apparently not." Baptiste sighed. "They're probably feeling pressure to settle things quickly so they can deal with the latest. As I said, not a happy business."

"That's their fucking problem." Fontaine's anger was palpable, and Baptiste found himself warmed by it.

The light turned green, and Fontaine accelerated through the intersection. As she did so, Baptiste stared out the side window—and saw a large suit of armor in the middle of the sidewalk facing a young man wearing a stylized sweatshirt. The latter was backed up against the brick wall of a large apartment building.

"You have got to be joking." He pointed ahead. "Look at that."

Fontaine followed his finger and said, "Oy."

When the suit of armor raised a lance and pointed it at the young man, that confirmed it. It was the self-proclaimed Knight Dude. "I do not believe this."

"What, that Valentine's back on the street or that he's doing something stupid again?"

"Pick one." He thumbed his radio. "PCD, this is 2205 with a signal 10 on the 6000 block of Simonson."

"Roger 2205."

Activating the siren, Fontaine and pulled over next to a fire hydrant that was about thirty feet from where Knight Dude was menacing the young man. As they got closer, Baptiste was able to make out the sweatshirt the boy was wearing: it was silkscreened with the image of Starling's costume on it, down to the hero's wings on his arms. It was probably an official piece of Superior Six merchandise—like all of it, sold by the McLean Foundation with proceeds going to charity—though it could just as easily have been one of the many knockoffs that were readily available.

The young man was actually a boy of about fourteen or fifteen; he appeared to be African American, though his dark skin had gone a bit gray at the sight of a man in a full suit of armor pointing a lance with a glowing tip at him. His back was to the wall, his palms pressed flat against the brick, his eyes wide as proverbial saucers. Having seen what that lance could do, Baptiste didn't begrudge the boy his fear. Besides the Starling sweatshirt, he wore the name-brand jeans and white sneakers that Baptiste saw on much of the black male youth of Super City.

"Officers!" Knight Dude's filtered voice echoed off the apartment buildings. "Thank goodness you're here! Behold, I have at last captured the Claw!"

Baptiste actually put his head in his hands.

Holding up his gauntleted left hand—his right still had what Baptiste hoped was a firm grip on the lance hilt—Knight Dude showed off a pair of gloves that looked like they were shaped like eagle talons. They were obviously supposed to go with the sweatshirt, though they didn't match up with Starling, as he had normal hands. Then again, the gloves were a different color than the sweatshirt as well, so they probably were purchased separately.

"See?" Knight Dude said enthusiastically, though the effect was muted by the helmet. "These are the claws he uses to kill his victims! I was about to dispatch him when you made your timely arrival!"

Fontaine almost snarled. "That's not the Claw, Englebert!"

"Of course it is!"

"The Claw is a mutated being, Englebert," Baptiste said, following his partner's lead by using Knight Dude's first name. "He does not wear gloves. The claws are his actual fingers."

"Really?" Knight Dude's voice went up an octave.

"Yes," Fontaine said, holding out a hand. "His victims all had

DNA on their cuts, not cloth. Now put the lance down and let the kid go."

Knight Dude just stood there for a second. The armor didn't give him a great deal of range of motion, so for a moment, he looked like a statue.

Then, with a metallic squeak, he turned to look at the young man. "My apologies, citizen. You are free to go. Here are your gloves back."

"*Keep* 'em, motherfucker, I'm out!" the boy said as he ran down the sidewalk.

Baptiste slowly walked up to Knight Dude. "I am afraid we are going to have to arrest you again, Englebert."

"How did you get back on the street again, anyhow?" Fontaine asked. "And get your armor back?"

"I have many spare suits of armor, Officer Fontaine," Knight Dude said proudly, "and I was released on bail this very morning! The judge did not deem me a flight risk—for where else would I go but the city I love?"

While Baptiste was trying to recall how they got his gauntlets off two days ago in order to put on the handcuffs, Fontaine said, "Let's just let it go, Trevor."

Shooting his partner a look, Baptiste asked, "Excuse me?"

"What's the point? We have to process him, deal with all the bullshit, and for what? It's not like that kid's gonna press charges." She shook her head. "And what if we bump into MacAvoy? I may have to punch him."

Baptiste couldn't help but burst out a quick laugh at that one.

"About time," Fontaine said with a grin of her own. "I was starting to think you'd forgotten how to smile."

"I do wonder sometimes." He shook his head. "Go, Englebert. And be careful, please?"

Raising his lance, Knight Dude started to say, "Tha—" then clunked the tip of his lance against his helmet, causing him to stumble backward. He pinwheeled his arms, dropped the lance, and fell backward in a very loud, clattering heap. The lance struck the sidewalk and fired.

Baptiste ducked as the air sizzled and a beam shot out from the lance's tip and struck their blue-and-white right in the grille. The metalwork shattered, the radiator pulverized, and steam came exploding outward.

Fontaine turned to look at Baptiste. Baptiste looked at Fontaine. Then Fontaine thumbed her radio. "PCD, this is Unit 2205. We have a signal 62 and require assistance."

Staring at the tattered remains of the grille, Baptiste shook his head. "Sergeant Taylor is going to kill us." Then he walked over to Knight Dude, who was struggling, loudly, to get to his feet and having very little success.

Looks like I'm going to have to get those gauntlets off. "Englebert Valentine, you're under arrest for the destruction of police property. You have the right to remain silent…"

2.10pm

`Javier Garcia didn't get` to go out to lunch very often. He generally didn't have the time, so he would bring his own in. Garcia was an excellent cook—he had originally romanced Maria by making empanadas—so he'd usually put something together on Sunday that was large enough to feed a family of ten, eat a bit of it for dinner that night, then pack the rest into a giant Tupperware container. That huge container was the one and only piece from his and Maria's kitchen that he kept in the divorce, for precisely this purpose. Each day, he'd scoop a bit out and put it into a smaller Tupperware that he'd bought after the divorce and take it in to sit in the refrigerator in HQ's kitchen until midday, when he'd toss it in the microwave. He generally did likewise when he got home, scooping out some onto a plate and nuking it.

Aside from the two weeks when HQ's microwave was busted, this plan had served him well in the days since he and Maria split up. For one thing, cooking a huge meal was a pleasant way for him to spend a relaxing Sunday after a stressful week on the job. There was an order to cooking, but also an art—the right proportions, the proper cooking time, getting the vegetables browned *just* right, frying the meat for *just* long enough.

More to the point, it was something he could control. He was responsible for a police force that barely was able to hold the city together in the face of a crime rate that was highest of any large city in the nation, coupled with a conviction rate that was the lowest (thanks to the costumes not testifying or filling out statements or doing much of anything useful beyond excess property damage). His marriage had come completely apart despite doing everything he could to keep it together.

And he couldn't stop *mami* from calling him a dozen times an hour.

But he could control what he cooked. It was the only time in the world that Garcia was at any kind of peace.

Today, though, he stumbled out of bed after yet *another* sleepless night. He guzzled down two cups of undrinkable coffee from his cheap percolator, as opposed to his usual single cup, bought a slightly less undrinkable cup from the sidewalk stand on the corner of Robbins and Nantier, and poured some squadroom sludge down his gullet upon arrival at HQ.

The coffee did very little to keep him alert, as it wasn't until he walked into the kitchen that he realized that he completely forgot to bring in his lunch. He had made a nice steak-and-shrimp stew, with tomatoes, onions, several types of peppers, and a ton of spices. It had come out particularly well, and he had been eagerly looking forward to eating it at lunch, so to find himself standing in the HQ kitchen like a moron looking around for a plastic bag that he'd forgotten to bring in was exceedingly annoying. Even Wednesday, when Fiorello was taken hostage and Garcia drove straight to the scene instead of taking STT into the office, he remembered his lunch.

Today, though, he forgot.

After that, the morning gauntlet of Taylor, assorted people from Chief Prosecutor's office, Merkle, the inevitable phone calls from *mami* and Dellamonica's office, and the nothing-new-to-report reports from MacAvoy and Milewski simply did him in.

He had to leave the building, if only for an hour.

So for the first time in he-couldn't-remember-how-long, he went out to lunch.

Both when he arrived at seven and when he'd gone back out at one, he'd had the presence of mind to use the side entrance, which had the advantage of having no press gathered around waiting to pounce on an unsuspecting police dumb enough to wander in that way. Zimmerman had gone in the front—however, she'd planned that ahead of time with Regina Dent, with prepared answers ready to go.

But after treating himself to a delicious lunch at the Argonaut, a nice Greek place on the corner of Nantier and 57th that he hadn't been to in ages, he decided to take a short walk. It was a nice spring day, not a cloud in the sky, in the low sixties with a mild breeze. Garcia liked the fact that Super City had tremendous variety in its weather—and in fact it was supposed to rain either tonight or tomorrow—but weather like this was what he lived for. He decided to take some time to enjoy it for once.

So distracted was he that he walked on autopilot, and found himself meandering down 61st toward the main entrance to HQ instead of around to the side entrance on Fox Place.

He didn't really notice until the phalanx of reporters and camera operators descended upon him like flies on a broken jar of honey.

At first he couldn't make out a single coherent syllable from the babble of questions that were thrown at him.

Holding up his hands, he cried out, "One at a time! One at a time!" Even as he was talking, he saw four unis noticing his presence and walking over.

Matt Barnett from *News 6 at 6* blurted out a question before anyone else could. "The *Gazette* has a source that says the FBI is going to take over the Claw case. Is this true?"

Garcia was about to say something that Barnett would have to seriously edit in order to use on *News 6 at 6* when his Zap rang.

The captain grabbed for the phone in his jacket like a drowning man clutching at a life preserver. The display indicated that it was his mother.

Promising to never again be annoyed at *mami* for calling him so often—a promise that had the same shelf-life as yesterday's promise to give up coffee, but what the hell—Garcia said, "I'm sorry, but this is an important call that I have to take."

He pressed TALK, turned around and walked quickly in the other direction. By this time, the four unis had shown up and were keeping the reporters at bay.

"Hello, *mami*," Garcia said.

For the next several minutes, Garcia's mother talked into his ear and Garcia made assorted grunts and vocalizations, some of which cohered into actual words like "yes, *mami*." All the while he walked around to Fox and the side entrance, where the press was not allowed.

The side door led into the kitchen—ironic, given Garcia's forgetfulness this morning—and Zimmerman was there, pouring grounds into the filter for the coffeemaker. "*Mami*, I gotta go."

"Well, you be careful, Javy, okay? I worry."

"I know you worry, and I *will* be careful, I promise."

Zimmerman smiled at him as he put the phone away. "How is Marisol doing?"

Garcia stared at the lieutenant. "She's been my mother all my life, and she hasn't changed a damn bit that whole time. You really think there's been a difference since you saw her last month?"

Recoiling as if Garcia had slapped her, Zimmerman said, "Sorry, Javier. I didn't mean—"

Closing his eyes and shaking his head, Garcia winced. "No, no, I should be apologizing. I got ambushed by the press outside."

Zimmerman frowned. "They were at the side?"

"No, I was an idiot and went to the front. *Mami*'s call actually rescued me. That reminds me, I need to call the *Gazette*." He explained what Matt Barnett said.

"It had to be Charlie," Zimmerman said.

"Of *course* it was Charlie." Garcia rolled his eyes. "*If* it's real, anyhow. Nobody else on the *Gazette* has that kind of juice. I gotta call him."

Zimmerman finished putting the coffee together. "The four Brutes that the Six captured are in the supers wing of Ellis Island. Lazzeri and Katzenberg are finishing up the paperwork—once that's done, we can put 'em back in rotation."

Garcia nodded, listening to the 1950s-monster-movie gurgle of the coffeemaker as the boiling water soaked through the grounds and the filter. The Ellis Penitentiary was located on a small island in the middle of the Thomas River, and had been jokingly nicknamed after the more famous immigration port in New York City.

"Bannon and Schiazza just got back from the M.E.'s," Zimmerman went on. "Donewitz's next-door neighbor—woman by the name of Adrienne Lashmar—was pretty ripe, but they were able to confirm that she was killed by something hot burning through her skin, which is consistent with the Bolt's MO."

"Good—maybe now he won't take out our drunk tank again." Garcia reached for one of the mugs in the cabinet over the coffeemaker. "The neighbor really was *still* next door?"

Zimmerman nodded. "Lashmar didn't have any family in town and she's unemployed and, according to Schiazza, her friends haven't heard much from her lately because she'd been depressed about not having any family in town and being unemployed."

"Yeah." The gurgles finished, and Garcia poured himself some coffee, then handed the pot to Zimmerman. "Where are we on the Claw?"

"Mac and Milewski haven't gotten back from the Cowan yet." The two detectives had gone back to the scene this morning to canvass the neighbors of the Claw's latest victim. To Garcia's annoyance, he couldn't remember the victim's name—which was the danger with multiples. One of the ways homicide cops dealt with more than one victim was to think of it, not as many murders, but one case. In those circumstances, however, it was easy to lose sight of the individuals.

Before Zimmerman could say anything further, a loud whoop and cry of "Hallelujah!" came from the entryway.

Turning, Garcia saw Bart Billinghurst and "King" Fischer walking into the kitchen. Fischer had his arms raised in triumph, and Billinghurst yelled out, "Angels and ministers of grace defend us, glory be, glory be!"

Unable to help himself, Garcia smiled. It felt good, and he resolved to try to do that more often.

Next to him, Zimmerman was out-and-out laughing. "What's going on?"

"Obviously," Garcia said, "King just saw a touchdown."

Putting his arms down quickly, Fischer said, "Sorry, Cap, but we're just in a good mood."

"You may ask," Billinghurst added, going to the refrigerator and opening it, "why we are in such a good mood, for we are murder police. By and large, we're a maudlin crew."

"Indeed," Fischer said. "We are prone to depression, gallows humor…"

"…smoking too much," Billinghurst added, liberating a Granny Smith apple from the bottom shelf of the fridge, "drinking too much."

"I don't smoke," Fischer said, "but I'll cop to the other one."

Billinghurst took a bite of his apple with verve and a very loud crunch. "Yet here we are—"

"Don't talk with your mouth full," Fischer said with a wince. "Let me do it. Here we are, triumphant and happy. And we are triumphant because—"

"And happy!" Billinghurst said through masticated apple.

"Yes, triumphant and happy," Fischer corrected himself with a nod to his partner, "because we just got word from Sergeant Taylor that the Clone Master has been sighted getting the shit kicked out of him by the Bruiser in Everett Square."

Having swallowed his bit of apple, Billinghurst added, "Which means he's alive which means there is little point in trying to solve his murder, which means we can go back to *real* police work!" He held up a hand, which Fischer obligingly high-fived.

Garcia's ZP500 chose that moment to ring. Pulling it out of his jacket pocket, the display told him that it was Dellamonica's office calling. *He never calls me on my cell*, Garcia thought as he hit TALK. The commissioner acting in an unprecedented manner almost always meant bad news.

"Yes, Enzo?"

"Merkle said you were out to lunch," Dellamonica said without preamble. "Since when do you go out to lunch?"

"Since I forgot my lunch at home and wanted to get the hell out of my office." Garcia wandered away from the coffeemaker to the relative privacy of one of the corners of the kitchen. "What is it, Enzo?"

"Catch the Claw yet?"

"No, not yet. MacAvoy and Milewski are out interviewing—"

"I don't care. I want him caught, Javier."

"So do I, Enzo. I—"

Garcia stopped talking when he realized that Dellamonica had hung up on him.

Zimmerman was staring at him as he put the Zap back in his pocket. "That must've been the shortest conversation ever with the commissioner."

"If only they were all like that." Even as he spoke, the phone rang again. This time it was the trunk line for City Hall on the display.

"This is Captain Garcia," he said after hitting TALK.

The voice of the mayor's assistant—Joan? Janet? something like that—came over the earpiece. "Hold for Mayor Sittler, please."

"Jesus," Garcia muttered, "did Merkle give *everyone* my damn cell number?"

"Captain Garcia," the mayor's voice said after a mercifully brief bit of bad hold music, "I'm calling in the hopes that you will have good news for me about the Claw."

"We're working on it, sir."

"Have the files from the Superior Six arrived yet?"

Garcia blinked. "I wasn't aware they *would* be arriving."

"I had a conversation with the Six on the subject," Sittler said in an annoyed tone, "and made it clear that *not* providing the files would have dire consequences. If they don't show up by end of business, call my assistant and let her know, will you please, Captain?"

"Of course, your honor."

"And if they *do* show up, call Jenny as well."

Jenny, that's it. "Absolutely, sir."

"Thank you, Captain. Good luck."

After again stowing his phone, Garcia looked over to see Fischer and Billinghurst still grinning, the former now with a mug of coffee of his own, the latter making short work of his apple.

"It's such a beautiful day, isn't it?" Fischer said.

Zimmerman said, "It's supposed to rain later."

Billinghurst snorted. "It will *still* be a beautiful day, because the Clone Master is alive—as he always was—and our long national nightmare is at last at an end!"

"Damn straight!" Fischer held up a hand this time, and it was

Billinghurst who delivered the high-five.

"What the fuck are *you* two so happy about?"

Garcia turned to see MacAvoy and Milewski, looking haggard, coming into the kitchen from the Fox Place entrance.

Frowning at Milewski, Zimmerman asked, "Kristin—isn't that the same suit you wore yesterday?"

Looking at the shorter detective, Garcia noted that the red pantsuit she wore was sufficiently wrinkled that it almost looked like she'd put the wrong size suit on that morning.

And, now that he thought about it, that *was* the same suit she had on yesterday.

Milewski started to say, "It's—" when her own Zap rang. She pulled it out of her purse, looked at the display, let out a noise very much like the sound of a pipe bursting, then tapped what had to have been IGNORE and put it back in her purse.

"Who was that?" Zimmerman asked.

"Don't even ask," MacAvoy said. "Whoever it is has been calling all day, and she won't say who it is."

"Fuck you, Mac," Milewski said with a dirty look at her partner.

Garcia asked, "Where are we with the Claw?"

"Same as always, Javy," MacAvoy said.

Milewski went over to the coffeemaker, taking one of the Styrofoam cups from the pile next to it. "We talked to the vic's family and neighbors. Nobody heard anything, nobody saw anything."

Taylor walked in then, her glasses dangling off the chain around her neck. She held a small envelope in her hand. "Hey, Detectives! You got something from the Schwartz Building."

MacAvoy and Milewski looked at each other. "Us?" Milewski asked, then pointed at Billinghurst and Fischer. "Or them?"

"You."

Walking toward Taylor, MacAvoy said, "If it's the Schwartz Building it better goddamn well be us." He took the envelope from the sergeant's hand and ripped it open, pulling out a small flash drive. "I'm gonna go out on a limb and say this has the Stupid Six's files on the Claw."

Billinghurst grinned. "See? It's a beautiful beautiful day!"

Garcia chuckled and shook his head. "Get to work on 'em. I'll be in my office."

Walking with Taylor, Garcia exited the kitchen. The former said: "Heard from Kane Memorial—they're gonna release Fiorello today. O'Malley's still in critical, though, and Fiorello's been spending all his time sittin' with him."

"Yeah." Garcia sighed. "Dammit, I should've gone to the hospital instead of getting all self-indulgent and going to the damn Argonaut."

Taylor stepped in front of Garcia just as they were nearing the reception area in the center of the squadroom, putting a hand on his chest. "Cut that out right *now*, Javier. You're the captain—you can *be* self-indulgent if you wanna, and you're entitled to have one lunch break where you say the hell with it and get Greek food. So stop all this nonsense, you feel me, *Captain?*"

Again, Garcia shook his head and chuckled. "Absolutely, *Sarge*. Now can I go to my office, please?"

Stepping aside, Taylor said, "Absolutely."

Barreling past any number of unis and deputy prosecutors, Garcia made it to his office, turned the knob, and proceeded to not open the door.

He turned to glare at Merkle, who shrugged. "I called maintenance. They said they'd be by this morning."

"It's after two in the afternoon," Garcia pointed out.

"I know, but that's what they said." Before Garcia could say anything else, Merkle quickly added, "I'll call them again" while reaching for the phone.

"Do that, but first get me Charlie Duffy at the *Gazette* and then call Jenny in the mayor's office and tell her that the Superior Six sent over their Claw files."

"Yes, sir," Merkle said, picking up the phone and starting to dial.

After shouldering his door open, Garcia shrugged out of his jacket and tossed it on the guest chair. He sat at his desk and stared at the green sheets that hadn't been there when he went to lunch. *Jesus Christ, is it time for annual personnel evaluations* again? *Didn't we just do this last year?*

Before he could start to flip through the new pile of paperwork, Merkle called out, "Charlie Duffy on two!"

Stabbing the button for line two on his phone as he picked up the receiver, Garcia said, "Hey, Charlie."

"Javier," said the scratchy voice on the other end. "To what do I owe the honor?"

"So I'm walking back from lunch, and Matt Barnett shoves a mic in my face and tells me the *Gazette* has a source that says the FBI's taking over the Claw investigation, and I'm thinking to myself, 'There's no way *that* can be true, because the only *Gazette* reporter who would have that kind of source is Charlie Duffy, and Charlie would *never* let something like that leak out to a TV reporter before he verified it with me or one of my people.' Especially since it's crap—no state lines have been crossed, and the feds can't do shit unless we invite them to, and if we had, I'd know about it."

"Since when do you go out to lunch?"

"Stop changing the subject, and—"

"Seriously, Javier? *This* is why you called me?"

"Yeah, this is why I called you, I wanna know—"

"For Christ's sake, Javier, how many years you known me? Do you *really* think that I'd let some dickless TV reporter know about a source of mine giving me police gossip before I ran it by you first?"

Garcia let out a sigh of relief.

"More likely, it was one of the thumb-suckers that Malmat brought over with him from the windy city last year," Duffy continued, referring to the *Gazette*'s new city editor, hired away from the *Chicago Tribune* a year and a half ago. "Either that or Barnett just pretended it was a *Gazette* source because he knew that you'd know it was bullshit if he said it was one'a *his* sources 'cause he don't actually *have* sources."

At that, Garcia laughed. "I had to be sure, Charlie. I get ambushed with shit like that—"

"Yeah, yeah. Hey, it's been a while, you wanna get a drink at Manny's after work?"

Remembering his promise to visit O'Malley in the hospital, Garcia said, "Not tonight—and not Manny's. No way am I letting you loose in a cop bar. Bad enough you're gonna try to pump *me* for dirt."

"Jesus, Javier, what do you take me for?"

"Exactly what you are, and don't even try to deny it," Garcia said with a big grin.

Duffy let out an exasperated sigh that sounded worse than it might have if the reporter hadn't been a chain-smoker since his teens. "All right, fine, we'll meet at the Blarney Stone."

"Always living the stereotype, aint'cha, Charlie?"

Putting on an exaggerated brogue, Duffy said, "Sure an' that's so, laddie." Then back in his normal gruff voice: "Tomorrow night when you get off-shift?"

"You got it."

Garcia hung up, chuckling. Duffy was part of a dying breed, and Garcia was fairly certain that the breed was dying for very good reason. But he'd seen and done pretty much everything, and was always fun to have a drink with and compare war stories. Duffy had turned out to be the last person to interview Old Glory—it was the fifth person to take on that mantle since World War II, and shortly after his sit-down with Duffy, he was killed fighting the Pantheon at the harbor. That interview had earned Duffy his second Pulitzer Prize.

Merkle stuck his head in the doorway. "Uh, I talked to the mayor's office, I left a message with maintenance, and your mother's on one."

Garcia closed his eyes and counted to ten in Spanish. *Hey, it's been ten whole minutes.* He picked up the phone again and tapped the button for line one. "Hello, *mami*."

4.32pm

`Peter MacAvoy smiled as` Milewski's Zap rang right at
half past, just like it had at *every* hour on the half-hour since their
shift started. She looked at the display, made that same disgusted
face she'd been making all day—the same one she usually made at
MacAvoy—and then hit IGNORE.

She then glared across their desks at him. "Aren't you gonna
ask who it is again?"

MacAvoy's smile widened into a grin. "Not much point, since
I know who it is."

For the third time since the Claw case, MacAvoy got to watch
Milewski go all crestfallen on him. When it was Garcia dressing
her down, MacAvoy was mildly entertained. When it was the news
that they had another victim, he was pissed.

This time, though, he felt full-on glee.

In a low, even monotone, she asked, "How the hell did you
find out?"

"His name's John Morgenstern."

Milewski's eyes went wide. "His last name's Morgenstern?"

The grin widened. "Never got to last names, huh?"

"Fuck you, Mac." Milewski turned back to her laptop.

That only served to keep the grin at full length. "So lemme
reconstruct the sequence of events. We just got finished processing
the scene at the Cowan. We hadda return our Malibu to the motor
pool, which you did so I could go straight home, since HQ ain't on
my way but was on yours. Thanks for that, by the way."

Milewski did not acknowledge the gratitude, but simply
continued to stare at the laptop.

"Anyhow, you dropped off the Malibu, and then decided
you were too wired to sleep after all this bullshit, so you went to
Maberry's Pub—"

Defiantly, Milewski asked, "How do you know I didn't go to Manny's?"

"Please—you *never* go to Manny's. You *hate* Manny's. And Maberry's is the closest place to Morgenstern's address that isn't a theme bar, which you also hate."

"You have his address?"

Now the grin became a chuckle. "Yup—474 85th Street, Apartment 3W. Anyhow, you met some guy named John, you had way too many Manhattans, you went back to his place, you had drunken sex, and then you woke up this morning feeling guilty as all shit because you think you're better than other police, even though we *all* fuck like bunnies on speed, and you slinked out and came straight to work wearing the same shitty suit you wore yesterday."

Clapping slowly and sardonically, Milewski said, "Let me guess, you saw his number on my Zap one of the eight hundred times he called me, and then ran the number while I was in the bathroom?"

"Bingo, Watson."

"Yeah, well, Holmes you ain't. For starters, I *did* go to Manny's—"

MacAvoy's jaw dropped. "Really?"

"—for about five minutes. You're right, I do hate it, but I needed a drink sooner rather than later. I left because everyone there wanted to talk about the damn case. So I went somewhere where nobody knew I was a cop."

"Maberry's."

Now it was her turn to grin. "No, the Bengal's Lair."

Shaking his head with disgust, MacAvoy said, "A costume bar?"

"It isn't, actually—the Bengal owns it, but it's a regular bar, except it's got pictures of costumes on the wall. And I didn't drink Manhattans because it's not 1918 and we weren't at the Ritz Carlton."

MacAvoy chuckled. "Fair enough. Gin fizzes?"

"Mojitos." She shuddered. "*Way* too many of them. And yeah, I did go back to John's place, but I didn't slink out."

"Hah!"

"I didn't!" she yelled, defensively, then shook her head. "No, in the sober light of morning, John I-didn't-know-his-last-name-is-Morgenstern decided to let me know that he's getting married next weekend, and he wanted one final fling. So, no, I didn't slink out, I stormed out. And it was already eight in the morning, so I came straight here." She shook her head. "I was an idiot."

"Whaddaya mean? We all been there, rook—there's always a case that makes you crazy and you need a release. Sometimes it's sex, sometimes it's booze, sometimes it's both. Billinghurst plays handball. Schiazza has his cigars. Jablonski used to go to the range."

Milewski frowned. "Jablonski?"

"He medical'd out after he got shot two years ago. Anyhow, you should be flattered."

Now Milewski glared at him. "Flattered? Seriously?"

"You were his final conquest."

"I doubt it. They're not even married, and he's already cheating on her."

"How you know she didn't let him?"

"She—" Milewski cut herself off and waved her hands back and forth. "No. I am *not* getting into this discussion with you." She stared intently at her laptop.

Chuckling, MacAvoy stared back at his.

Once he finished the file he was reading—which didn't have any information on the Claw's second appearance in Super City that wasn't in Blue-Blue's case file—he got to his feet. "I'm gonna get a cigarette."

"Hang on, Mac."

MacAvoy winced. He was having a serious nicotine craving, and his triumph over Milewski was just intensifying it. There wasn't much that sustained MacAvoy in these agonizing final months before he hit his thirty, but messing with Milewski was second on the list after cigarettes. After achieving one, he wanted the other to celebrate.

"I'll just be a few—"

"No, *look* at this." She looked up. No longer was she glaring; instead she had a look on her face that, after three decades, MacAvoy knew to trust in the face of another police. "It's file 377A5."

With a dramatic sigh—he wasn't about to let on to Milewski that she had done anything other than annoy him—he sat back down and called up the file in question. They had copied the contents of the flash drive onto each of their department-issue laptops, after which the flash drive could no longer be accessed in any way. The files were still fine on the laptop, though. Milewski had handed the flash drive over to the tech department in the hopes that they could work their magic on it, and he and Milewski had spent the two hours since learning all kinds of things about the Six's encounters with the Claw, though nothing useful like, say, a name.

After a quick glance at it, MacAvoy looked across the two desks at his partner. "Yeah, so? It says that the first time they faced the Claw was right after the mission to Dimension X. Besides sounding like the title of a crappy old movie serial, I don't see what—"

"I just got finished reading up on Dimension X."

Rising once again, MacAvoy said, "For *this*, you're keeping me from a cigare—"

Milewski waved one arm. "Just *give* me a sec, okay, Mac?" She turned her laptop toward MacAvoy, who peered down at it.

One window on her computer had an article from *The Journal of Paranormal Studies*, written by a Dr. Stanley Lieber, about the properties of "what has been popularly referred to as Dimension X, but is properly called the Augustyn-Waid Dimension." A quick perusal revealed some quotes from Dr. Sera Markham, a.k.a. Ms. Terrific, and more besides.

"I don't expect you to get the whole article," Milewski said with a sardonic smile, which MacAvoy ignored, "but the gist of it is that people who go there undergo a metamorphosis. They turn into the evil versions of themselves."

"What, like on that old *Star Trek* episode?"

Smiling sheepishly this time, Milewski said, "Actually, it was a whole bunch of *Star Trek* episodes, but the point is, no, it isn't. On the TV show they met their evil counterparts. Here, they actually *turn into* their evil counterparts. They mutate and, according to Dr. Lieber, the baser instincts of their minds take over and they no longer have a conscience."

"Okay." MacAvoy sat back down. "But this only happens in Dimension X, right? And for the record, I can't fucking *believe* I just said 'Dimension X' out loud and meant it seriously."

Milewski nodded while leaning over and tapping on the track pad to bring another window to the front. This was an article from *SC Magazine* called "Twenty Questions with the Flame." "Look at the fifth question," she said.

MacAvoy leaned over the desk. Question number five asked what the strangest adventure was that he'd ever had as a member of the Terrific Trio.

Aloud, MacAvoy read the answer: "'That would have to be when we went to Dimension X—or as my older sister prefers to call it, 'the Augustyn-Waid Dimension,' even though those two jerks didn't discover it, they just stumbled across it by accident and the Superior Six had to save their butts. About a year later, we wound up going there, and it was *nasty*. Sera tried to shield us from the effects, and it did work on me and her—but it didn't help Clyde. I've never seen him like that, and I sure as hell hope I never see him like that again. He was twice his usual size, and *vicious*.'" MacAvoy stood upright and blinked several times. "Jesus."

"Well, that confirms one theory." Milewski was smiling again.

"What?"

"That you can't read without moving your lips. Anyhow," she added quickly before MacAvoy could respond, "look at the file from the Six again."

MacAvoy stared at her for a second. He wanted to give her some kind of comeback to that lip-reading comment, but he found he couldn't actually come up with one, which annoyed him no end. So he peered at his screen instead. "I ain't seein' nothin' I didn't see an hour ago."

"Look who was facing the Claw in that fight. *Five* of the Six. The original roster was still together back then: Old Glory, Spectacular Man, the Bengal, Mercury, and Herakles. Notice who's missing?"

Shaking his head, MacAvoy said, "Starling—or, rather, 'the Starling.' That's how he's listed in all their files. Was wondering why the kimono lady used a 'the' when no one else does. Anyhow, he's listed as being on 'temporarily inactive duty due to illness.'"

"Not only that, but there are three other images of various members of the Six fighting the Claw. In *none* of them is Starling present." Milewski leaned forward. "Think about it. Dimension X—or Augustyn-Waid, whatever—mutates whoever goes there and makes them lose their conscience. Now take Starling, add what Augustyn-Waid does—"

"And you get the Claw. Christ." MacAvoy leaned back in his char. "Now I *really* need a cigarette."

"It gets better. Remember Elwood's theory about the proximity to the blimp? What if it wasn't a villain drawing the Six out?"

MacAvoy saw where she was going. "What if the Claw *was* one of the Six and he just flew down from on high?" He frowned. "But wait—the last two times, the bodies didn't fall anywhere near their floating gasbag."

Milewski held up a finger. "Yeah, but the last two times were after the Six went to the planet Zagnar and got their shiny new teleporter with its proprietary design."

"Sonofabitch." MacAvoy had to admit to being impressed. "We've got him."

"Let's not get ahead of ourselves here," Milewski said quickly. "Right now we've got a theory that fits the facts, but none of it is anything like real evidence."

Getting to his feet for the third time in five minutes, MacAvoy said, "Okay, I'm goin' outside and I'm gonna smoke at least one, maybe twelve cigarettes. When I get back, you and me are talkin' to Zim."

5.46pm

`Judge Eleanora Velasquez looked` down at the warrant, then looked up at Milewski and MacAvoy, sitting in the guest chairs of her chambers. The chairs were uncomfortable wood-on-metal seats, the desk an industrial metal monstrosity, both reflective of the fact that this was a converted classroom. The county had taken over DeCarlo Middle School as a temporary courthouse while the original was being reconstructed following a pitched battle between Prism and the Uzi two months ago.

Wooden bookshelves designed to hold art supplies and textbooks were laden with law books, while either the judge or her clerk had decided to use the blackboard for a calendar, with the month laid out in white chalk, appointments written in blue, and court dates in yellow.

Rain pounded a staccato beat against the flip-down windows behind the judge as she peered over her glasses in a move that made her look entirely too much like Sergeant Taylor, especially since Velasquez also kept hers on a chain around her neck.

After one final glance at the warrant, she removed the glasses, leaving them to dangle over her black robes, and tossed the papers back across the desk toward them. "There's no way I can sign this warrant, Detectives."

While Milewski had been expecting exactly this response, she still felt a flush of disappointment. When she and MacAvoy had sold this to Zimmerman—barely—one of the arguments was Milewski's good relationship with this particular judge. Ellie Velasquez and Krissie Milewski were both on the school newspaper when they went to Mayor Colletta High School together, and they'd remained friends.

MacAvoy gritted his teeth. "C'mon, Judge, we've got—"

"You got nothing, Detective," Velasquez said with a sharp look at Mac. "I don't see a *shred* of evidence here."

"We're askin' for a DNA sample," MacAvoy said, "so we can *get* the evidence. That's the whole damn point."

Milewski quickly added, "The PC is good, your honor."

The sharp look moved to Milewski, though the detective took solace in the fact that it was softer on her. "Kris, this isn't probable cause, it's highly *im*probable cause. You're trying to create a chain of evidence, but for a chain, you need links. All you've got here is a bunch of rocks in a stream. You slip on one, you'll be in up to your neck."

MacAvoy looked at the ceiling. "Who the hell decided it was Cute Metaphor Day?"

"Watch your tone, Detective. I see a lot of supposition here."

Pointing at the warrant, MacAvoy said, "We got a scientific article backin' us up!"

"With all due respect to *The Journal of Paranormal Studies*, all the accounts in it are secondhand. We don't actually *know* what happened to Starling in that other dimension, we just know what Dr. Lieber was *told* happened to the entire team, with a pretty appalling lack of specifics. If we had any kind of *evidence* that Starling was altered into something *like* the descriptions we have of the Claw, then, maybe, I could see it."

Before MacAvoy could say something else impolitic, Milewski jumped in. "What if we can get that evidence?" She had no idea how to do so, but she was officially at the grasping-at-straws stage.

Velasquez folded her hands together. "I still couldn't sign it, because I *also* don't have enough specifics about whose DNA you're asking for."

Milewski blinked. "Sorry?"

"You're asking for Starling's DNA. Tell me—who is that?"

Now Milewski winced, seeing where she was going with this.

However, Velasquez kept going. "Let's say I do sign this, and you go up to that blimp, and you get DNA from a guy in Starling's costume. First off, what if the DNA doesn't match? It'll be a political and a PR nightmare, and your lieutenant, captain, and commissioner will all be getting it from on high, and you know that abuse'll kick down on both of you."

"The DNA'll match," MacAvoy said. "It's him."

"How do you know?"

"Because I been doin' this a while. I know when somethin' feels right, and this does. Your buddy here, my partner? She's a royal pain, and she don't always know her ass from her elbow, but one day she's gonna be good police, an' I know this 'cause she nailed this one. Starling's the Claw."

Milewski felt her jaw drop almost to the floor.

"Besides," Mac added, "if I'm wrong, I can take the heat. I'm three months from my thirty, I could give a shit if Dellamonica gets pissed at me."

Velasquez tilted her head in acknowledgment. "Fine. Now, let's say you *are* right, and the Claw *is* Starling, and the DNA you get from the guy in Starling's costume matches what you've found on the Claw's victims. So you go back to the blimp and arrest a guy in Starling's costume. How do you know it's the same guy? See, I've had McLean Foundation lawyers in my courtroom before. This goes to trial, first thing they'll do is move for a dismissal, because the deputy prosecutor won't have any proof that the Starling you took your DNA from is the same guy in the courtroom."

"That's nuts," MacAvoy said.

"Is it? Five people have been called Old Glory, and we only know two of their real names, and we didn't find those out until after they died. Hell, we don't have definitive proof that there were as many as five, or that there were *only* five."

MacAvoy exhaled through his teeth. "We'll have Starling's real name once we arrest him."

"Yeah, but that still won't *necessarily* be who you got the DNA from." She pointed at the piece of paper. "And that name isn't on your warrant. I need a real person to put there, and we don't have it."

"We could make it a material witness warrant," Milewski said. "Then we can not only take the DNA, but hold him until the results came in."

Velasquez shook her head. "You don't have enough for a material-witness warrant."

"Why not?" MacAvoy asked. "He's a person of interest, and he's an *actual* flight risk—he can fly and everything."

"Because we're back to the problem of your lousy PC."

Milewski shook her head. "What if we can get his real name?"

"I can issue a court order," Velasquez said with a sigh, "but only if you can get a DP to come up with a good legal argument to justify suspending his fourth- and fifth-amendment rights."

Standing up, MacAvoy said, "This is fucking insane."

The sharp look returned as Velasquez looked up at MacAvoy. "Watch your mouth, Detective."

MacAvoy smiled. "Sorry. This is fucking ridiculous."

"Mac—" Milewski started, but her partner was on a roll.

He started pacing the classroom-turned-chambers. "It'll take *weeks* to get all that, *if* we can find a DP with enough balls to take on the Six and *if* those fucking McLean Foundation lawyers you're talkin' about don't rip it to shreds. Meanwhile the Claw'll prob'ly kill a buncha other people, and the Six'll keep covering his ass."

"I don't like it anymore than you do, Detective MacAvoy, but this is what we have to deal with. You've been on the job for thirty years, you know the drill."

MacAvoy moved toward the door—a wooden door with a small square window that the judge had covered with a cloth to preserve privacy. "Twenty-nine years, nine months, and three weeks. And lemme tell ya, that last three months and one week can't come fast enough."

He threw the door open and left.

With a sigh, Milewski stood up. "I'd better go catch up to him before he does something stupid."

Velasquez smiled. "You mean besides being too dumb to realize he has *two* months and one week to retirement?"

Almost involuntarily, Milewski laughed. "No, it really is three months, he's just been on the job a month shorter than he's counted it. I stopped correcting him a couple days into our partnership."

"He's an ass, but he's a good cop—his testimonies in my court have always been solid, and he makes good cases." She smiled. "And he seems to like you."

"This isn't any definition of 'like' I'm familiar with. Mostly, I get saddled with the him-being-an-ass part." She shook her head. "Whatever, it's only three more months. I'll tough it out. Thanks, anyhow."

Velasquez got up and walked around the desk. "No problem. And it's good to see you—but next time, could you wear a suit you haven't slept in?"

"I didn't sleep in it, I just—" Milewski felt her cheeks flush. "Never mind—let's just say that I never made it home last night."

Now Velasquez's pleasant smile modulated into a mischievous grin that no one ever saw in her courtroom. "Was he any good?"

Shuddering, Milewski said, "He was engaged."

"That wasn't what I asked." At Milewski's look of disbelief, Velasquez added, "Hey, c'mon, us old married types have to live vicariously through you single ladies."

"Gimme a break." Milewski shook her head. "Speaking of which, how *are* Pablo and the kids?"

"Pablo's got a job interview tomorrow, and the kids're fine. Giaconda asked about her aunt Krissie the other day."

Milewski got a warm smile at that. Gia was a sweet kid. "Tell her I'm fine, and I'd love to see her if her Mom ever invited me over to dinner."

Her face growing serious, Velasquez said, "Let's see how the interview goes."

"Yeah."

They briefly hugged and kissed each other on the cheek. Then Milewski went to the door. In a plastic garbage can next to the door were both her and MacAvoy's umbrellas. Somehow it didn't surprise Milewski that her partner was so busy storming out in a huff that he forgot his umbrella. "Take care, your honor."

"You too, Detective."

After pulling open the door, Milewski jogged down the linoleum hallway toward the corner staircase, in the hopes that she didn't play catch-up with Velasquez for so long that she lost her partner.

She chastised herself for thinking that her friendship with the judge would get her any special treatment. Velasquez wasn't one to do that. The pair of them had spent many a night at a bar bemoaning the old boys' network, and she wasn't about to engage in that kind of behavior, not even for her old high-school buddy.

As Milewski went down the wide staircase, she thought about poor Pablo. The small tech consulting firm he'd worked for since graduating college had their offices trashed by the Pantheon six months earlier, and the owners took the insurance money and disappeared to Costa Rica, leaving their dozen employees— including Pablo—suddenly unemployed. He hadn't been taking it well, which was why Velasquez had deferred inviting Milewski over for dinner. Pablo wasn't fit company when he was in a bad mood.

MacAvoy wasn't anywhere to be seen on the ground floor, but Milewski figured he was standing outside the big metal doors sucking nicotine.

Sure enough, when she pushed the horizontal bar in to release the door, it opened to reveal MacAvoy standing under the overhang with a cigarette in his mouth.

"'Bout time you got down here," MacAvoy said, taking one final drag before dropping the cigarette and stepping on it. He grabbed his umbrella out of Milewski's hands and opened it. "C'mon, we're goin' to the Schwartz Building."

Milewski opened her own umbrella. "What?"

"We can't get a court order for DNA, 'cause we need a name. Fine, no problem. Y'know what we don't need a court order to do? Talk."

"Talk?"

MacAvoy nodded. "Talk. We go to the Schwartz Building, and ask to speak to Starling as a person of interest in the Claw case. And then we sit down with him and ask him questions."

"Which he probably won't answer." The pair of them turned into the parking lot, heading for their Malibu.

"Maybe. But he *definitely* ain't gonna answer 'em if we don't *ask*. 'Sides, if it's a choice between talkin' to another costume or tryin'a get one of the limp-dick DPs to get that court order before I retire, I'm gonna go back to the blimp."

Milewski wanted to argue with MacAvoy, but found she actually agreed with his logic.

Disgusted by the very thought, she went to the passenger side, hoping she remembered to stick a protein bar in there.

She closed and shook the umbrella as she clambered into the car, then dropped it on the floor in front of her. As she leaned down to open the glove compartment in the hopes of finding food, she caught a flash of light out of the corner of her eye.

Looking up and out the windshield, she saw a speck of light in the sky that seemed to be growing larger.

Within the space of two seconds, it grew incredibly large, showing itself to be a round metal object that seemed to be plummeting toward the ground. It kept getting closer and closer, bigger and bigger, plowing through the cumulous clouds. For a moment, Milewski thought it was going to crash right into the city. In fact, she reached for the Malibu's radio, just in case—though she was sure PCD was being flooded with contacts from cops on the street at this point.

Suddenly, the UFO—for that was what the thing truly was, an unidentified flying object—decelerated with frightening speed and efficiency, settling about a thousand feet over the city. From the looks of it, the thing was hovering right over the Thomas River. A massive sonic boom rocked the car briefly, shattering glass all up and down the street, and setting off at least three nearby car alarms.

Holy shit.

MacAvoy sat in the driver's side, looking out at the same tableau. Reaching nonchalantly into his jacket pocket, he took out his pack of cigarettes. "Great. Another damned alien invasion…"

6.17pm

`The rain was pounding` against the windshield as Trevor Baptiste heard the sound of Rhonda Fontaine's favorite TV show theme coming from his partner's pocket.

He was behind the wheel this time. To Baptiste's relief, she actually offered to let him drive, as she was in a bad mood. Since her last bad mood involved treating 13th Street like a slalom course, he was more than happy to accede to that particular request.

At present, they were sitting on the shoulder of the Goodwin Expressway, watching the traffic go by. With the big alien ship in the sky, and nobody yet knowing who or what it was about, people often panicked, and panic on highways with cars going sixty-five miles-an-hour or more could get dangerous. Right now, the ship wasn't doing anything, and Baptiste had seen one of the Superior Six—he wasn't sure which—flying toward it to investigate.

Fontaine took out her phone and said, "Yeah, Yasmin?"

Baptiste could hear the babysitter's voice. "I am very sorry, Miss Mara, but Rhonda needs to speak to you right away. I know you do not like to be bothered while at work, but—"

"It's okay," Fontaine said quickly. "Put her on."

Sounding incredibly relieved, Yasmin said, "Thank you, Miss Mara. Here she is."

Now the voice on the phone was shakier and quieter. "M—Mommy?"

"I'm here, Rhonda-bear. It's okay."

"Mommy, I'm scared."

Baptiste winced. Fontaine leaned forward in the passenger seat. "I know you're scared. But it's gonna be okay."

"No, it's not! The aliens are gonna kill us all! I know it!"

"They're not. Don't worry, Rhonda-bear, it'll be just like the last time, and the time before that. Everything will be fine."

Shaking his head, Baptiste tried not to think too hard about the fact that, at age seven, his partner's daughter was already on her third alien invasion.

"Can you come home?"

"Unit 2205, this is PCD. We have a signal 10 at 472 82nd Street. There's blood dripping from the ceiling of the ground-floor apartment."

Baptiste gave Fontaine a look. They were on the shoulder right near the 81st Street exit on the expressway, which would put them just a few blocks from that address.

"I'm sorry, but Uncle Trevor and I just got a call. We need to go protect people, okay? But I promise, right afterward? We'll come by and say hi, all righty?" She glanced at Baptiste, who smiled and nodded as he put the cruiser into gear and merged into the traffic on the Goodwin.

"All righty, Mommy." Rhonda sounded less shaky.

"Take care, Rhonda-bear," she said as Baptiste exited the expressway and took the left turn onto 81st. "I love you lots."

"I love you more than lots!"

With a smile, Fontaine put the phone away. "Rhonda was scared because of—"

"Yeah, I heard. You keep your phone's volume far too loud."

"Sorry." She sighed. "I'm starting to think we should've put off that call."

"Taylor'd be on our asses if we did that. We'll swing by to see your girl afterward." Baptiste smiled, then. "'Sides, I ain't tickled her in way too long."

Baptiste turned onto Cornell Place, which brought them quickly over to 82nd. The 400 block of 82nd Street was entirely three-story brownstones. He double-parked the cruiser in front of 472.

Fontaine called into PCD that they'd arrived, and then both officers climbed out of the blue-and-white, their police hats protecting them from the rain. She glowered at him as they approached the building. "You know she hates being tickled, right?"

Chuckling, he replied, "Nah, she loves it, she just pretends to hate it to maintain her dignity."

"She's seven, Trevor, she doesn't *have* dignity."

Like most of the brownstones, 472 had a big stone staircase leading up to the main door, which had two doorbells—likely for the first- and second-floor apartments. To the right was a gate to a tiny verandah that had a door recessed into the staircase, which led to the ground-floor apartment, from which the call had come.

Baptiste opened the gate, which creaked open, walked across the verandah, and rang the doorbell next to the door under the stairs. It had a laminated piece of paper with the words HAO & XUE HSU in the slot beneath it.

The door opened to reveal an older Asian woman, with short, paper-white hair and heavy wrinkles down to her jowls. She wore a shabby white housedress and large fuzzy white slippers. Baptiste assumed this was Xue Hsu.

"Hello," she said in a low, accented voice. "Thank you for coming. There is dripping from the place upstairs."

A male voice from inside the apartment screamed out something in what Baptiste figured to be Mandarin or Cantonese, given the last name on the doorbell. That was probably Hao Hsu. The woman turned around and yelled back into the apartment in the same language, her voice an octave higher, several decibels louder, and considerably faster.

Then she turned back. "Please excuse my husband. He cannot hear very well, and he wants to know if mail came."

Baptiste asked, "We were told it might be blood?"

Xue nodded. "At first we think it's rain—the ceiling has leaked before—but this is *red*. We call upstairs, but she not answer."

"You know your neighbor personally?" Fontaine asked. That wasn't a given, after all. In fact, Baptiste didn't know any of the other people in his own building, aside from the superintendant.

Again, the old woman nodded. "We feed her cat when she go out of town. But she not answer cell phone."

"You sure she's home?" Fontaine asked.

"We hear walking around—floors lousy here. That why it leaks." This time she shook her head. "We know every time she home."

"What is her name?" Baptiste asked.

"Joan." She gave a small, sheepish smile. "I not pronounce her last name."

Baptiste gave her a reassuring smile back. "That's fine, ma'am. We will check it out."

"Thank you." She retreated back inside, shouting something back to her husband in the high-pitched wail she used for her native tongue.

Baptiste looked at Fontaine, shrugged, and then walked out of the verandah, again opening the creaky gate.

The rain was getting harder. "Christ," Fontaine muttered, "if that damn spaceship has to be there, couldn't it at least block some of the rain?"

That earned her a chuckle from Baptiste as the pair of them walked up the steep stone steps to the large wooden double doors with etched glass. The downstairs doorbell had the name ANKHMENI under it—like the Hsus, the paper was laminated—while the top one had a regular piece of paper that had been water damaged, smudging the ink and rendering the name illegible.

"Damn," Fontaine said, "no wonder she couldn't pronounce it. *I* sure as hell can't."

Smugly, Baptiste said, "It's 'onc-MEN-ee'."

Fontaine just stared at him sourly, and ruined all his fun by dismissing him with a, "Whatever." She rang the bell.

After a few seconds, nobody answered. Baptiste reached for the doorknob of the rightmost of the double doors, and was surprised to find that it turned and the door came open, swinging out toward him.

He and Fontaine exchanged shrugs, and then they went in, each pulling out their Berettas.

The double doors led to a small foyer. On the left wall were two small unlabelled metal mailboxes set into the wall. Neither looked like they'd been used for years. Under them was a small radiator, and there was a big pile of mail on top of the metal radiator cover. The single interior door was large and wooden, with more etched glass in a similar design to what was on the front; it was also ajar.

Fontaine nudged the door open with her left foot, the Beretta still at the ready.

The hallway had a dark wooden staircase leading upward, a small hallway to the right of the staircase with what appeared to be a closet door at the end, and a large metal door on the right. The latter had obviously been a more recent addition, as the gray metal didn't match the dark brown wood of the rest of the décor. Like the interior door, it was ajar. A golden tabby cat was curled up in the far corner next to the closet. Baptiste figured this to be the cat that the Hsu woman had mentioned. It probably had made a break for freedom through the partly open door.

Baptiste was liking this less and less.

Fontaine stood back a distance from the door. Baptiste called out, "Ms. Ankhmeni? This is the police. Are you home?"

All Baptiste could hear inside was a strange rustling sound. The cat woke up at the sound of Baptiste's voice, lifted its head, then settled back down into its nap.

He looked at Fontaine, who nodded. Both officers undid the safeties on the slides of their respective Berettas.

Kicking the door the rest of the way open, Baptiste went in.

The metal door led into a big living room, with windows on the right that looked out onto 82nd Street. To the left was a large entryway that led to the dining room, which had a window that looked into the airshaft between this building and the brownstone next door. A small door on the side of the dining room led to a hallway that took you to the rear of the apartment—presumably the bedrooms and bathroom. Matching furniture covered in plastic slipcovers made Baptiste feel as if he'd entered a time-warp. Some of the ugliest abstract paintings he had ever seen in his life hung on the walls between the windows.

Now the rustling sound was louder, and seemed to be coming from the dining room area.

Fontaine pointed at the entryway to the dining room and moved past the slipcovered couch.

Baptiste looked in to see a small, round dining-room table and a china closet in a room that opened on the near end to the living room and the far end to the kitchen.

Between the dining room and the china closet, he saw a large man covered in feathers kneeling over a bloody, messy female figure. He'd seen the former before, on Tuesday in an alley off Esposito.

Jesus shit!

Everything happened very quickly after that.

Fontaine cried out "Fuck!" as soon as she saw the Claw and what was probably the dead body of Joan Ankhmeni.

The Claw leapt up toward the living room, going from a

kneeling position to airborne in less than a second.

Baptiste found himself deafened by the reports of two Berettas throwing multiple shots. In fact, he didn't consciously register that his finger had squeezed on the trigger until he heard the noise in his ears.

Turning in midair toward Fontaine, the Claw landed on Baptiste's partner.

Now Baptiste hesitated, the bitter taste of almonds in his mouth, as the Claw was right on top of Fontaine, and Baptiste couldn't fire without risking hitting her.

The Claw swiped at Fontaine's throat with a taloned hand, and blood spurted in all directions.

"No!" Baptiste screamed and then started squeezing the trigger again and again, continuing to throw shots into the Claw, until the clip emptied and the Beretta's slide tore into his hand.

Dropping the Beretta in shock from the pain of the slide, Baptiste reached for his billy club. He was having trouble breathing and his chest was tight, but he was goddammit going to do his job and do what he could to stop the Claw from—

He realized as he yanked his club out from its strap on his belt that neither the Claw nor Fontaine were moving, as both were in a bloody heap on the floor.

For several seconds, Baptiste just stood there, staring at the two dead bodies tangled up in each other.

Then the Claw started to shimmer and glow. *What the—?*

Baptiste was forced to shield his eyes with his hand as the glow intensified for just a second before fading again. Blinking the spots out of his eyes, he saw that the Claw had shrunk and looked a bit more normal. Still covered in feathers, with wings and talons and the rest of it.

To his shock, Baptiste recognized what the Claw had turned into.

"Jesus shit," he muttered, "that's Starling."

The Claw was one of the founding members of the Superior Six.

And Mara Fontaine was dead. Taking a closer look, there was no doubt about it. Her eyes were wide open, staring blankly at the ceiling, and her throat had been completely torn open. Baptiste had seen far too many corpses in his five years on the job not to know one when he saw it.

This wasn't supposed to happen. It was supposed to be a simple call, and then they'd go visit Rhonda.

Oh Jesus shit, Rhonda's never going to see her Mommy again. Just like I'm never going to see Sylvia again. And now that sonofabitch ex of hers is going to get custody, and—

Focus, Trevor. He was standing in a room with three bodies, one of whom was his partner, another of whom was a killer that had been at the top of the city's most-wanted list for six years. The third was some poor woman wouldn't have been found for who knew how long if it weren't for the crummy floors leaking blood to her downstairs neighbors' place.

He needed to call this in.

Grabbing his radio, he started to speak, but it came out as a croak.

Clearing his throat, he tried again.

"PCD, this is—this is Unit 2205 with a signal 13. Officer down. Suspect down. Need Homicide, crime-scene, M.E."

"What the hell happened, 2205?"

"Mara is—" He couldn't say it. "We—we got the Claw."

Before PCD could reply, the ground shook hard enough to cause Baptiste to lose his footing and the lamp on the end table next to the slip-covered easy chair fall to the floor with the snap of shattered glass.

Super City didn't get earthquakes. Baptiste had a feeling the alien invasion had finally started in earnest.

Perfect timing…

7.07pm

For Charlie Duffy, the roof of City Hall was a haven. The mayor's security detail didn't like people loitering outside to smoke cigarettes, and of course the entire concept of smoking indoors had been rooted out in pretty much every public location and half the private ones. The Blarney Stone had held out longer than most of the bars, but two years ago, they finally gave in. Charlie's own shabby-but-rent-controlled one-bedroom apartment was the only indoor spot he lit up in anymore.

However, the roof of City Hall had a heliport that was open to anyone with credentials to be inside the Hall, which included staff, city government, and the press, so the reporters would come up here to smoke. There was even an overhang for days like today when it was pouring rain.

Everyone had been in a kind of holding pattern since the UFO appeared in the sky. Charlie didn't recognize it. There were a few aliens who'd shown up more than once, like the Hlakkins—shape-changers who'd taken over the McLean Foundation, leading directly to Charlie's first Pulitzer—and the Brin-Lavi—one of whom, Lavi-3-Zel, had joined the Superior Six before being kicked out for experimenting on humans as if they were lab rats, something that wasn't actually a crime by Brin-Lavi standards, and sent back home. A few others had arrived briefly, including the Omnivore more than once, but this ship didn't look like any of them.

Then again, Charlie could barely tell the difference between a Ford and a Chevy, so what the hell did *he* know? It was a gray, oval ship with four weird shapes jutting out of it.

In any case, whoever these guys were, they were just hovering, floating, *sitting* there. From his vantage point near the heliport, he'd seen, at different times, three of the capes—Spectacular Man,

Prism, and Amethyst—fly toward the ship to investigate, only to depart again for no obvious reason.

He was alone up here. None of the other smokers had joined him, citing a lack of desire to get wet—Charlie reminded them of the overhang, to no avail—and the weather also meant that the mayor's helicopter wasn't going anywhere anytime soon.

Having no one to talk to, he found his thoughts went to Javier Garcia. It had been good to hear from him, even if the captain had only even called because Matt Barnett was a lying sack of shit. It would be good to catch up with him. Garcia had been a good deep-background source back when Charlie was covering the police beat full-time, and maybe after pouring a few bourbons down the captain's throat, he would get something juicy. Of course, Garcia had been expecting that—which was why he'd insisted on the venue not being Manny's—but Charlie had faith in his abilities.

Suddenly, lights came on all around the alien ship. Shoving the cigarette between his lips, Charlie dug into his pocket for his ZP500. Take one last drag on the cigarette, he opened his mouth to let it drop to the roof and stepped on it as he activated the video and audio recording functions on the Zap. He also tried to set it up so that what he recorded would stream directly to the *Gazette*'s web site, but he wasn't sure if he was doing that right, and he doubted the opportunity to call tech support was going to present itself.

Then the entire roof shook, and Charlie stumbled. Holding onto the Zap with his left hand, he tried to brace himself with his right, slamming his hand into the concrete. Pain shot through the heel of his right hand, as well as his arthritic knees, which made a noise like Rice Krispies in milk as he fell.

Though he'd lived his entire adult life in Super City since moving here to attend Busiek University, Charlie grew up in Los Angeles, so he was familiar with earthquakes. In fact, one of the reasons why he left Southern California was to get away from them...

The four protrusions on the ship revealed themselves to be gun turrets of some kind, as red beams shot out from each of them in different directions. His Zap's lens pointed squarely at the ship, Charlie started to say something, but wound up with a phlegmy coughing fit.

In the background he heard several explosions. Closing his eyes briefly, he tried to picture the map of Super City he had in his head. Getting his coughing under control and clearing his throat, he said, "The beams that just fired from the alien ship appear to have hit Kirby Park, Hamilton Island, the middle of downtown, and somewhere in Simon Valley. Christ, I hope they didn't hit the south lawn of the park..."

The protrusions rotated on the top of the ship, moving to different spots. "Looks like they're repositioning to fire on different locations."

Suddenly, a purple sphere appeared around the ship and the red beams—which looked green now—expended harmlessly against it.

Looking around, Charlie soon spied the form of Amethyst, the gem buried in his chest being the source of the purple sphere. Moving his Zap to point at the cape, Charlie zoomed in to see that Amethyst had a weird helmet on.

Sonic booms heralded more capes, and Charlie zoomed back out to take in the other new arrivals: Prism, Major Marine, and five of the Superior Six. Charlie couldn't see Starling, but Spectacular Man (carrying Suricata), Komodo Dragon (carrying the Bengal), and Olorun were all flying toward the ship, and they *all* had the weird helmets.

"Looks like the Superior Six, Major Marine, Prism, *and*

Amethyst are all ganging up to stop these guys. And they've all got funny helmets on. Half expect 'em to be made outta tin foil, but now I know why Spec Man, Prism, and Amethyst all flew away from the ship without doing anything before. Probably some kinda weird mind-control thingie."

The turrets all shifted position so they were next to each other, and then one big red-but-looking-green beam fired at a single spot on the purple sphere.

A moment later, the sphere just disappeared, and Amethyst started to fall toward the ground. However, Olorun swooped down and caught him in his bare, muscular arms.

Prism then pointed at the ship and a laser beam sizzled from her finger, hitting all four gun turrets at once and melting their apertures.

Charlie was recording all of it on his Zap. "Nicely done. Setting it up, knocking it down."

An explosion rocked that section of the ship. Charlie guessed that Prism had been hoping the beams would try to fire after she melted the muzzles, with the power feeding back. He really hoped that he'd set up the web link properly, because this was going to send the *Gazette*'s web traffic through the roof. Much as he hated a lot of what he found on the Internet, Charlie also appreciated that he was able to reach readers through the web that he never would have in the print-only days.

Small cubes came zipping out of the ship a moment later, and they started firing red beams of their own.

The scene after that was chaos, and Charlie found himself unable to take it in. He just recorded it and hoped that he'd be able to sort it out later. All eight heroes—Amethyst appeared to be back in the game now, too, based on the purple shapes that kept appearing out of nowhere—took on the cubes, trying to keep the beams from striking the ground, and mostly succeeding.

One beam got past Olorun and slammed into the copter on the helipad, slicing right through the propeller, which then crashed to the roof, shattering the glass of the cockpit in the process. It made a tremendous noise that rang in Charlie's ears.

Two cubes managed to sneak through the gauntlet and headed toward the ground. In fact, they were headed straight for City Hall, and Charlie felt a lump in his throat.

Just as he was starting to make peace with the fact that he was going to die as he lived, working on a story, and with a plan in place to haunt tech support if the web link from his Zap wasn't working, he saw something he never expected to see again.

Two red-white-and-blue balls went flying through the air toward the two errant cubes, both having been preceded by a familiar fwoomp of compressed air. When they hit the cubes—both aimed perfectly—the balls unravelled into American flags that wrapped around the cubes.

A muffled explosion later, and the flags started to collapse, having apparently destroyed the cubes. Then the flags themselves distintegrated with a flash of red, white, and blue sparkles.

Charlie couldn't believe it. He thought for sure that after the last one—the one he interviewed, the one he got his second Pulitzer for—there wouldn't be another.

But he could see, standing on the lawn in front of City Hall, holding the miniature cannon that fired the flags, yet another person who had taken on the mantle of Old Glory.

Now Charlie *really* hoped that the Zap was linked to the *Gazette*'s web server, because he was getting exclusive real-time footage of first known appearance of the sixth Old Glory.

He zoomed in. This new OG had the same flag-themed costume that had not significantly changed since the Second World

War—but it looked different somehow. Zooming in further, he saw that this new cape was lithe, curvy, and *feminine*.

She turned to aim the mini-cannon again—it appeared to be a T-shirt cannon of the type used at sporting events, but modified to look like the famous cannon that was also called "old glory"—and now Charlie saw the outline of two breasts on the chest.

"Sonofabitch," he muttered. Then, remembering that he was recording, he added in a louder tone: "Ladies and gentlemen, there's a new Old Glory in Super City, and she's a woman!"

Suricata leapt onto one of the cubes and did a midair backflip, tossing it toward the City Hall roof. Once again Charlie's throat became lumpy, and this time he didn't think that the new Old Glory was going to be any help. Of course, the stupid cape probably thought that nobody was on the roof, especially after the helicopter was trashed.

Trying to make his weakened legs move, Charlie tried to get to the large metal roof access door, propped open as always by a small brick that had been serving the purpose of keeping that door open for the tobacco hounds since the new indoor-smoking laws were passed.

He put his hand on the side of the door in the hopes of prying it open just as the world exploded all around him.

PART FIVE
FRIDAY

6am

"Good morning Super City! And welcome to *News 6 at 6*. I'm Mindy Ling."

"And I'm Chuck Ortiz. Later on, we'll have Ian Michaelson with the latest from the Capes in sports, Debra Fine letting us know when the rain will finally stop on the weather, and Donna Brodsky with how the aftermath of the alien invasion snarled the morning rush hour on traffic. But first our top story. Mindy?"

"Thanks, Chuck. Obviously the story on everyone's mind is last night's attack by the alien race identified this morning by the Terrific Trio as the Children of Yarfor. One of their ships appeared near City Hall last night and remained in the air for an hour before it attacked, destroying the Moore Building, sinking Hamilton Island, and doing considerable damage to Kirby Park's north lawn and the intersection of 23rd and Ayers in Simon Valley. The Superior Six, aided by Prism, Major Marine, Amethyst, and what appears to be a new Old Glory—about whom we'll have more later in the program—were able to destroy the ship and its attack drones. Spectacular Man and Olorun dragged the hulk of the ship into orbit, where it will be studied by United Nations scientists on the International Space Station in conjunction with Ms. Terrific. The Terrific Trio released a statement this morning that they briefly encountered the Children of Yarfor during a mission to Brin-Lavi two years ago, and that this drone ship matched their design. Chuck?"

"The invasion was brutal for many, Mindy. Two people were killed in City Hall, including *Super City Gazette* reporter Charlie Duffy, who was on the roof reporting on the attack, and mayoral staff member Olga Bludeau, who was on the top floor retrieving files. Dozens more were injured. While the Moore Building was officially closed for business, there were several people inside, including maintenance, security, and office workers—a full casualty list has yet to be released. Emergency workers are still at Kirby Park, but the latest reports have five dead with many more injured. No one was killed in Simon Valley, though about a dozen injured were taken to Kane Memorial Hospital. Thankfully, the Hamilton Island Museum was still closed for repairs, and because of the weather, there were no workers on the island during the attack yesterday. Mindy?"

"Mayor Sittler held a press conference late last night, and had this to say…"

"First of all, I want to express my condolences to the families of all of those who lost their lives tonight. Two of those were very dear to me personally. Olga Bludeau has been a valued member of my team since my City Council days, and she will be sorely missed not only by her husband and children, but by everyone in City Hall. As for Charlie Duffy, he's been a fixture in the press room since long before people started calling me 'your honor,' and I figured he'd still be there long after I'd moved on. I got to know him very well when he followed my mayoral campaign for the *Gazette*, and he was a true man of the people and a tribute to his profession. It won't be the same in this building without either of those two. Second of all, I want to express my gratitude to the Superior Six, as well as the others who aided them in driving off these invaders, and also to the Terrific Trio, the Bruiser, and the Cowboy, who were all assisting emergency services in rescue operations in Kirby Park and in Simon Valley. The world would be a much worse place and a lot more people would have lost their lives if it hadn't been for their intervention, and I cannot begin to express how much Super City appreciates the continued presence and good work of these costumed heroes."

"The mayor went on to announce that a parade in honor of those who participated in the battle against the aliens will be held

Monday morning on Nantier Boulevard. Channel 6 will be showing the parade live, with coverage beginning at nine a.m. with Matt Barnett and Judi Bari."

"Congressman F. Richard Wert of Montana, author of new legislation that would compel people with enhanced abilities to register with the government, had no comment last night or this morning regarding the attack or the fact that we owe or lives to the heroes whose activities would be curtailed by his bill."

"One of those heroes is a new face in a familiar costume, Chuck. Several witnesses to the alien attack claimed that a new Old Glory was on the scene aiding the Superior Six and their allies. Some only saw the trademark flags being fired into the air and destroying the alien attack drones, but a few saw Old Glory in the flesh—and with an important difference. This Old Glory…is a woman! Adriana Berardi has the story."

"Before his tragic death, *Super City Gazette* reporter Charlie Duffy was making cell phone recordings of the fight against the alien ship, which was being streamed live on the *Gazette*'s web site. It's become the most-viewed video both on the paper's site and on YouTube."

"SonofaBEEP. Ladies and gentlemen, there's a new Old Glory in Super City, and she's a woman!"

"The new Old Glory was able to stop several of the attack drones from reaching ground level before the ship was taken care of, and she disappeared after that. While the Superior Six has yet to make a formal statement, I was able to talk briefly with Sharon Parsons, the Six's spokesperson, who told me that the Six is very grateful for the new Old Glory's assistance and is looking forward to working with her further. On a personal note, Charlie Duffy was a good friend and colleague, and we're all going to miss him a lot. He won a well-deserved Pulitzer Prize for his interview with the last person to wear Old Glory's costume, and it's only fitting that his final act was to break the story of his successor—and the first woman ever to take on the mantle. For *News 6 at 6*, I'm Adriana Berardi."

"Thanks, Adriana. The first Old Glory fought with the Allies in World War II, and continued to fight enemies foreign and domestic until 1956, when he was killed on Nantier Boulevard by the Red Menace. His true identity remains classified by the U.S. government. Four more men took up the mantle over the years, including Jack Burke from 1959 until he was killed in Viet Nam in 1968; two more, one from 1971 until he simply stopped appearing sometime after 1980, and another who was seen sporadically throughout the eighties and nineties; and then Samuel Teeo, who took on the costume after the events of September 11th, 2001, and who was a founding member of the Superior Six until his death five years ago. Chuck?"

"We've got plenty more, including details on the Terrific Trio's saving of an apartment building that borders Kirby Park, the end of the Claw's reign of terror, and more on what last night's events mean for Congressman Wert's controversial bill."

"We'll be right back."

8.25am

Under other circumstances, Peter MacAvoy would've enjoyed his partner staying quiet for an extended period of time. But Milewski had been close-mouthed ever since last night when they cut short their planned trip to the Schwartz Building after being summoned by Zimmerman to the Ankhmeni residence on 82nd Street. Expecting a proper crime scene, they instead found Zimmerman already there, along with Commissioner Dellamonica and Regina Dent, of all people, waiting for them with detailed instructions on how to proceed.

Crime scenes with brass at them always were pains in the ass. Crime scenes with brass *and* the department spokesperson were absolute nightmares. MacAvoy's thirty couldn't possibly come fast enough.

Now they were finally sitting in the butt-ugly waiting room on the fourth floor of the Schwartz Building. A different woman was sitting at the reception desk—she was much younger, looking like she was barely out of high school, and had half the hair and twice the makeup of the other one.

Unfortunately, staring at her was all MacAvoy had to do, since Milewski was just sitting on the cracked leather couch staring straight ahead with her eyes hard and nasty, and her lips pursed in that annoying way of hers. MacAvoy's last two trips here had enabled him to exhaust the waiting room's reading matter, such as it was. So he paced the floor, trying not to look at the picture of Starling at the Shuster Bridge that was still on the wall.

Finally, the painted lady answered a buzz from the phone in front of her with a thick Southern accent. "Yeah? Okay." She hung up. "Y'all can head on up."

"Joy of joys. You comin', rook?"

Milewski just rose from the couch quickly enough that the

cracked leather didn't even make the farting noise, which MacAvoy found oddly disappointing.

Once they were teleported up to the blimp, Milewski actually took the lead, storming out into the fancy reception area.

But nobody was waiting for them. That disembodied female voice said, "Welcome to the Superior Six's flying headquarters. Someone will be with you shortly. Please make yourself comfortable."

"Like hell," Milewski muttered. "After all this bullshit, we have to wait *longer*?"

For his part, MacAvoy was staring at the flat screen, watching it cycle through various images. One of the images now was from the alien invasion last night. While they waited, it went through the entire run of images before cycling back to the alien invasion, and MacAvoy noted that there were no images of Starling anywhere to be found.

Spectacular Man strode in from the same rear door that Komodo Dragon had come through the last time MacAvoy and Milewski came up here. MacAvoy didn't feel all that intimidated by the costume this time, though.

"Greetings, Detectives. What can the Superior Six do for you this morning?"

"You can kiss my ass!"

To MacAvoy's surprise, he wasn't the one who said that, though he wouldn't deny thinking it.

No, it was Milewski. Her eyes had gone from hard to blazing, and she was walking right up to Spectacular Man, pointing an accusatory finger up at his face, and looking at least as unintimidated as MacAvoy, even though the costume had well over a foot of height on her.

"You knew—the whole time, you *knew* that Starling was the Claw!"

Spectacular Man just stared down at Milewski, his jaw set. MacAvoy found himself wondering what, exactly, he was thinking at that moment. He often went through that with suspects, trying to discern what was going through their minds based on their facial expressions, but it was harder in this case thanks to the mask that covered the costume's eyes.

But then Spectacular Man turned away, and MacAvoy had no trouble reading *that*.

"Not the whole time." Usually, Spectacular Man spoke with a deep, booming voice, but now he sounded subdued—which was almost ridiculous coming from a behemoth in a red-and-blue skintight outfit.

He continued: "At first, we…. But I should explain. You see, when you travel to a place called Dimension X—"

MacAvoy interrupted. "We know. Read *all* about it—turns you into your evil self, gobby gobby, whatever."

"All right." The costume seemed nonplussed. "When the Claw first appeared, we had no idea it was the Starling's Dimension X analogue. We—"

Milewski rolled her eyes and stomped away from the costume, apparently not wanting to be that close anymore. "It wasn't an 'analogue.' That means it wasn't *really* Starling, just his counterpart in that other dimension—like Spock with a goatee. But when Officer Baptiste shot him—after your 'hero' teammate killed an innocent woman *and* Officer Fontaine—he turned back into Starling, with bullet wounds in the exact same spot. And we *read* the article, we know that it changes people. Also? We ran Starling's DNA. It's the same that was on *every single one* of the Claw's eighteen victims. So don't give me this 'analogue' shit, all right?"

MacAvoy tried not to grin.

"My apologies," Spectacular Man said after a moment. "My

point is—we didn't know at first. When the Claw didn't come back for so long, we assumed him to be a one-shot."

Frowning, MacAvoy asked, "A what?"

"A one-shot. Someone tries on a uniform to see what it's like, or someone who had enhanced abilities and only uses them once before realizing that being a villain—or a hero, in some cases—isn't all it's cracked up to be."

"He killed *five* people that first time," Milewski said through clenched teeth, "including one of ours. That isn't 'one.'"

MacAvoy stared at his partner's second semantic rant in as many minutes. "You really were an English major, weren't you, rook?"

"Fuck you, Mac." She didn't even look at him, as she was back to staring daggers at the costume. "So what happened when he did come back?"

Tersely, Spectacular Man said, "He killed one of *ours*." Then he let out a sigh, which felt like a stiff summer breeze. "That was when we found out it was the Starling. We tried to stop him. Herakles felt that we should go public, but the damage to our ability to function would be tremendous. The balance of the membership voted on it, and we agreed three to two to keep it quiet for now. Herakles then quit, and went after the Claw himself."

"Are you serious?" Milewski walked back toward him, again pointing a finger in his masked face. "Are you *serious*? Your 'ability to function' is based entirely upon the fact that you go ahead and function without any oversight, any regulation, any *anything*."

"But we do have the good will of the general public, Detective Milewski," Spectacular Man said sharply. "The public trusts us to help them, and that enables us to do our jobs."

"They're not 'jobs'!" Milewski snapped. "They're, at best, hobbies that you—"

MacAvoy stepped in before she could continue. "Before my

partner goes off on *another* language rant, lemme ask—why'dja keep the secret *after* Herakles was killed?"

"We thought we cured him. Komodo Dragon came up with a treatment that would stop him turning into the Claw, but—" Another stiff-breeze sigh. "Two years later, it happened again. The Bengal tried to reason with him, but in that form…"

"So you just swept it under the rug?" Milewski was sneering now.

"Tell me, Detective," Spectacular Man snapped, and for the first time since he walked in, MacAvoy was a little scared of him, "what would you have done if it was one of yours? If, say, Detective MacAvoy here turned into a serial killer by a force out of his control?"

"I'd put his ass away," Milewski said. "Or, at the very least, keep him from ever killing anyone ever again. But you didn't do that."

"We *tried*."

"You should've tried harder!" Milewski screamed.

"All right, that's enough." MacAvoy stepped in between the costume and his partner. "Just calm down."

Milewski chuckled bitterly at that. "I'm barely getting started."

"Just shut up, already, okay? You've made your point."

"No, honestly, Mac, I don't think I have." Now she was pointing in *his* face. "You realize what we *should* be doing up here?"

"Which raises a rather pointed question." Spectacular Man now stood with his massive arms folded over his expansive chest. "What *are* you doing here? I assume you didn't simply come here to upbraid us for our role in this rather unfortunate affair."

"Don't!" MacAvoy said, putting a hand on Milewski's shoulder, since he just *knew* she would start to pick on his use of the word *unfortunate*.

Letting out a quick breath, Milewski said, "We're here to let you know what we're *not* doing. We're *not* arresting you—and Komodo Dragon, Bengal, Olorun, and Suricata—as accessories to fifteen counts of murder. We're also *not* arresting you all for obstruction of justice. Mind you, we *could* do that. We could build an airtight case against you so good that the chief prosecutor's office would have a collective orgasm. And I really really *really* want to do all of that—but we're under orders not to."

"Y'see," MacAvoy said, "the commissioner himself was at our crime scene last night. Since he became top cop, Enzo Dellamonica don't show up at crime scenes unless there's a problem. And the problem we got is you guys. See, you just stopped an alien invasion. Saved the whole fucking planet. Sittler's givin' you guys the keys to the city—*again*—there's gonna be a parade, the whole nine. Everyone on the damn planet's ready to give you all blow jobs in the middle of Everett Square. We stick you guys in the middle of a nasty murder investigation, and it all goes sideways. It's a PR fucking nightmare. It'll give that stupid bill that guy in Montana's pushing through all the traction that last night took away. Besides, the Claw's dead, anyhow. So we're here to tell you that you dodged a bullet—or, I guess in your case, let it bounce off those six-pack abs of yours."

"We would also prefer," Spectacular Man said slowly, "to have the public remember the Starling as a hero. He did a great deal of good for the world, and he had no control over this transformation. He—"

"Yeah, yeah," MacAvoy said, waving him off, "we already got the spiel from our own spokesperson. Starling died while helping Fontaine and Baptiste stop the Claw. Baptiste is on board, since he wasn't thrilled at the idea of being known as a costume-killer, even if that costume did rip open his partner's throat. Anyhow, you're in the clear."

"For now," Milewski added. She had wandered back to the

window, and was looking out at the view of Super City while she spoke. "But we know what you're capable of. We know you're even more arrogant than could possibly be believed, and even more dangerous to innocent people than we could ever have imagined. Yes, when you guys acted last night, you saved *a lot* of lives, and I can admit that I'm grateful for that." She turned around to face Spectacular Man. "But by failing to act when you goddamn well should have, you allowed more than a dozen people to die, including two of your teammates."

"Only one of our teammates was killed by the Claw."

Milewski walked toward the costume. "No, it's two. Herakles—*and* Starling. If you'd gone public, if you'd *explained* what was happening, maybe Starling would still be alive."

To MacAvoy's shock, Spectacular Man had nothing to say to that. Milewski just stared at him for a few seconds, then turned on her heel and walked toward the teleporter.

MacAvoy smiled at the costume. "Guess you're gonna have to change your name—I suggest the Fucked-Up Five, myself."

"Actually, we've invited the new Old Glory to join our ranks."

Milewski turned back around. "Seriously? Do you even *know* anything about her?"

"We do now. Our charter requires a consistent membership." Spectacular Man gave a slight smile. "We can hardly call ourselves the Superior Six if there are only five of us, after all."

With a scowl, Milewski said, "You can hardly call yourselves *superior* at all." She went on into the teleporter.

Hesitating, MacAvoy asked, "Who was the other vote?"

"Excuse me?"

"You said Herakles voted to go public with Starling being the Claw, and that he lost, three to two. I wanna know who the other yes vote was."

Spectacular Man hesitated for a couple of seconds before finally saying: "It doesn't matter. The vote was final."

"It matters to me. I wanna know which one of the surviving members of your little team I might almost respect a little."

Impatiently from the inside of the teleporter, Milewski said, "You coming, Mac, or what?"

"Yeah." MacAvoy ambled over to the teleporter, suddenly overcome with a massive desire for nicotine.

To MacAvoy's relief, Milewski went back to being stony and silent once they stepped into the teleporter, and she barrelled ahead after the glow dimmed, storming past the over-made-up receptionist to the elevator. MacAvoy took his time on the theory that he had the keys to the Malibu, so she had to wait for him.

The elevator didn't even arrive until after he caught up to her at the bank. As they rode down, he reached into his jacket pocket for his pack of cigarettes, only then remembering that he smoked the last one on his way here.

Still, there should have been a spare pack in the car. Homicide always took their cars from a particular set of the ones in the motor pool, and since all but three of the detectives in the unit were cigarette smokers—the exceptions being Milewski and her asthma, Fischer and his perfect teeth, and Schiazza, who stuck with cigars—there was almost always a spare pack in the well of any given Malibu signed out to them.

They exited the Schwartz Building, and MacAvoy was hit with a sticky coldness. There was still some humidity in the air from the rainstorm, and it remained cloudy. The whole city was dank, like it was covered in a haze. Milewski would probably call it a *miasma*, if she'd been in the mood to talk.

When they got to the spot where they'd parked three blocks down, MacAvoy climbed into the driver's side and found a fresh, unopened pack. Not his brand, but at this point, he could give a damn.

Turning the car on, he tapped the button to put down the driver's side window all the way, then undid the plastic wrap of the pack. Cool sticky air wafted into the car, but it would also vent his puffs.

Next to him, Milewski sat in the passenger seat, listlessly putting on her seatbelt and staring straight ahead.

Lighting up, MacAvoy took a long, wonderful drag on the cigarette, immediately calming down from the annoyance of Spectacular Douche and his merry band of tights-wearing loonies.

Then he pulled out into traffic, making a quick U-turn, driving down to Kanigher, and making a left.

That last action got Milewski's attention. "Where the hell are you going?"

"We're heading to Monty's. Best diner in town. We're gonna have breakfast—my treat."

Milewski blinked and stared at MacAvoy. "Who are you, and what have you done with Peter MacAvoy?"

Grinning, MacAvoy said, "C'mon, we're celebrating."

Now she looked away. "What the hell do we have to celebrate?"

"You kidding me?" He shook his head. "What happened Sunday night when we caught the call for the Claw case?"

"My life as I know it came to an end?"

MacAvoy chuckled. "Besides that."

"Four open cases got shoved under our names."

"Actually, it was fifteen, since the eleven open cases got lumped in with it."

Squirming in her seat, Milewski said, "Right, and then we got three more added."

"Yeah, but those last two were literally open-and-shut. And that's my poi—"

"Oh, for Christ's sake!" Milewski threw up her hands as she shouted. "They are not *literally* open-and-shut! In order for that to be true, you'd have had to actually *taken* the physical case files and opened them and then immediately shut them. When you use the adverb 'literally,' it is *not* a term of fucking emphasis!"

"Jesus, who died and made you William Safire?"

Milewski rubbed her temples. "Just get to the fucking diner already. I haven't eaten all day."

Given how conscientious his partner had been about keeping her blood sugars up, it was a statement as to how messed up Milewski was that she'd let it go this far. She wasn't even rummaging for a protein bar in the glove, something she'd done with the motor-pool cars with even more obsessiveness than the smokers had with the spare pack.

"My point is—"

"You have a point? That's a first."

MacAvoy ignored that. "—that we now have eighteen closed cases, eleven of which were colder than a well-digger's ass. And by closing one of those eleven, we've finally cured the department of its biggest black eye."

That got Milewski's attention. "Huh?"

"Mulroney." MacAvoy stopped for a red light at 64th. "Up until six years ago, there'd never been an unsolved murder of a police in this town. Thanks to us, that's true again."

Letting out a snort, Milewski said, "Please. We didn't *do* anything. Only reason this case is solved is because the Claw made the mistake of choosing a victim with leaky floorboards. We were lousy cops on this one."

"And yet, we closed the case—one of the biggest cases in the city's history—which means we're great ones."

Milewski shook her head. "I guess that's supposed to make sense now, huh?"

"Hey, listen, if it makes you feel better, you *solved* the case way back when you found that file on Dimension X—which I *still* can't believe I'm saying with a straight face." The light turned green and MacAvoy accelerated. "And see, this is why you still got a shitload to learn, rook—we don't *solve* cases, we *close* cases. Solving cases is what they do in books. You wanna solve a case, read Agatha Christie. Us, we *close* cases. Maybe it's 'cause somebody ran a light with a murder weapon in his back seat. Maybe it's 'cause he bragged about it to somebody who got popped that night for a B&E and wants to plead out. And maybe it's 'cause he kills again and this time gets caught and shot by a uni. The point is, it's *closed*, and we got eighteen cases down, which is gonna put our shift's clearance rate through the roof, and *that* is cause for celebration."

"I guess," Milewski muttered.

"Oh, and did I call it? That fed profile was less than useless. Starling's in his early twenties, he was raised by both his parents, and we don't know *what* the biannual—or biennial, whatever— occurrence was that turned him back into the Claw." MacAvoy grinned. "But hey, at least they got the 'white male' part right."

"Whatever." Milewski stared out the window, her elbow resting on the door and her fingers rubbing her forehead.

MacAvoy sighed. Schooling rookies was always slow work. Obviously, he was going to need the entire three months he had left....

9.47am

"—I cannot begin to express how much Super City appreciates the continued presence and good work of these costumed heroes. On Monday morning, a parade will be held on Nantier Boulevard between 3rd and 29th Streets to honor all the heroes who helped save our planet tonight. Furthermore—"

"Turn that shit *off!*" Captain Garcia snapped as he entered the kitchen from HQ's rear entrance.

Therese Zimmerman was standing with a cup of coffee watching the battered old television set that sat atop the refrigerator in the kitchen, which was currently on CNN's Headline News, which was doing a story on the events of Super City. So was MSNBC, C-SPAN, Fox News, and pretty much every local channel in the state, as well as the main CNN station. Headline News was the first one she'd found that was running the entirety of Sittler's press conference from the night before.

She grabbed the remote from one of the Formica tables and hit the POWER button. Sittler's face winked out.

Turning, she saw that Garcia was dressed in an actual suit instead of a shirt-tie-slacks combination that more-or-less matched. It was charcoal, with a white shirt and dark blue patterned tie.

Remembering why he was wearing the suit, she asked quietly, "How was the wake?"

"Anybody who has a problem with freedom of the press shoulda bombed the funeral home. Never seen so many journalists in one place." Garcia went to the coffeemaker.

"Charlie was good people." Therese personally had very little use for the elderly reporter. He was old-fashioned in all the worst ways, his articles were sensationalist garbage, and he always smelled of cheap cigarettes, cheaper booze, and bad coffee. But she knew that he and the captain had been friends, and besides, he hardly deserved to die.

"Yeah." Garcia poured himself some coffee into one of the Styrofoam cups. "Makes you wonder what tomorrow'll be like. And the funeral oughtta be a zoo." He swallowed some coffee.

"I stopped by Kane Memorial on my way in this morning," Therese said. "They've moved O'Malley from critical to serious."

"Really? That's great!" Garcia's eyes widened like he wanted to smile, but couldn't bring himself to do it. "I never got there last night thanks to aliens and dead cops," he added bitterly.

Sergeant Paula Taylor entered, her glasses dangling over her chest. "Javier, Zim—we just got official word. Mara's funeral *will* have the full honor guard, and both she and Trevor'll get medals of honor."

"You call Baptiste and tell him?" Garcia asked.

Paula shook her head. "I figured you'd wanna."

"Thanks." Garcia guzzled the rest of his coffee, then crumpled the cup and tossed it in the garbage can. "I'll be in my office."

After nodding to Garcia as he departed, Paula said to Therese: "Oh, Zim, we got a coupla dead bodies on Jaffee and 19th. Mac and Kristin aren't back yet, so who do I send? King and Bart are up next, right?"

Therese shook her head. "I gave them City Hall." Fischer and Billinghurst needed a dunker after dealing with another one of the Clone Master's wild goose chases, so she gave them the City Hall roundup. They'd all be ruled accidental in any event, but the mindless paperwork needed to be handled. "And I wouldn't give Mac and Milewski a double after the Claw. CC are in court—" Cordova and Cacciatore were generally referred to by the abbreviation. "—so give it to Olivares and Pavlack."

"Okee dokee."

Once the sergeant left, Therese turned the TV back on. She was curious.

However, Sittler was no longer on the screen. The chyron said LIVE and it was now the mayor's press officer. "—oint out that, in addition to their public heroics, one member of the Superior Six gave his life to stop the Claw's reign of terror."

Oh hey, don't mention the cop that died, too. Therese almost turned it back off, but decided she wanted to hear more.

The perky press officer went on: "Super City no longer needs to live in fear of the Claw thanks to that sacrifice. This proves what the mayor has always said—we need costumed heroes to keep our city safe."

Disgusted, Therese did finally turn it back off. Fontaine dead, the Six covering up more than a dozen murders, but the guy who actually committed those murders winds up the big hero, at the expense of poor Baptiste, who was the one who deserved having the mayor's office singing his praises, not that costumed maniac.

But it would get votes, and probably strike a huge nail into Congressman Wert's bill. Therese was no fan of Wert—and the bill was, at best, completely impractical and impossible to enforce—but that two cops were being cast aside like this…

Therese sighed. It was politics as usual, and she knew it. It was how she made rank so young, after all.

But she didn't have to like it.

Maybe she and Marc could argue about it at lunch today. He'd decided to make up for all the busted dates by taking her to Simon Says, a theme restaurant run by a reformed super-villain called Simple Simon. She was supposed to meet him there at one-thirty.

And then a thought occurred to her that made the coffee taste bitter—well, more bitter—in her mouth.

What did Marc know about the cover-up?

Leaving the kitchen, she headed for the wide staircase that would take her to the second floor. Intellectually, she knew that

Marc probably knew nothing about it. He was the Six's financier, after all. There was no reason for him *to* know that the Claw was actually Starling.

But what if he did?

As she hit the landing and entered the detectives' bullpen, she glanced over at Homicide's section. Milewski and MacAvoy's desks were still empty—which tracked with what Paula had said. Their meeting at the Superior Six should've been done by now. Elsewhere, Bannon and Schiazza were screaming at each other about something—it was either the Lashmar case or that stupid argument about whether or not costumes should be allowed to play professional sports. Nobody else was around.

Looking over at the door to the interrogation rooms, she saw that one door was closed—which meant either someone was being questioned or Dickerson wanted a quiet place to have breakfast again.

Nearer by, Billinghurst and Fischer both sitting at their laptops, doing the very mindless paperwork she'd mentioned to Paula.

Rather, Billinghurst was doing it. Fischer was on the phone.

"Oh, hold on," he said when he saw Therese enter. Removing the phone from his ear, he said, "Mr. Clean's secretary for you, boss."

Billinghurst stared at his partner. "Now now, King, it's not nice to call Zim's boyfriend Mr. Marc McLean by such a silly, frivolous nickname. His proper nickname, after all, is 'sweetness.'"

"Right, of course," Fischer said with a solemn nod. "Sweetness's secretary is on line three, boss."

Rolling her eyes, Therese said, "There are times when you two are really funny. And then there's now."

She went into her office and closed the door, not wanting any of her conversation with Marc to be overheard. Billinghurst's hearing "sweetness" the other day was going to continually bite her on the ass as it was.

Grabbing her phone and stabbing at the "3" button, she said, "Hi, Beth."

"Hello, Therese. Hold for Mr. McLean."

A moment later: "Hello, sweetness. Just wanted to make sure we're still on for lunch. It's just been an *awful* day so far, and I could really use your company."

Therese had been expecting to have to protest his cancelling lunch, which she quickly swallowed. Having been denied her conversational opener, she just went straight for the throat. "Marc, there's something I need to ask you."

"Of course, sweetness. You can ask me anything, you know that."

Somehow, that didn't make her feel better. "I need to know—" She took a deep breath. "I need to know if you knew about Starling being the Claw."

"I'm sorry? The Starling helped defeat—"

"Marc, I *know* the truth. I was standing there in Joan Ankhmeni's apartment when we decided on the story. And I know that the Superior Six have been covering this up for *years*. So I need to know, for my own peace of mind, whether or not *you* knew about this."

"The McLean Foundation handles the Superior Six's finances and trademarks. That's *it*. We're not involved in the day-to-day of the team."

Therese frowned. She couldn't help but notice he provided a canned, corporate answer to what should have been a simple yes-or-no question.

More to the point, the answer wasn't "no."

"I'm sorry, Marc, but I'm afraid I can't do lunch today. Way too much paperwork piling up. Maybe next week?"

"Sweetness, I—"

"Gotta go. I'll set something up with Beth." She slammed the phone down.

Then it startled her by ringing right away. Once she got her heart rate down a bit, she snatched it back and said, "Zimmerman."

"It's me," Paula Taylor said. "Just got a call. There's a dead body in a Dumpster on 29th."

She hesitated, needing a moment to reboot her brain back to work. The only Homicide cops around had cases. She was going to have to give it to either Bannon and Schiazza, or to Billinghurst and Fischer.

Then Paula added: "It's yet another Clone Master."

Therese let out a very long breath. It would be cruel and unusual punishment to do that to Billinghurst and Fischer again.

Grinning, she said, "Give it to Bart and King."

Trevor Baptiste was sitting on an uncomfortable chair in a drab waiting room when his cell phone rang. The display indicated that it was HQ's trunk line.

"This is Officer Baptiste," he said, flipping open the phone.

"Trevor, this is Captain Garcia."

Baptiste found himself sitting up straight at the sound of Javier Garcia's voice. "Yes, sir!"

"Calm down, Trevor, I'm just checking in to see if you're okay."

"I'm fine, sir," Baptiste said automatically.

Skeptically, Garcia asked, "Really?"

Baptiste blew out a breath. "No, sir, not really, but I do not know what else to say."

"I can understand that. You're going to talk to Dr. Feldhusen, right?"

"Yes. In fact, I'm in her waiting room right now."

"She's a good counselor. Trust me, I know from shitty shrinks, but she's a good one."

"Yes, sir, I know, she—" Baptiste hesitated. "She was who I spoke to after—after Sylvia."

There was a bit of a pause before Garcia said quietly, "Of course. Look, Sergeant Taylor just told me that the commissioner's office has officially stated that Mara's gonna get an honor guard at her funeral Tuesday."

"Good," Baptiste said emphatically. *If anyone ever deserved it…*

"And," Garcia added, "you're both getting medals. The ceremony'll be Monday morning—right before the parade they're giving the costumes."

Baptiste didn't feel like he deserved a medal, but knew better than to say that out loud. Besides, the brass liked it when unis got medals. It made good copy—and God knew the department liked good copy. Why else was the spokesperson at the crime scene last night?

So he simply said, "Thank you, sir."

"I'm just sorry that Mara's has to be posthumous. You take care, okay, Trevor? You need anything, call me—or call Merkle, and he'll find me."

"I will, sir." Again, the words were automatic, though he doubted he would take the captain up on his offer. What would *he* be able to do?

"Take care, Trevor."

"Thank you, sir."

After the captain disconnected, Baptiste closed the phone and put it back in his pocket.

The waiting room had three doors. One led to the hallway, one to the counselor's office, and one to a restroom. Baptiste was considering getting up to use the third door when the second one opened to reveal a short, elderly woman with curly white hair, wearing a white blouse and plaid skirt. "Officer Baptiste? Please, come in."

Nodding, Baptiste got to his feet and followed Dr. Feldhusen into a room that was just as drab as the waiting room, but bigger, with a dull painting over a couch on one wall, two chairs in the center of the room, and file cabinets and an old-fashioned roll-top desk on the facing wall. A coffee table was situated between the two chairs.

Feldhusen indicated one chair while sitting in the other. "Have a seat, please, Officer Baptiste. I'm sorry to have to see you again."

As he sat, Baptiste's eyes widened in mild surprise. "You remember me?"

"I didn't at first, but when I read your file..." She straightened her plaid skirt. "How are you doing?"

"The lawsuit is still pending, though they have been moving to try to settle things. I spoke with my lawyer on the way here, and she suspects that after—after what happened last night, they might be more amenable to a settlement. We shall see."

"Okay, but what I actually was asking about *was* what happened last night."

Baptiste put his head in his hands. "What about it?"

"How does it make you feel?"

At that, Baptiste shook his head, and chuckled mirthlessly. "It is funny, I've been asking myself that same question since it happened, and throughout a very sleepless night. And honestly, I feel nothing. Empty. Mara's dead, Sylvia's dead, the Claw is dead, Starling is dead..."

"And you're alive," Feldhusen said after Baptiste trailed off.

"Yes." He shook his head again. "And I have no idea how that happened. The Superior Six and the rest of them—they fight monsters and aliens and powerful creatures and people with incredible technology. And I shot and killed one of them with a Beretta nine-millimeter pistol. That makes no sense to me. It—it shouldn't have been that *easy*. And now I'm going to get a medal for this."

"Really?"

He nodded. "Captain Garcia told me before you called me in. I'm to receive a medal, as is Mara, posthumously, and she will get an honor guard."

"Do you think she deserves one?"

"Of course! Why wouldn't she? She was a good officer, and a good friend—and a good mother. Her daughter deserves to see her honored." He sighed. "Especially since no one else is honoring her. All anyone wishes to discuss is the alien invasion, and when the Claw is mentioned, it's said that Starling helped us stop him to prevent bad publicity."

"And you're all right with that?"

"I don't know." Baptiste slumped into the chair. "I'm just empty about that as well. I don't know what to do next. I don't think I can go out onto the street again."

"There are jobs you can do in the police without being assigned to a cruiser."

"Oh, of course. But I do not feel I will be a police officer anymore if I am at a desk." He sighed again. "Nor do I feel I will be if I am on the street. I feel a fraud."

"How are you a fraud? You're a hero, Trevor. You stopped one of the most notorious serial killers in the city's history."

"Did I? Or did I murder a hero?"

"That's ridiculous."

Baptiste stood up. "So is this session."

Feldhusen stared up at him, a hard look suddenly on her face.

"This session is mandatory if you are to go back to work."

"Then perhaps I will not go back to work."

With that, Baptiste departed the office, unsure where he was going to go next.

Garcia hung up with Baptiste and then just stared at the phone. He had a pile of paperwork on his desk, and a ton of other things to deal with, but he found himself unable to even think about it. All he could focus on were Baptiste, and on Fontaine and Charlie Duffy both being dead.

The phone buzzed and Merkle's voice came over the speaker. "The commissioner on one."

"Yippee." With a desultory poke at the "1" button, Garcia picked up the phone. "Yeah?"

"What's wrong, Javier, you sound like your pet died."

Garcia felt his jaw drop. "Seriously, Enzo? This is the comment you make when I just got back from Charlie Duffy's wake and just got off the phone with Officer Baptiste to talk about his partner's funeral arrangements?"

To his credit, Dellamonica sounded contrite in response. "Sorry, Javier. Seriously, that was crappy of me to say. I'm just in a good mood—we beat off an alien invasion, the Claw's a done deal, and people are happy to live here again."

"I can hardly contain myself, I'm so excited," Garcia deadpanned.

"Oh, cut it out, Javier. This is a win for the department, and it happened on your watch. That'll mean something down the line, trust me."

Garcia didn't believe that for a second. At best it would mean something for Dellamonica, who would parlay this into a raise and a major point of whatever political campaign he decided to run in a few years—City Council, Congress, mayor, governor, whatever. But Garcia didn't suck up to Dellamonica nearly enough for this to be of any benefit to him. He undid the top button on his white dress shirt and loosened his tie.

"I want you to pin the medal on Officer Baptiste," the commissioner said. Before Garcia could object, Dellamonica added, "Don't worry, I'll still give the speech and answer press questions, but I think you should be the one to do it. Remind the people who the guy on the front lines is."

Since Garcia despised talking to the press, he had to grudgingly admit that this offer was a nice gesture on the commissioner's part, allowing him to honor Baptiste—and, by extension, Fontaine—without having to make an ass of himself by chowing down on his foot on camera.

"Oh, and I just got word from the comptroller's office—no more OT for the rest of the fiscal."

What meager goodwill Garcia had managed to dredge up toward his boss evaporated in an instant. "What?"

"Don't get your bowels in an uproar, we'll revisit at the third quarter, but for now, the money ain't there. Sorry, Javier."

"You can't—" Garcia started, but Dellamonica had already hung up.

For a second, Garcia just stared at the phone in disbelief. The city was perfectly content to spend hundreds of thousands of dollars on a stupid parade that would snarl up traffic on Nantier and suck up a huge number of uniforms—all of whom had to be taken away from their usual on-shift duties, since the city was perfectly discontent to spend the money to pay his unis overtime. *Sonofabitch*...

A triple-tap came from the closed door to his office.

"Javier?" The muffled voice belonged to Michael Spila, one of the deputy prosecutors.

"C'mon in," Garcia said with a sigh.

Garcia saw the doorknob turn and then heard the wooden clunk of the door colliding with the doorjamb and not actually opening, at which point he closed his eyes and counted to ten in Spanish.

Spila took another shot at it and this time managed to push the door open. Waddling in, Spila reached up to put his comb-over back into place, the action of ramming the door open having disturbed it rather badly.

"You really should get that door fixed, Javier."

Garcia managed to resist giving that the response it deserved. "What is it, Michael?"

"Just wanted to give you a heads-up that I'm taking Reddington to the grand jury."

Garcia frowned. "You told me yesterday you didn't have enough."

"Yesterday, I didn't," Spila said with a wide smile showing crooked teeth. "Yesterday, I had no physical evidence and just one witness."

"So what changed this morning?"

"I still have no physical evidence, but my one witness saved dozens of lives in Simon Valley last night during an alien invasion and is having a parade partly in his honor Monday morning."

Nodding, Garcia recalled that Spila's witness was the Bruiser. "I guess alien invasions make everything better."

"Hey, if it means I can get Reddington to flip on his bosses, I'm a happy camper." Reddington had remained silent on the theory that Spila didn't have enough to indict him. Spila obviously now felt differently.

"Glad somebody is. Thanks, Michael."

Spila nodded. "Close the door?"

Shaking his head, Garcia said, "Best not."

"Okay." Spila disappeared down the corridor.

Garcia let out a long breath. *Yeah, alien invasions make everything better as long as you're not an actual cop in this town. Politician, costume, deputy prosecutor—everything's fine. If you're a police, well, then you're totally fucked. But hey, at least you get an honor guard at your funeral.*

Merkle called out, "Captain, your mother's on three."

Closing his eyes, Garcia counted from ten to one in Spanish. Then he hit "3" on his phone and picked it back up. "Hi, *mami.*"

About the Author

Keith R.A. DeCandido's first published fiction was a Spider-Man short story in 1994 entitled "An Evening in the Bronx with Venom," which had the Marvel Comics hero working in tandem with the NYPD. He has returned to the theme of mixing police procedure with elements of the fantastic several times, including in two Spider-Man novels (*Venom's Wrath* and *Down These Mean Streets*), other licensed universes (*Supernatural: Nevermore, Buffy the Vampire Slayer: Blackout*), and in his other original fiction (the high-fantasy police procedural *Dragon Precinct*, which has spawned a half-dozen short stories and the sequel novels *Unicorn Precinct* and the forthcoming *Goblin Precinct*)—plus, of course, in the novel you're reading.

Keith has written more than forty-five novels, plus dozens of novellas, short stories, comic books, essays, and articles. When he isn't writing, he's editing (he has ten anthologies to his credit), practicing karate (he achieved his first-degree black belt in 2009), meandering around the Internet (his web site is DeCandido. net, his blog is kradical.livejournal.com, and he is on Twitter and Facebook under the username KRADeC), and following his beloved New York Yankees. He lives in New York City with several humans and animals.

CHAPTER ONE

MIDSHIPMAN NATHANIEL DEMMING GLANCED AT his pocket watch again, the luminous face easily readable through the water. T minus four to launch. No worries, old boy, he told himself. After all, we're about to attempt the first launch of an untested ship with an untried crew and an uninformed captain, on a mission to an unexplored domain after an unexplained target.

Why fret?

"T minus four to launch," Lizette Mills reported from the helm. Demming hid a smile. She was half a second off in her count, but what did that matter? And what would he possibly gain by pointing that out now? Far better to keep silent and rib her about it later, in the officers' mess. Lizette was always a fun one to rib.

"Roger that," Captain Mendez replied, sitting tall in the command chair. From his position behind her Demming could still make out the topknot of her dark blond braid beneath her cap. Not a hair out of place, as usual. "Are we secure?"

That last was directed at him, Demming realized after a heartbeat, and scanned his console, studying the readouts. "Secure, captain," he confirmed a few seconds later. His heart was thudding so loudly it was a wonder the water was rippling all around him. "All crew in their harnesses, all ports locked down."

"Good. Mister Dittmer?"

"All secure, Captain," the quartermaster replied right away, his voice as lazy as always. With any other man Demming would have assumed he had taken the time to double-check while the captain was waiting for his answer first, but with Dittmer he knew that wasn't the case. Dittmer didn't need extra time. He already knew where every scrap of material was on this ship. The man had a memory like a clamshell, latched on tight.

"T minus three," Lizette updated. Everyone on the foredeck tensed with anticipation. Behind him Demming heard someone, most likely one of the ensigns, gasp for breath—and start choking as water filled his lungs. Classic rookie mistake. A wave of quiet laughter filled the cabin. Demming could hardly blame the ensign, though. It was all he could do to keep his own mouth closed, nostrils clamped shut, gills narrowed. What he really wanted was to start gasping himself, but that would never do. He was a midshipman of the line, for current's sake! He had not only his own dignity but the dignity of the entire ship and the entire Royal Navy to maintain!

Plus the others would laugh at him just as they were all laughing at the ensign now. And that was no way to begin a mission. Especially this mission.

"T minus two."

"Throttle us up, Miss Mills," Mendez ordered. Lizette nodded, her hand going to the smooth coral inlay of the throttle and easing it down a quarter toward the console. Beneath and all around him Demming could feel the thrum as the ship's engines started to spin.

Soon. Very soon.

"T minus one."

"Ready on my mark," the captain warned. She reached

for the speaking tube built into the arm of her chair, and her next words echoed faintly, as they repeated from speakers all throughout the ship. "Ladies and gentlemen, we are about to embark on our mission. I consider it an honor and a privilege to lead you into history. May the waves grant us success, and water save the queen."

"Water save the queen," Demming repeated softly, along with the other officers and, no doubt, the seamen in their compartments. And water save us, he thought. But did not say out loud.

"Mark!" Mendez hissed, and Lizette's quick fingers tapped controls, releasing the clamps that bound them to the docks and slamming the throttle down full. With a roar and a twist the ship's engines boomed to life, revving instantly to full speed, and with a mighty rushing sound the *HMES Remora* shot up from the ocean floor, her long, tapered prow pointed up at the air and at the stars beyond.

The force of their acceleration slammed Demming back in his seat, and he was grateful for the webbing that secured him there. He gripped the armrests on either side, feet planted flat on the floor, and kept his eyes squarely on the narrow windows that sliced down over the foredeck and arced along it toward its nose. For now all he could see was water, lit by the *Remora's* powerful searchlights but shifting past too quickly to leave any real impression. This was the easy part, however. He had seen all of this before.

It was what came next that would be a shock.

In what seemed only moments but Demming knew had to be closer to an hour the water began to lighten. He could make out fish and reefs rushing by. They were nearing the surface. He felt his lungs constrict at the very thought of it.

The surface!

"Prepare for wave breach!" Lizette announced, her hand tightening on the throttle to one side and her fingers poised over the sonic pulse array to the other.

"All hands, hold fast!" Captain Mendez ordered through the speakers.

The water continued to brighten, forcing Demming to squint against the glare. He fought the instinct to turn away, or close his eyes. He had to watch this. After all, how many could say they had experienced true wave breach? And he wanted to remember all of this journey, every second, so that he could chronicle it later. For posterity.

Or for those who wondered what became of them.

With a surge of sound that set the hull ringing, the *Remora's* prow burst upward through the waves. The light was blinding. Demming blinked, trying to clear his sight, and after a few seconds he found he could see again. It was so bright! And so empty!

His body pushed back in his chair, feeling heavy and sluggish. The *Remora* groaned around them. The noise had increased when they'd broken through, but the sense of momentum had dimmed rapidly. Now it felt as if they were barely moving, yet he could make out strange white shapes, filmy like jellyfish but puffed out like ink clouds, appearing in view and then vanishing below. So they must still be rising.

But for how long? Even now the waters exerted their hold, attempting to draw the ship back into the deeps.

"Sonic pulse on my mark!" Captain Mendez told Lizette. She didn't shout—their two chairs were less than a body-length apart—but every word was crisp and clear.

"Aye aye, captain!" Lizette tensed at the ready.

"Mark!"

The pilot's fingers jabbed down on the array, and the *Remora* shuddered as a rush of energy exploded behind her. Demming held his breath. All of this had worked in theory, and on the probe, but they had never had the chance to test it on a real ship, with a real crew.

This was the test.

Right now.

With them in it.

He waited, not sure what he was expecting. But after a second he realized that the *Remora* was still rising. If anything, her velocity had increased. It had worked!

"Again!" Mendez ordered, and Lizette complied. The ship shook again, though some of that faded as Lizette throttled down the impellers to three-quarter speed, and the *Remora* leaped skyward again, forced upward by the focused sonic burst it had just released behind.

And above—

Demming peered through the window. The sky was lighter and lighter in color as they rose, approaching pure white now, and through it he could just make out the twinkling of lights.

The stars.

They were close.

"How soon?" Mendez demanded. The question didn't seem aimed at anyone in particular, so it was her first lieutenant, Daniel Holst, who answered.

"Fifty kilometers and closing, captain," he reported. "And all systems are performing admirably."

"Thank you, Mister Holst." Demming could hear the smile in her voice. "Miss Mills, please continue."

"Yes, captain." Lizette fired off another sonic pulse, the

energy wave pushing off the waves and earth below and propelling the *Remora* further. The pressure was immense, slamming everyone into their seats, causing whines and creaks from spots along the hull and around the inner port, making it hard to breathe, hard to focus, hard to think. Demming kept his eyes trained on the stars beyond and took short, shallow breaths, letting the water filter into his gills almost of its own accord. The scientists had all agreed this pressure would let up once they breached the air. And they were so close! Almost— almost—

Wham!

The *Remora* lurched as if she had slammed into a strong current head-on. The ship flipped onto its side, all its momentum spent, listing and drifting with the dregs of that lost velocity. Water buffeted Demming, slapping his face and hands and chest and legs, and again he resisted the impulse to gulp for breath. Beyond the window, the glare had suddenly winked out, replaced by a darkness as deep as any abyss. There had been no lights in the cabin—none had seemed necessary—and in the sudden darkness only the telltales on various consoles could be seen. And here and there the gleam of those lights reflected in wide, terrified eyes.

And there was silence.

Demming had found the noise deafening as they'd shot through the air, but its absence was far worse. He had expected normal sounds, if slightly diminish—the roll of the waves, the rush of water through the impellers, the hum of the engines, the song of whales and chatter of dolphins and flutter of fish.

Here? Here there was nothing.

Everyone, it seemed, was holding their collective breath.

And then the sounds came all at once. But only from within

the *Remora* herself.

Shouting. Whispering. Cursing. Whimpering. Even crying.

The ship generated its own wave of noise as crew and officers alike began to panic.

Demming fought down his own urge to do likewise. This would not do! This was a ship of the line! They had their honor to maintain!

He forced himself to calm down, to breathe slowly and evenly. He unclenched his hands where they had dug into the armrests. He uncurled his toes and set his feet flat against the floor once more. And he waited.

Waited for the captain to tell them what to do.

Captain Mendez was an experienced captain. Not of a ship like this, of course—no one was. But she had years of training handling other vessels, and crews this size and even larger. She was quiet and competent and very much by-the-books. He knew that, once she had taken time to collect herself, she would regain control and restore order.

So Demming waited.

The seconds seemed to stretch on. The cacophony did not diminish. If anything, it grew in volume and diversity as more of his shipmates found their voice. There was thrashing as many wrestled with their harnesses, and banging throughout the *Remora* indicated that at least some had already worked their way free, though to what end Demming could not imagine.

He was content to sit and await orders.

Until he heard the one thing he had feared the most.

It began as a whisper. Rapidly it grew into a wail, a single ululation that sound spread into words.

Words that chilled him to the very soul.

"Oh, great wave!" were the words that struck terror into his heart and blood. "Great wave, we're lost! We've been consumed by the abyss! Our souls will be devoured by the darkness!"

All other sounds on the foredeck ceased, then, as every officer turned to stare at the command chair—and their tall, blond captain, who curled up in it, sobbing and crying out in despair.

A NEW SERIES FROM CROSSROAD PRESS

O. C. L. T.

THERE ARE INCIDENTS AND EMERGENCIES IN THE WORLD that defy logical explanation, events that could be defined as supernatural, extraterrestrial, or simply otherworldly. Standard laws do not allow for such instances, nor are most officials or authorities trained to handle them. In recognition of these fact, one organization has been created that can. Assembled by a loose international coalition, their mission is to deal with these situations using diplomacy, guile, force, and strategy as necessary. They shield the rest of the world from their own actions, and clean up the messes left in their wake. They are our protection, our guide, our sword, and our voice, all rolled into one.

They are O.C.L.T.

Following is Chapter One of the first full-length O. C. L. T. novel, *The Parting*, by David Niall Wilson. Other works in this series include a novel, *Incursion*, by Aaron Rosenberg and novellas by both Wilson and Rosenberg. Watch for these titles and many more at http://www.crossroadpress.com

From *The Parting*, by David Niall Wilson

Chapter One

IN A LOW BUNKER IN THE DESERT near the border of Jordan and the Dead Sea, a dozen men have gathered. They arrived over a period of hours, none too close to the other to avoid being seen together. They were not men given to solitary excursions, but each had left comrades and security behind in the interest of security. They were robed, and their faces were covered against the whipping desert sand. Far above, the moon shone pale and cloaked in clouds.

Salt clusters along the bank of the water glimmered oddly, almost glowing in the dim light. The water was as flat and lifeless as a sheet of glass. None of the twelve even glanced at it, though the last of them stopped and gazed directly across the surface toward Jerusalem. He stood there for only a moment, and then passed between the two squat, expressionless guards stationed outside the door. The two were associated with none of the twelve. They were carefully vetted mercenaries without affiliation. They did now know who they guarded, or why, and they didn't care, as long as they were paid well, and on time.

Inside the building was a single long room. There was a small kitchenette, and a bathroom, but these were sealed. The room was centered by a long rectangular table set very low to the ground. The twelve gathered around it. There were drinks, but for the most part they were ignored. The room was lit by a single lamp on the table, as if those present weren't even comfortable knowing one another, let alone getting a good look.

When they were all seated, the man at the head of the table leaned back, glanced around at the others, and shook his head.

"We represent," he began, "an incredible gathering of power. The resources we command should be able to move mountains—with or without faith. We can, and have, bought kings and ambassadors."

"And for all of that," one of those to his left growled, "we have failed once again at the one task we must accomplish before all others."

There were mumbles of agreement all around. None of those gathered was happy, and each secretly blamed the others for their failure. They were not men accustomed to failure, or the denial of their desires. They dealt in blood, fortunes, and power. The one thing they shared—the one central binding power—was the passion of their faith. They were from a variety of nationalities, but theirs was a common enemy and a holy cause.

"Sometimes," the man who'd first spoken continued, "I feel as if we have lost our way. Allah places more obstacles in our way than he removes, and despite our unwavering loyalty, the Holy City is yet in the hands of the unclean. They have proclaimed themselves God's People to the world. What have we been proclaimed?"

"Killers," one of the others said.

"Terrorists," a third cut in. "They say that we care about nothing but the shedding of innocent blood. No matter that our beliefs are those of our fathers, and our father's fathers. No matter that the blasphemy of our most Holy City being handed by Western dogs to the unclean cuts us to the very soul."

He slammed his fist on the table. As sturdy as it was, the

glasses and lamp jumped. Still, none of them rose. Their passion simmered, but it did not boil over. Nothing that had been said was new. Theirs was an old hatred, and it burned slowly, but with great heat. It was fueled by frustration and the futility of their efforts.

"There must be a way," the first man spoke again. "Allah will lead show us that way."

The grim semi-silence of the gathering was broken by a peal of rich, feminine laughter. They spun as a single unit, drawing blades, and guns and diving back from the table with cries of surprise. They were leaders, but each of them had earned their position through years in the field. None of them was privileged by birth, and if they'd been compromised, every man of them would fight to the death.

There was no invading force. There was only a lone woman, swathed from head to foot in traditional robes of an Arab woman. Her head was swathed in a dark Hijab, covering all but her face. It was a remarkable face. Despite the dim light, her eyes glittered, and the grim line of her mouth was bent in a scornful frown. She stood with her arms crossed in front of her, glaring down at them as if she belonged –as if her presence did not break every law of their faith. As if all their security was so much dust in the desert.

"So," she said at last. "You have come to wallow in your defeat. How clever of you. How proud you must be. Allah would be pleased."

The first of the men back to his feet closed on her, his dagger raised.

The woman cocked her head and watched him, making no move to retreat.

"Who are you?" he asked. "How do you come here?"

The Parting

"I came on the wind," she replied. "I come because you have called me. I come—because you have failed."

"You will not leave this place alive," the man said.

"I will," she said. "I will leave as I came, and I will leave with your promise, and your aid. You may call me Amunet."

The man closed on her quickly. He was not in the mood for idle chatter. He drove the dagger straight at her heart, but she only smiled. She spoke a single word—a word none of them heard clearly, and that none of them would have understood had they heard it.

The dagger shimmered and lost its rigidity. It coiled and turned back on itself, writhed and squirmed in the man's grip. He screamed, and tried to release it, but—now a serpent—it had coiled back around his wrist and moved up his arm toward his face. It was fast, and he staggered back, crashing into the table and falling across it, reaching to grab the snake behind its head and prevent it from reaching his face.

Two of the others ran to his side. One gripped the serpent behind its head, and the other dragged it free of his wrist. They held it—and then—with a cry of his own, the man gripping the neck cried out and backed away. His hand dripped blood, and he stared in shock.

The dagger fell to the floor between them. The twelve turned and stared. Amunet gazed back at them, unperturbed.

"You will listen to me," she said. "You will help me, and I will help you. Though I am certain that my words are wasted, I will tell you this—there is nothing you can do to prevent it."

"Sorceress!" one of the men cried. "Allah protect us!"

Despite what they'd just witnessed, these were hard men. They were not going to be taken down by a simple illusion, and they were unused to being spoken to as lackeys- or for that matter, by women whom they had not addressed first. The frustration of their recent endeavors, coupled with the ignominy of the situation was too much. They spread out and moved in quickly. They did not speak, they acted, but the woman, Amunet, did not back away. She raised both of her hands and spoke in clear, cutting tones.

Again, her words were lost to them. She seemed to speak in tongues, though now and then a phrase made the ghost of sense. The already dim light darkened, and there was a rising wail from outside the building. They ignored it. Before any of them could reach where the woman stood, the wailing was joined by twin screams.

They hesitated and turned toward the single door. There were no further screams, but the wail had grown to a roar, as if the desert had lifted up to sweep them away.

"What is it?" one of them cried. "What is happening?"

"Sandstorm!" another yelled. "It must be a storm. What else could…"

The door slammed inward as if struck by a huge hammer. It crashed open and hit the wall so hard the stout wood cracked. A dark cloud roared through and spread like smoke. The wail they'd heard was now a droning, pulsing wall of sound. Before they could even back away, the wall of locusts struck them. They were driven back, pounded into the walls, covered head to foot in biting, buzzing death. They screamed, and as they did, their mouths were filled. They tumbled back, scrambled for cover that did not exist, and through it all, Amunet stood, untouched, unmoving.

When the twelve were down, covered and helpless, crawling with her plague, she clapped her hands and shouted a single word.

The Parting

In that second, there was absolute silence. The locusts had vanished. The door swung loose on its hinges. The light flickered once, threatened to go out, and then grew steady once more. Amunet walked to the table and straightened it. The twelve scuttled back against the walls, watching her in terror-stricken awe. She met their gaze, not smiling, not angry. When she saw they would not speak again, she nodded very slightly.

"Now," she said, "you will listen. There is work to be done, and if you hope to know the glory of your vision, you will act swiftly and exactly as I command. You have prayed, and you have maintained your faith. I am here. Your ancestors, long ago, faced off with the Hebrew sorcerer Moses—and their hearts were weak. Mine is strong, and I offer that strength to you. In exchange, you will bring me what I need. The Holy land will grow strong—you will be great in the eyes of Allah, and of the world. I will have what is mine."

One by one, the men rose from where they'd fallen. They checked themselves for dangers that were not there. One of them walked to the door and, after glancing out to see that the two guards lay dead in the sand, closed it as well as he could. They righted the chairs and returned to their seats. When they were ready, Amunet began to speak, and they listened very carefully. They listened long into the night, and then, when she was finished, they dispersed as randomly and as quietly as they'd arrived.

When she was alone in the room, Amunet finally allowed her lip to curl in a dark, enigmatic smile. She turned out the lamp, and as the light drained from the room—she was gone.

Curious about other Crossroad Press books?
Stop by our site:
http://store.crossroadpress.com
We offer quality writing
in digital, audio, and print formats.

Enter the code FIRSTBOOK
to get 20% off your first order from our store!
Stop by today!